Penny's

Diner

A Novel

By Marianne Gowers

Copyright c. 2016 by Marianne Gowers
All rights reserved.
This is a work of fiction. Characters and events in this book are
a product of the author's imagination or are represented fictitiously.

Books by Marianne Gowers:

Remember Me Series
Return to Chelsey Falls
Natalie's Gift
Ripples

In the Quiet Heart
In the Quiet Heart
Penny's Diner

Chapter 1

Brock sipped at his soda, willing the caffeine to help him feel more alert as he headed toward his remodeling job. He'd had a late night repairing a neighbor's broken faucet, making it doubly hard to get out of bed this morning. He would have preferred to call in sick, but owning your own business didn't allow for that. If he didn't show up, no one else would do the work. Besides, he had promised Mrs. Fennick that he would get the painting done today. She had a family party planned for the weekend and wanted a few days to clean and rearrange furniture.

The truck in front of him suddenly hit its brakes causing Brock to stomp on his own. His old truck squealed as he came to a halt a few feet behind the other vehicle.

"What's going on?" he leaned to the side hoping to see around the other truck. He considered honking the horn when he spied a biker swerving into the road to avoid a garbage can. The guy on the bike wasn't wearing any reflective gear, and with the early hour of the day, he was hard to see. "You're gonna get killed," Brock said as he slowly drove past the biker.

He checked his rearview mirror and saw that several cars were lined up behind him. The driver in front of him picked up his speed and continued up the windy road. Brock grabbed his drink and finished it off. He went to set it back in the cup holder and missed. The cup tipped and fell onto the passenger seat of his truck. He swore softly under his breath and reached for the cup, but couldn't quite reach it without taking his eyes off the road.

"Dadgum cup!" he said watching it roll against the door.

He hit the brakes again as the truck in front came to a stop behind a bus with its lights blinking red. Taking advantage of the stop, Brock leaned toward the cup and grabbed it firmly, accidentally popping the lid off. He mumbled a few more choice words as the ice tumbled out onto the seat.

A honk from behind forced him to abandon the ice and continue down the road. Brock grumbled to himself. "Honking ain't gonna help. Can you see the truck and bus in front of me? I'd go faster if I could."

He checked his mirror and realized the car behind him was full of impatient teenagers most likely heading to the high school, which was about another mile up the two-lane road. There were intermittent cars coming in the other direction, so he and the rest of the cars had no choice but to follow at a much slower speed than was posted.

Finally, the bus turned down a side street and the truck he'd been following pulled into a driveway. He increased his speed, relieved to have open road ahead. The car full of kids apparently was not satisfied with his speed and went even faster to pass him. Brock shook his head, and let off the gas to let them go by. "Be careful," he said thinking of his own son that was about to turn sixteen.

His breath caught and his heart beat erratically in his chest as he watched the young driver pull quickly back into his own lane to avoid a car that suddenly appeared around a curve in the road. The oncoming car honked and gestured at the young man behind the wheel.

The high school campus came into view and the students pulled into the parking lot. He was relieved to know that one less car full of crazy teenagers was off the road at least for a few hours.

He continued on his way to the Fennick home, checking the clock as he approached the upscale neighborhood. He had hoped to have an earlier start, but things weren't going his way this morning. He thought of the couple that had hired him just two weeks ago. They seemed pleased so far with his work although Mrs. Fennick watched him like a hawk and asked him a million questions while he worked. The couple had asked him to repair several walls in the front hallway and living room that had been damaged from an earlier water leak. It was a small job, but it was work.

Brock checked the street sign to his left. The Fennicks were just one more block down. He slowed as he came to the next street, a garbage truck heading the other way blocked his left hand turn as it collected the trash. He checked for oncoming cars, and waited as the garbage truck pulled forward. He began his turn, but was surprised when a pair of headlights came around the curve. He hit the gas as a large delivery truck came barreling toward him from the opposite direction.

The speeding truck slammed into the bed of his truck spinning him around and forcing him into the side of the garbage truck. He heard a horrible squeal of metal on metal as he collided with the two vehicles. He grunted in pain as his body was thrown first into the steering column and then ripped backward against the seat as his truck came to an abrupt stop and everything went black.

***

> MIDVALE —Local man, Brock Carver, was injured in a car accident Wednesday morning when his pickup was struck by a delivery van and forced into the rear end of a garbage truck. Carver, a handyman by trade, was taken to the hospital with serious, but stable injuries. The driver of the other vehicle was also taken to the hospital, but sustained only minor injuries. The driver of the garbage truck was not injured. The crash is still under investigation, but speed and low visibility seem to be factors in the accident.

"Oh my. How sad," she mumbled as she circled the article with a neon green marker and continued to peruse the newspaper. "So much heartache in the world."

Chapter 2

"Happy Birthday, dear Megan, Happy Birthday to you!" Janae, the baby's thirteen-year-old stepsister sang out joyously before kissing her little sister on the head.

The baby looked around at the large group of extended family with a smile, thrilled to be the center of attention on this warm July day. The Lundquist family was gathered in their backyard under a canopy to celebrate the first birthday of Kate and Jay's daughter Megan.

"Should we take her dress off before I give her the cake, Mom?" Janae asked holding a piece of cake with one unlit candle in it.

"Yes. Let's do that." She lifted the baby's dress over her head as Janae set the plate in front of Megan. Kate folded the dress and stepped to her husband's side.

"That year flew by, didn't it?" Jay asked as he wrapped his arms around his bride of two years and nuzzled her neck.

"Yes it did. I'm not sure I like my baby growing up so fast," Kate said softly as she leaned back into her husband's embrace. She drew in a sharp breath and then laughed as the birthday girl stuck her whole hand into the pink frosted cake.

"Well, maybe we should think about having another one," Jay whispered softly, turning his wife around and kissing her lightly on the lips.

"Are you two going to just stand there, making out or are we going to get some cake too?" fifteen-year-old Mitch asked with a smirk.

Jay leaned forward and kissed the boy's stepmother a second time with even more passion, sending a happy thrill through Kate, and leaving her heart racing. He grinned and looked over at his son who was rolling his eyes. "Kissing or eating cake? Hmm. That's a hard choice."

Kate giggled and stepped to the table where the birthday cake waited. "Mitch will you go bring the ice cream out?" she asked as she began cutting into the pretty pink cake she'd gotten from the local bakery.

The boy hurried to do her bidding, pausing at the back door of the house. "Do you need a scoop?"

"No. I have that," she answered as she slid the first piece onto a paper plate.

"How can I help?" Penny asked as she came to stand beside Kate.

"I think I've got it. You can sit down in the shade and just relax," Kate said to the grey haired woman.

Penny had been Kate's client at the hair salon for the last two and a half years, but since Megan had been born, Penny had become like another grandmother to the child. She brought dresses and toys, continuously doting on the child as if she were truly her own grandchild.

With no children of her own, and a husband who passed away just over two years ago, Penny had seemed to need a family and Kate was happy to include her in many of the family gatherings.

"Let me get a picture of you with Megan," Kate's mother, Jen, said as she motioned for Penny to stand beside the sticky half naked child in the high chair.

"I'll take the picture," Jay said taking the camera from his mother-in-law. "Let's get all the grandmothers in it together. Winslow, will you bring a couple of chairs over?" Jay asked his father-in-law.

"Certainly." Kate's father set up three chairs next to the baby in the high chair.

"Thank you," Penny said as she sat down beside the baby.

Jen smiled and took a seat next to Penny. "Diane come get in the picture too," she called to Jay's mother who was chatting with Janae.

"Oh. Of course." Diane sat in the seat on the other side of the baby and smiled as Jay took several pictures of the group. "Now son, give me that and I'll get one of you and your sweet little family. Mitch, Janae, come stand by your sister. Kate put down that knife."

Kate obediently stepped behind the antique high chair, her eyes resting on the word engraved across the back of the baby seat. Blessed. Yes she truly was blessed. She placed her arm around her husband's waist and gathered her stepchildren under her other arm and smiled as Diane took the picture.

"Thanks, Mom," Jay said, retrieving the camera and hugging his mother. "I'm so glad you made it."

"I wouldn't miss it for the world. Just like I hated missing your wedding, but I guess I understand why you couldn't wait . . ."

Jay and Kate were married two years ago this month and his mother was still harping on him for getting married while she was out of the country on a mission. "I said I was sorry, Mother. You know you could have come, but we didn't want to burden you with the expense of flying home. Will you ever forgive me?"

"I suppose I should." She laughed and gave her son a hug. "Especially now that you've given me another beautiful grandbaby. Oh how I love this grandmother business." She hurried to help Kate with the baby who was now covered in pink frosting.

"Jay, let's take one more picture of her before I run her in to wash her hands and face . . . and hair." Kate laughed and turned the child around in her arms.

"Look up here, Sugar," Penny called to the baby as Jay snapped the picture. Megan clapped her sticky hands together as her mother carried her into the house.

"Should I take the ice cream back into the house?" Mitch asked as his father stepped to the table to find a piece of cake. "It's melting."

"I just need some and then you can run it in." Mitch scooped his father a large mound of ice cream and placed it next to his cake. "Thanks Son."

The boy snapped the lid on the bucket and took it back to the house, returning a few moments later with a freshly scrubbed and dressed Megan on his hip, Kate following closely behind.

"It's time for presents," Janae announced lifting a gift bag and kneeling in front of the baby who was sitting on Kate's lap. "This one's from me."

The baby looked at her sister unsure what to do with the bright colored bag with the tissue coming out the top. "Pull this out and see what's underneath," Janae explained, as she tugged at the tissue paper.

Kate helped Megan remove the tissue and lifted a toy phone from the bag.

"It plays music. See, you turn it on here and then you push the buttons." Janae showed the baby how to work the phone and smiled as the toy began to sing. Megan giggled and took the phone in her own chubby hands.

"I knew she'd like it. She's always stealing Mom's phone," Janae said as she turned to get another gift.

Kate loved that Janae called her Mom. Mitch had hesitated to make the transition from Kate to Mom, but this last year he had begun calling her Mom as well. She hoped Renee, the children's deceased mother, was pleased with the way she was trying to raise her children. There had been challenges that Kate had not anticipated, like having to discipline the children when Jay was gone. Her husband still served as the stake president at church, leaving Kate as sole caregiver at times.

The stepchildren were really quite easy for the most part, only giving her trouble occasionally. Mitch would be driving soon and Kate had already told Jay that he was in charge of that. She had her hands full with a new baby and although she'd been a stepmother now for two years, she was still getting used to the idea of having two teenagers under her care.

"This one's from Mitch," Janae said handing the baby another bag. Mitch looked up as a polka dot dress was pulled from the bag.

"You have mighty fine taste, Mitch. It matches my shirt," Penny said as she pointed at her blouse.

The boy smiled. "Okay, so maybe I can't take credit for picking it out, but Mom had me wrap it."

The group chuckled, and then oohed and aahed over the rest of the presents as the little girl began to understand the idea of pulling the wrapping paper from the pretty packages.

"Thank you for inviting us, honey," Kate's mother said as her parents each gave her a hug. "We should be going, but we'll see you on Sunday afternoon for dinner."

Kate nodded and lifted Megan up to tell her grandma goodbye. "Wave bye-bye, Megan." The little girl grinned before turning into her mother's shoulder to hide. "We're still working on it." Kate kissed her baby's head.

"You are so cute," Kate's mother said as she tickled the baby on the back.

Winslow, Kate's father, took his wife's hand and waved goodbye to the remaining group. "Have a good evening, it was good to see you all."

Jay's parents stood and said their goodbyes as well. "We've got an early morning tomorrow, so we better head out too."

Janae hugged each of her grandparents and Mitch waved as the two couples left through the back gate.

"Are you saving the plastic forks," Penny called to Kate as she began clearing the table of the used plates and cups.

"No. You can toss them, but Penny you don't need to do that," Kate handed the baby to Janae and moved to the old woman's side. "We'll get it later."

Penny continued to gather trash and stuff it into the garbage bag in her hand. "I want to help. A body needs to feel useful."

Kate nodded and picked up the leftover cake and took it into the house. Mitch followed with the punch bowl and Jay started folding up chairs.

"Look at all these toys, Megan," Janae said as she sat down in the grass with the baby. "Should we feed your dolly?" The thirteen year old showed her sister how to hold the baby bottle against the doll's mouth. "Yum yum."

"Janae," Penny called as she tied up the garbage bag. "Will you run in the house and bring me my purse. I left my gift for Megan in it."

"Sure, Grandma P." Janae ran into the house and returned a moment later with Kate and their little dog Rudi in tow.

"Leave a few chairs up, Jay. I need to talk to you and Kate for a few minutes," Penny said as she lifted Megan onto her lap. "I know it's your birthday little one, but I have gifts for your brother and sister too."

Janae handed the purse to Penny and stood by her side. "They must be pretty small to fit inside your purse," Janae said with a laugh as she sat on the ground and pulled the little dog into her lap.

Penny took the purse and lifted a large envelope from inside. "It's not as fun as the toys and the pretty clothes she got today, but it will be something for your future."

Jay and Kate pulled up a chair and Mitch came from the house and sat on the grass.

"You didn't need to get them anything, Penny. We're just glad you could come celebrate with us." Kate reached for the baby who was trying to eat the envelope.

"I know, but I'm getting older and I don't have any family of my own." She paused and removed several pages from the envelope and nodded at the three children that surrounded her. "I've set up college funds for each of the kids."

"Really? How mu—" Mitch began to ask, pausing when he caught a stern look from his father.

Kate sat up straighter and drew in a breath. "Can you really afford to do that?"

Penny smiled at Kate. "Yes, I can." She handed the papers to Jay. "My Del took care of me very well over the years. I'll be fine for the remaining years I have left in this world." The woman looked Kate in the eye. "And besides, it's something I want to do." Penny took a cleansing breath and smiled at the children. "You have become the family I never had." The elderly woman reached up and wiped a tear from her eye and added, "I love you all more than you'll ever know."

Janae leaned down to hug Penny. "We love you too, Grandma P."

Chapter 3

Kate gazed out the window as she finished up with another client. Her children were eager to go to the community pool this afternoon. She hoped they'd have time before dinner and that the weather would hold. These warm days often included thunderstorms by afternoon. She shut off the hair dryer and returned her attention to the woman in the chair.

"How's that?" She handed a mirror to the young lady and swiveled the chair around.

"Thanks. It looks great."

Kate followed her client to the front and collected payment. "Have a good day."

"You too." The door chimed as the woman walked out into the sunshine and held the door for Kate's next customer—Penny.

The older woman greeted Kate. "Hi, honey. How's your day going?"

"Good. How was your walk?" Kate asked.

"Marvelous. I feel so much better after a long walk." Penny stepped to Kate's salon chair and waited as the hairdresser snapped the shield in place. The two women walked back to the sink area.

Kate turned on the water and tested the temperature. She smiled down at Penny who already had her eyes closed. Penny enjoyed the wash more than anything and Kate always spent some extra time with it, massaging longer than she would for others.

Several minutes later, Kate said, "Sit up and I'll towel dry it a bit." She shut off the water as Penny sighed and did as she was told. "Are you going to wait around for me after we're done, so I can run you home?" Kate asked as she squeezed the water from Penny's hair.

"Yes. I may run a few errands in town while you finish up here, but I'll be back by three o'clock."

The women returned to the chair and Kate proceeded to trim Penny's hair. She and Penny had worked out a system over the last few months. When the weather was nice, Penny walked to the salon for her appointments, but then Kate always insisted on driving her home. Penny would have her hair done just after lunch and then would either sit and visit or walk around town doing errands until Kate finished up for the day.

"How's your brother doing, Robin," Penny asked the hairdresser in the station next to Kate's.

"He's good. He is so much happier now that he's in school. I just can't believe the change." Robin smiled and continued working on her client.

"Did you say he was doing something with cars?" Kate looked at Robin as she fingered through Penny's hair.

"Yeah. Guy's been at UVU since January in their auto body program. It's perfect for him. He's always enjoyed working on cars. He's even applied to work at a shop up in Provo. Hopefully he'll get it so he can quit the pizza place."

"I'm sure he will," Penny said with a slight nod. "He's a good worker."

"How do you know Robin's brother?" Kate asked pausing in her work.

"Oh, I've seen him working at the pizza shop. He's always so polite and makes the best pizza." Penny looked up as Kate reached for the hair dryer. "Have you tried that new stuffed pizza crust? That's one of the reasons I have to take a walk everyday." The woman laughed.

Kate shook her head, turned on the dryer and shared a smile with Robin as she dried Penny's hair. The younger hair stylist had taken over Kate's fulltime position when Megan had been born. Kate only worked one day a week now, and she had finally gotten to know Robin better.

Although Kate had never met Robin's brother, she had discovered through some very interesting conversations, that the siblings had been in the foster care system for most of their lives, shuttled from one home to another.

Connie, one of the salon's other hairdressers, said that Robin's parents had been in and out of jail for various reasons and had no contact with their children. Connie also mentioned something about Robin's brother having spent some time in juvenile detention, but the two were currently holding down jobs and living in an apartment together. Kate was glad to hear that the brother seemed to be turning his life around and both were doing well considering their difficult start in life.

"There you go Penny. Anything else?" Kate asked as she sprayed a light coat of hairspray on the woman's new do.

"Nope. Looks perfect as always." Penny waited as Kate removed the drape. The woman stood up and brushed at her clothes. "Connie," Penny waved at the woman behind the cash register. "I meant to ask you about your brother as well. How is he? Is he recovering from the accident?" Penny stepped toward the front where Connie had just been on the phone.

"It's been hard. His wife Emily says that the insurance company is only going to cover part of what a new truck will cost and they won't pay for any of the tools to be replaced. He will probably have to take out a second mortgage on his home."

"I am so sorry to hear that, dear." Penny patted Connie's hand. "And how is his leg healing?"

Connie frowned. "He's still on crutches, but in another couple of weeks the doctor hopes to put him in a walking cast. It's pretty hard for him to do anything though." Connie shook her head. "Chris and I offered to help with his house payments for a couple of months, but we can't do much else."

"Shouldn't the guy that hit him pay for stuff?" Kate asked.

"That's what we had hoped, but the police say it was Brock's fault. He apparently turned in front of the other truck."

The phone rang and Connie reached to answer it.

"Here you go Kate," Penny said as she handed the hairdresser a check. "I guess I'll walk up the street and do some window shopping."

"Are you sure? It's getting pretty warm out there," Kate said with concern.

"Oh, I'll be alright. I'll just step inside one of the shops if I get overheated." The older woman put her checkbook back into her fanny pack and smiled. The salon door opened and a young man in a baseball cap stepped inside holding the door wide as Penny exited.

"Hi, Chase, right? How are you today?" Kate said recognizing the young man as Robin's next client. "Robin is almost done. You can have a seat and she'll be right with you."

"Sounds good, thanks." The dark haired man slumped into a chair near the hairdryers and waved at Robin who grinned in his direction.

"They're going out," Connie said softly next to Kate's ear. "Don't they make the perfect couple?"

Kate raised her eyebrow and looked between the two twenty-somethings. "Oh yeah? Since when?"

Connie checked the appointment book and continued to speak in soft tones. "He took her to a BYU concert last week. She wasn't sure he was her type, but I think she really likes him."

"Did they just meet here at the salon?" Kate asked as she straightened the pens.

"Uh huh." The bell at the front door chimed and Connie motioned toward the woman coming in, calling in a louder voice, "Hello, Lisa. Come on over."

Kate moved back to her station, eyeing the clean-cut young man skimming though a magazine. She had been here a few months ago when Chase had first come in. She'd had her own client at the time so Robin had done his hair. The bell chimed again and Kate looked up to see her own patron come through the door. "Good afternoon, Debbie. Come have a seat."

As Debbie set her purse down, Kate watched Robin remove the drape from her customer and lead her to the front. "Would you like to buy any product today?" Robin asked as she stood behind the register and sneaked a peek in Chase's direction.

"No thanks."

The woman handed Robin some cash and slipped out the door.

Robin closed the register and walked back toward her salon chair. "Next?" She smiled as Chase stood and removed his hat, a pile of dark curly hair spilling out.

"You must be breaking all kinds of rules over at BYU with that mop of hair." Connie commented as she paused to watch Chase slide into the salon chair.

"Yeah." He said with a nod. "I let it get too long." He looked up at Robin. "But I have a great hairdresser that will make me look sharp again in no time."

The younger woman blushed and covered the man with the drape. "Should I wash it first?" she asked.

"Of course." The man stood up and followed Robin to the sink. Kate heard the girl giggle at something the handsome man said.

"Are we coloring today, Debbie?" Kate asked turning her attention back to her own client.

"Yes, please and I'd like it a bit shorter than last time." Kate nodded and stepped to the back to mix the color for Debbie. Robin and Chase were still at the sink deep in conversation. Kate squirted the gel into the bowl and began to mix, trying not to eavesdrop.

"I guess I can. I'll have to get the day off," Robin said as she rinsed Chase's hair.

"Hey, Kate would you be able to trade me days next week?" Robin asked.

Kate paused in thought. "What day do you need me to take?"

"Wednesday and I'll work Tuesday for you." Robin shut off the water and grabbed a towel.

"That should be fine. I don't have anything going on as far as I know. Are you doing something fun?" Kate asked.

"Chase and some of his friends are going waterskiing. He's asked me to come," Robin said as she towel dried the man's hair.

"Sure. I'll plan on it." Kate smiled as Chase stood up and wandered back to Robin's chair. "I love his dimples." Kate whispered as she glanced in Chase's direction.

Robin tossed the used towel into the laundry bin, her cheeks turning pink as she grinned toward the man in her chair. "Me too."

Kate returned to Debbie and began applying the color.

"How's that baby of yours?" Debbie asked.

"She just turned one. If you can believe it." Kate pointed at her youngest daughter's picture on the mirror.

"Time flies, doesn't it? My babies are fourteen, sixteen and eighteen. Which is just unbelievable to me." Debbie sighed deeply.

"How was Megan's party?" Connie asked from across the room.

"It was fun. All the grandparents were able to come, so we took lots of pictures. Even Penny came," Kate explained as she brushed the dye onto Debbie's hair. "She brought a present for all the kids, not just Megan."

"Well that was nice of her," Connie said.

"Yeah right? She actually set up an account for each of them for college. I don't know how she could afford that. As far as I know, her husband was a rancher all his life and Penny worked at a diner. So I would think she's living on a limited income."

"Ranchers actually do pretty well sometimes," Debbie added to the conversation.

"I just get the impression that they lived a simple life." Kate shrugged and set the remaining dye on the counter. "Okay, Debbie let's have you sit under the dryer for twenty minutes. Do you want a magazine?" Kate helped her client get situated before stepping to the back of the salon.

She took out her phone and sent herself a text about switching days with Robin. Then she sent a text to her mother who had the baby today. Her mother answered that Megan was sleeping.

As she waited for the timer, her mind drifted to Penny and the money she'd set aside for her kids. She really didn't know where the money had come from. Penny hardly talked about her past, but Kate knew she never had children of her own. She'd probably been saving money for years. Kate hoped she wasn't giving away her life savings. Penny should hang onto that in case she needed the money for medical bills or something in the future? The paperwork that Penny had given them didn't say how much was in the accounts, but Jay said he would look into it and get more details.

She sent off a text to her husband.

"Hey sweetie. Did you have a chance to check on the college funds?"

She watched the clock, wondering if he was too busy to reply. Jay was an attorney and some days he hardly had time to breathe, let alone find time to text her. Just as the timer began to ring for Debbie's hair, Kate's phone chimed with a brief message from Jay.

"No time today. Sorry."

Chapter 4

Penny wandered down the block passing the music store and a bakery, pausing at several windows along her way. Spanish Fork reminded her of Ephraim, the small town where she'd spent her entire married life. Her husband, Del had been a ranch hand as a young man in Arizona and had decided that ranching was the life he wanted. Just days before their wedding in 1961 he'd announced that he was considering a job in Utah. Penny had never been to the Beehive State, but after a short discussion, they agreed that if he were offered the job, they would make the move.

On the next block Penny paused in front of the antique store and stepped inside. The large store was crowded with furniture and household items from years gone by. She walked past a shelf full of knickknacks and glassware. She stopped to touch an old set of china on a table brimming with decorative serving plates and teacups. As she handled a delicate cup, Penny smiled at a young woman seated on a couch against the wall. An older woman was settled in an adjacent armchair discussing the suitability of the furniture for the younger woman's home.

Penny continued her perusal, touching the spine of a book as she read the title. As she stepped further into the store, her attention was drawn to a speed limit sign and several soda pop logos that hung on the walls above an old armoire. Just above her head a small biplane was suspended in the air by a length of string. Del would have liked that, she thought. Her husband had made a similar model airplane many years ago with Roberto, the grandson of his ranch hand.

A familiar ache surfaced instantly, making Penny sigh. She had always been saddened by the fact that she had never given Del children of his own. He would have been a wonderful father. But as fate had left them little choice, they had looked for and found many other children to love and fill that void in their lives.

"Can I help you find anything?" the proprietor asked as Penny passed the register counter.

"Oh no. I'm just looking. Your store always brings back a lot of memories for me." Penny smiled.

"You're not the first one to tell me that." The man nodded, a smile lighting his face. "Let me know if you have any questions."

The aisles at the back of the store were almost too clogged to pass through. Penny walked around a curio cabinet and past a shelf holding an assortment of small ceramic animals. As she stepped around a corner, she found herself in front of a wrought iron garden table with two matching chairs. Behind the lawn furniture was a small wooden cradle in disrepair. Penny ran her hand along the peeling paint and carefully touched a broken spindle.

"What a shame," she murmured softly. "This is almost like the one we gave to Helen."

The fifty-year-old memory came flooding into her mind and Penny was suddenly transported back in time.

February 1962
Ephraim, Utah

"I think we should get a smaller table. We don't really have room for such a . . . ." Del paused as he noticed his wife's attention was drawn to a couple across the showroom. A man and his expectant wife were standing beside a beautiful white cradle. The pregnant woman reached out and caressed the curved headboard, a smile touching her lips. The woman's husband gave the tiny bed a push, putting it in motion.

Del touched Penny's arm. "Hey, honey. What about this one?" he asked steering her thoughts back to the reason they'd come into the furniture store in the first place.

"It would fit along the wall in the kitchen and it has an extra . . . uh . . . piece that we can put in when we have visitors." Del pulled out a chair and tested the seat for comfort. He looked up at Penny waiting for her opinion.

"A leaf," Penny said as she pulled out another chair and sat down. "It's called a leaf." Penny's gaze wandered back to the couple still discussing the baby bed.

"Yeah, right." Del stood and pushed the chair under the table. "It's just what we're looking for, don't you think?"

Penny ran her hand over the wood finish and nodded. "We'll only need four chairs."

Del took Penny's hand and pulled her up beside himself. "Let's see if they can have it delivered." He leaned down and kissed his wife's head, placing his arm across her shoulders. He motioned to the salesman that now stood beside the other couple. "I guess Dan is the only one working today."

They stood a few feet from Dan as he discussed payment options with the other couple. "Yes, we do have financing and for $20 down I can have it hand delivered next week."

The dark haired woman rested her hand across her protruding belly as she looked hopefully up at her husband. "What do you think, Artie?"

The man took a deep breath and lifted the price tag. "I don't know Helen." He studied the amount, apparently calculating in his head. Several uncomfortable moments passed as the man debated whether they could afford the cradle. A sad expression crossed his face as he looked at his anxious wife. "I really think we should wait." Helen's shoulders sagged, but she slowly nodded in agreement. Artie looked up at the shopkeeper. "Sorry. Maybe we'll be back."

Artie took his wife's hand and led her toward the front door. Penny watched as the disheartened woman and her husband left without the baby bed.

The salesman sighed and stepped closer to Del and Penny. "Hello folks," he said as he extended his hand. "How's the new house?" The couple had met Dan last month when they'd bought a bedroom set.

"Great, but now we need a table. We're looking at this dining set over here." The two men moved in the direction of the table as Del asked about delivery options.

Penny stepped to the side of the cradle and lifted a toy bunny from the mattress. She held the soft fur against her cheek and stared at the glass door that Artie and Helen had just departed through. She turned back to the cradle and studied the price tag before letting it drop. She ran her hand across the wood and pursed her lips together. After another moment she dropped the bunny back into the small bed and hurried to find Del and Dan who were now at the cash register.

"Penny. He says we'll have it by Wednesday next week. That should work right?" Del asked as Penny stopped beside him.

"Sure." She looked up at the clerk and motioned to the baby bed. "And we'll take that cradle too."

Dan blinked several times and looked up at Del who seemed as mystified as Penny's husband.

Penny tapped the counter. "Do you have any bedding for it?"

Dan regained his composure and answered with a smile. "No we don't, but I'm sure they have some at the shop on the corner."

Penny nodded and strolled back to the children's area with a smile on her face.

Del paid for their purchases and escorted his wife out to the truck. "I suppose you know someone that needs a cradle?" he asked as he climbed behind the wheel.

"Why . . . Helen and Artie," Penny said with a mischievous grin.

"The couple we've never really met, but saw for the first time in the store?" Del asked as he started the engine.

Penny bobbed her head. "Don't worry. I'll pay for it with the money Mother sent."

Clarinda, Penny's mother, had sent money to the newly married couple the week before, expressing concern for her daughter's welfare. Penny sighed loudly. "She won't come see us, but she is absolutely certain that we can never survive on a rancher's income." Penny rolled her eyes. "I haven't even told her about my job at the diner. She would probably have a heart attack if she knew I was waiting tables."

Del chuckled. "The money is just her way of showing she cares." He reached across and took Penny's hand. "I do like the idea of using her money for a new cradle though." He placed his hand back on the steering wheel and turned toward home.

After several minutes he asked, "And just how do you plan on finding out where Helen and Artie live?"

"I'll ask around. How many Helen and Artie's can there be?" Penny said, confident that someone in this small town new the expectant couple.

Chapter 5

"Can I make cookies for family night?" Janae asked as she climbed into the car.

"Yes. What kind? I don't think we have any chocolate chips, but we could stop at the store on the way home," Kate said as they left the school parking lot. Megan babbled in the back seat as they turned toward home.

"Maybe we should do raisin oatmeal. Dad likes those."

"Those sound good and I am pretty sure we have everything we need for that recipe." Kate made her way through town, pausing at a stop sign. "How did the class go today?"

"It was good. We're practicing drawing people and I still can't make hands very well. Mrs. Green helped me, but Tori needed more help than I did."

Kate nodded. Janae was starting the second week of a four-week course at the high school where they were offering a community class on art. The girl seemed to be thriving under Mrs. Green's instruction.

"Is Grandma P coming over tonight?" Janae asked as they pulled into the driveway and into the garage.

"I haven't talked to her for several days. I'll have to call her after I put Megan down. Can you unbuckle her from her car seat while I get the mail?"

Kate walked to the mailbox, finding a stack of bills and several catalogs. She read the return address from the last envelope and thought the name looked familiar. She ripped open the letter as she stepped into the kitchen. It was from Penny's attorney about the college funds that had been set up for the kids. Kate continued to wonder how this woman who had to live on a limited income could afford to give money to her three kids. When she'd questioned Penny about it, the woman had just smiled and said, "Don't look a gift-horse in the mouth, Sweetie."

Megan and Janae were sitting on the floor in the living room watching a cartoon with their little dog, Rudi, in the older girl's lap.

"Are you ready for lunch?" she asked the two girls as she pulled open the fridge. "Would you like a quesadilla or leftover potato soup?"

"Quesadilla please with chicken and barbecue sauce on it," Janae called over her shoulder.

"That does sound good. I wonder if Mitch would like one. Will you please go ask him?"

Janae pushed the dog off her lap and walked down the hallway, returning a moment later. "He's not here." Janae stepped into the kitchen and stood by the island. "His music was on, but he wasn't in his room."

Kate furrowed her brow. She had told Mitch that she would be right back. "Was he in the bathroom?"

"Nope. The light was off and the door was open. Maybe he went to Joe's house."

Her stepmother nodded and pulled the cheese from the drawer in the fridge. "Maybe. Would you grate this while I chop the chicken?"

Kate began to worry about her stepson. Mitch knew he was supposed to ask before going anywhere. It wasn't normal for him to just leave. If he had a phone she could call him, but they had decided not to get him one until he started driving. Kate thought that was a good idea, but at times like this she'd like to be able to reach him. How had they managed before cell phones?

"Is this enough?" Janae asked lifting the grater from the pile of cheese.

"Yes, thanks. I'll have these ready in just a minute. Go see where Megan has gone," Kate said as she realized the baby had lost interest in the television and wandered off.

After lunch Kate put the baby down for a nap and stepped out into the front yard wondering where Mitch might be. She thought about calling some of his friends' homes, but he might resent her checking up on him. She considered calling Jay, but wasn't sure she should do that either. "Where are you Mitch?" she asked as she walked back into the house.

"Did you call Grandma P yet?" Janae asked as Kate joined her at the dining room table.

"No. I forgot. I guess I'll do that now." She pulled her phone from her purse and dialed Penny's number. She let it ring several times, hanging up when no one answered. "She's not answering. I guess I'll try later," she said setting the phone on the table as she leaned over Janae's shoulder. "That's a nice drawing. Is that Megan and Rudi?"

The little girl nodded and smiled brightly. "Yep." The girl stood up and hung it on the fridge amidst her other drawings.

"You should make those cookies now before I have to use the oven for dinner," Kate said.

"Okay." Janae pulled the cookbook from the shelf and turned to the well-worn page for the cookie recipe. "Should we make extra for Grandma P?"

"Sure. That's a great idea. Let's double it." Kate set the sugar and flour canisters on the counter and pulled the eggs from the fridge. "How much butter do you need?"

"Two cubes."

An hour later the house smelled like vanilla and two plates of cookies were cooling on the counter. "I think the cookie baker and her assistant need to make sure they taste alright, don't you?" Kate asked as she lifted two cookies and handed one to Janae. They quickly bit into the sweet treats. "Perfect," Kate said as she wiped crumbs from her mouth. "Now to start dinner."

Kate's phone chimed as she started the microwave to defrost the chicken for dinner. "Will you see who that is?" she asked Janae.

Her stepdaughter picked up the phone and read the text. "Daddy says hi and asked if he needs to pick up anything at the store."

Kate smiled and took the phone and dialed her husband's number. She stepped into her bedroom to speak with him privately.

"Hey there. How's your day going?" she asked.

"Busy, but that's a good thing. How are you?"

"Fine. Just starting dinner. I don't need anything from the store, but it was nice of you to offer." Kate sat on the bed. "I am worried about Mitch though. He's gone somewhere and he didn't really tell me where he was going."

Jay was quiet for a moment. "How long has he been gone? Maybe he's shooting hoops with Tyson."

"It's been two hours. I guess I could call Tyson's house. I just wish he'd told me before he left."

"Yeah. I'll have a talk with him when I get home. He shouldn't make you worry like this." Jay covered the phone and Kate heard him speak to someone else in the room. "I'm sorry, honey. I have to go. Call me later if he doesn't get back soon. Love you." He hung up and Kate sighed.

The baby woke and Janae took her out to the backyard to play while Kate put the dinner in the oven.

"Let's go for a walk and see if we can find your brother. Maybe he's at the Millers."

Kate grabbed her phone and a hat for herself and the baby. She strapped Megan into the stroller and shut the garage door. It had been more than three hours since she had discovered Mitch was missing. She had never been so worried about anyone like she was about her stepson right now. Motherhood was harder than she'd anticipated. Having teenagers and a baby made her feel like she was being pulled apart at the seams sometimes. She didn't have the luxury of getting used to the idea of her children growing up and making decisions on their own.

As they turned the corner, Kate paused in front of the Miller's house and saw a basketball resting against the fence, but no boys around. "Would you go ring the bell and see if he's inside?"

The girl obediently went to the front door and knocked, waving back at her little sister as she waited. Megan pointed and babbled, happy to be outside. The door opened and Kate could hear Janae asking for Mitch. Mrs. Miller nodded and called to Kate. "I'll go get him."

"Okay, thanks." Kate sighed in relief and walked the stroller back and forth until Mitch appeared.

"What's up?" he asked as he came out to the porch. "We're in the middle of a game."

Kate lifted her eyebrows at the tone of his voice. "Uh, well. I was worried about you. You didn't even tell me where you'd gone."

"Oh well, Tyson called and asked me to come over. I didn't think you'd mind." Kate was glad to see his stance soften a bit. "I'm sorry."

"That's okay, I guess. You just need to let me know next time. Can you come home in about fifteen minutes?" she asked. "Dinner will be ready and your dad will be home soon."

"Yeah sure. I'll come as soon as I can." Mitch ran back into the house and closed the door.

Janae joined Kate on the sidewalk and they circled the block, returning to their home. "Here we go little one," Kate said as she lifted her daughter from the stroller. "Let's feed you first. Janae do you want to feed Megan or set the table?"

"I'll feed her."

"There's yogurt in the fridge and maybe we'll try some toast tonight." Kate smiled as the older girl hefted the baby onto her hip and placed her in the high chair.

"In you go, little Miss Megan. Are you hungry? Want some yogurt and toast?" the girl asked in a silly voice. "Sissy's going to feed you tonight."

Janae was quickly becoming a second mother to the child, which was a great help to Kate. Having teenagers wasn't all bad, she had to admit as she checked the oven. She quickly grabbed a stack of plates from the cupboard as Mitch came walking into the house.

"Hey," he said in greeting as he reached for a cookie.

"Uh, hold it. Have you washed your hands? We're going to be eating soon too. Maybe you should wait." Kate was surprised at how mother like she sounded. The teenage boy sighed and stepped to the sink. "Would you finish setting the table, Mitch? I need to make the sauce for the chicken."

The boy counted out the silverware and grabbed several cups. He arranged the table and headed down the hallway. "I'll be in my room."

"Thanks for setting the table," Kate called as she stirred the sauce and checked the clock on the stove. Jay should be arriving any minute.

As the thought left her mind, Kate heard the garage door open and Janae say excitedly, "Daddy's here, Megan!"

All three females looked up expectantly as Jay walked through the door.

"How are my girls today," he said as he kissed the two little girls on the head and stepped to the stove. "Mmm, something smells good." He placed his arm around Kate's waist and kissed her soundly. "I love having you standing in my kitchen when I get home." He whispered against her ear.

"I love being here." Kate smiled and returned to her pot.

"Did Mitch ever come home?" Jay asked as he wandered toward the hall.

"Yes, just now." Kate wondered if he would talk to the boy now or later. She didn't like getting Mitch in trouble, but she had been truly worried. "Dinner's ready by the way."

"I think she's done, Mom." Janae stood and placed the spoon in the sink. "Did you ever talk to Grandma P?"

"No. She didn't answer. I'll try her again after dinner. It might be too late for her to come now, but we can always take her the cookies tomorrow."

Kate set the food on the table and filled the glasses with ice water. She was about to send Janae to find her dad and brother when they appeared in the doorway. Her husband had a serious look on his face and Mitch was wearing a frown.

"I'm sorry for not telling you where I was today. I shouldn't have done that and made you worry," Mitch said in a quiet voice.

Kate smiled. "That's alright, Mitch. I forgive you. I just was anxious not knowing where you were, that's all."

The boy nodded and took his place at the table. Jay took Kate's hand and moved to his chair. "Janae will you bless the food tonight?"

After the dinner, Kate started helping Mitch load the dishwasher, but paused as he took the bowl from her hand and waved her away.

"I got it. You can go do . . . whatever. Thanks for dinner. It was good," Mitch said as he continued to load the dishes.

Kate set one last cup in the dishwasher and smiled. "Well, okay. I guess I'll put the baby in bed and then call Penny. We'll have family night as soon as I'm done."

Megan went down easily and Kate went to the kitchen to find her phone. She dialed Penny for the third time today and let it ring and ring, but the woman still didn't answer. Kate walked into her husband's office and found him reading a book. "I'm a bit worried about Penny. Janae made some cookies for her and we thought we'd invite her over tonight, but she hasn't answered her phone all day. I wonder if I should go check on her."

"I'm sure she's fine," Jay said as he pulled his reading glasses from his face. "But maybe you could check on her tomorrow after work."

"Actually, I don't work tomorrow. Robin and I traded this week. I guess I could make a trip down to Spanish Fork in the morning though."

Jay twirled his glasses and pursed his lips. "We could take a drive down tonight after family night," Jay said. "Is it my week to teach?"

Kate nodded. "I can find something to teach . . . if you want me to. I know you're busy." She stepped beside her husband's chair and touched his hair.

"Never too busy for you," he said pulling her into his lap. "Let's read a conference talk and call it good." He wrapped his arms around her and kissed her gently.

"Excuse me?" Mitch called from the doorway. "Can we have the lesson? I have things to do."

"Yes we can." Jay pushed his wife from his lap and led her down the hall. He rapped softly at Janae's door. "Come join us for family night, Janae."

The family gathered in the living room for a brief lesson and a prayer. After eating a cookie, Jay said, "Your mother and I are going to check on Penny. You two stay here and listen for the baby. We'll be back soon."

Kate grabbed the plate of cookies and headed to the garage with her husband, excited to be out of the house and away from kids even for an hour.

Chapter 6

Penny's house was completely dark which seemed odd since it was only seven thirty. Jay took the plate of cookies as Kate climbed from the car. He took her hand as they walked up the path to the house. She rang the bell and knocked loudly. Penny didn't always hear the bell. A shiver ran down Kate's spine as she waited for the woman to answer the door. Jay looked out at the street as she knocked a second time and waited.

"Maybe she's at the store or something," he said.

Kate shook her head. "No. She only shops on Thursdays because she says the store is less busy that day. Besides she doesn't like to go out at night. Her vision isn't as good in the dark." She knocked again even louder.

Jay walked down the stairs of the porch and motioned to the garage. "Let's see if there's a window into the garage and find out if her car is here." Kate followed him to the side of the garage and took the plate of cookies as he pushed through the bushes below the window. He rubbed at the dirty window and leaned against the glass. "Well, her car is in there. I wonder if she went walking or if she's visiting a neighbor," he said as he stepped away from the window.

"What if she's fallen . . ." She paused.

" . . . And can't get up." Jay said with a tiny snicker.

"I'm serious, Jay. She could be lying on the floor in her bathroom." Kate shook her head.

Jay looked apologetic. "I know, but I couldn't resist."

"She's probably sick in bed and too weak to answer the door." Kate turned to move to the back yard. "Maybe the back door is unlocked." As she stepped around the corner of the house a little dog came bounding up to her. "Hey Corky. How are you?"

"Corky? Do you know this dog?" Jay asked as the dog sniffed at his shoe.

"Yes, he lives nearby. Penny says he comes to visit her all the time."

The couple climbed the stairs to the back door with the little dog in tow. Jay rapped sharply. Kate let out a sigh as they waited another minute. "I don't like this," she said.

"Hello?" a voice called from the side of the house. "Kate is that you?" Kim, Penny's neighbor, came around the corner. "Hi, I wondered whose car that was." The neighbor pointed to the curb. "I was just coming to check on Penny. I haven't seen her for a couple of days. I was away at a tennis tournament over the weekend."

"She's not answering. I tried calling her several times today and never got an answer." Kate shook her head. "I'm starting to worry. Her car's in the garage, so I don't think she went anywhere. I wish we could get inside somehow."

"Maybe I can jimmy the lock open," Jay said as he rattled the knob.

Kim took a breath and shifted her purse on her shoulder, then paused. "Oh hey. I have a key. What was I thinking? She gave it to me about a year ago. I hope I can find it," she turned toward the street. "I just live two houses down. I'll be right back."

Kim hurried away.

"Should we call the police?" Kate asked as she sat down on the steps near the back door.

Jay sat down beside his wife and took her hand. "Let's see if we can get in first and see what we find. She's probably just gone for a walk. You know how she loves to walk." They sat together for several more minutes waiting for Kim to return, the little neighbor dog sniffing around in the yard.

"I found it. Sorry it took so long," Kim said as she hurried around the house and handed the key to Jay. "Here try the door. I think it's the right key. I should have marked it."

Jay stood up and climbed the stairs and inserted the key in the deadbolt. It turned easily. "Looks like it works." He paused and waited for the women to come up the stairs. "Kate why don't you call to her and announce yourself. We don't want to frighten her."

Kate stepped through the door. "Penny? Hello? It's me . . . Kate. Are you home?"

The small group stepped into the dark kitchen. Kim reached for the light switch and flipped it on. "Penny, honey. I'm here too," Kim called as she hesitantly moved into the living room. "I guess I'll check the bedroom."

Kim carefully pushed the door open to the bedroom and let out an audible sigh of relief. "She's in bed. Should we wake her?" Kim asked.

Kate turned to her husband. "What do think Jay? I thought all the knocking would have awakened her, but maybe she's a heavy sleeper."

"Well, let's wake her carefully." Jay admonished as he flipped on the light in the hall. "Quietly call to her and see if you can rouse her." He watched as Kate and Kim walked into the old woman's bedroom.

"Penny?" Kate called softly. "We're sorry to wake you, but we wanted to make sure . . ." Her words trailed off as she touched the woman's hand. She squealed and recoiled. "She's freezing."

Kim turned on the bedside lamp and groaned. "Oh my! She doesn't look right." The neighbor fell against the wall her hand over her mouth and her face completely pale.

Jay hurried into the room and took the shaken woman by the arm. "Come out. It's okay. Come with me." He escorted both women back outside and pulled out his phone. "I think we better call the police."

Jay spoke to the dispatcher and then hung up his phone and turned to Kate. "They'll send someone over. They said to just wait outside."

As the three adults stood on the lawn, a policeman arrived and Jay talked to him in hushed tones about what had happened. Then the medical examiner arrived and both officials went into the house. Ten minutes later, the police officer stepped back into the yard and moved toward Jay and the women who were huddled together under the tree in front of Penny's house.

"It looks like she died at least a day ago, maybe more. It doesn't look like there was any foul play, but there will need to be an investigation." The officer stepped to his car and began talking on his radio.

Kim sniffed. "I should tell my husband." She took out her phone and called her husband, explaining where she was and what had happened. Her husband stepped out onto the porch of their home down the block and waved. "Don't let the kids come out, Jeremy," she said as she returned his wave. "I'll come home in a few minutes." She hung up and looked up at Penny's home. "This is nuts. I've never had to deal with this sort of thing. We have to tell someone that she died, but I don't think she has any family. No one's ever come to visit at least."

The group nodded silently.

An ambulance arrived a few minutes later. Two men climbed out, removed a gurney from the back and followed the policeman into the house. Kate shivered and Jay wrapped his arms around his wife and kissed her on the cheek. "I should probably call the kids and tell them we'll be later than we thought."

Kate drew in a sharp breath. "Oh no! What are we going to tell the children? Don't tell them she died yet. We can tell them tomorrow or sometime later."

Jay pulled out his phone and dialed the home number. "Hey Mitch. This is Dad. How's everything? Is Megan still sleeping?"

He waited a moment.

"Great. Well . . . uh, we are going to be here for another half an hour I think. So I just wanted you to know that we aren't coming as soon as we thought. Okay. We'll see you later. Bye."

"How are they?" Kate asked as he slipped the phone back into the holster on his belt.

"Fine. Just watching a movie." Jay turned as a noise at the front door caught his attention. A covered gurney was being lifted down the steps by the two men and was quickly whisked into the back of the ambulance.

Kate wrapped her arms around herself. "I can't believe she's gone. Just like that."

"Yeah." Kim nodded and swiped at tears on her cheeks. Several other neighbors were now standing on their lawns as the ambulance drove silently away.

The officer stepped back out of the house and paused in front of the small group. "So do you have any idea who the next of kin would be?"

Kate shook her head and looked at Kim.

"I don't think she had any family. Not living close by at least," Kim said softly.

"Well until we can find out for sure, they'll most likely take her to a funeral home here in town." The officer shook Jay's hand and smiled at Kate and Kim. "Sorry for your loss folks."

Kim sighed. "I think I'll go home. My husband says the kids are still up, so I need to take care of them. If you want to just lock up when you're done or whatever . . . maybe you should just keep the key, until you talk to her family or whatever. I don't know . . ." She stopped and shook her head.

"We'll take care of it, Kim. Thanks for your help," Kate said as the neighbor headed down the block.

Jay walked up to the house and slipped the key into the lock. "We can hold onto the key right?" he asked the officer that stood at the foot of the stairs. "We'll call her attorney in the morning."

The officer nodded. "Sure."

"Did you lock the back door?" Kate asked.

"Yep. I did it myself." The officer nodded and Kate sighed, turning toward the street. Her head was still reeling from the night's events. Jay waved to the officer and climbed behind the wheel.

"I'll contact Ron in the morning and see if he can meet with us," Jay said as he headed for the freeway. "I'm really glad Penny updated her will last year and left instructions for her death. I hated making her think about it, but it will make things much easier for the next of kin."

Kate nodded and stared out the window. She was glad Jay had come with her. She would have never known what to do if she'd discovered Penny on her own. That was a tender mercy that she could be grateful for at least. She would miss Penny, but she suspected her friend was having a wonderful reunion with her husband, Del. The old woman had been so lonely these last two years without him.

Chapter 7

Kate and her husband stepped off the elevator and turned toward the glass doors of the law office. Jay swung the door opened and followed his wife into the plush waiting area of the attorney's office.

The woman behind the front desk smiled. "Good morning? How can I help you?"

"We're the Lundquists. We have an appointment with Ron."

"Of course. Have a seat and I'll let him know you're here."

Jay nodded and ushered Kate to a group of chairs to his right. The impeccably dressed woman picked up the receiver and spoke softly into the phone.

A moment later, the receptionist stood and asked them to follow her down the hall to Ron's office. She knocked lightly on the door before opening it and motioning for Jay and Kate to enter.

The couple passed through the door and Kate heard it close gently behind her.

"How are you, Kate?" Ron asked stepping around the large desk, taking her hand in his. "I wish we were meeting under more favorable circumstances." The attorney welcomed them warmly into his office and turned to shake Jay's hand as well.

"Thank you. I'm doing okay. It was quite a shock. I'm a little worried about telling the kids. They loved Penny so much."

"And she loved them. Whenever she and I met she always had such wonderful things to say about you and your children." Ron offered the couple a seat in the chairs facing the mahogany desk before he slipped into his own seat.

"Well, Jay, I'm sure you know how this goes, but Penny left very specific instructions." The attorney lifted a file folder and flipped it open, and read the document. "She wishes to be cremated and have her remains buried next to her husband in Ephraim. That will be taken care of very soon and you won't need to do anything for that. She did ask that you have a small memorial for her in Ephraim where they spent most of their lives."

Kate nodded.

"I have notified the funeral home in Ephraim that you would be contacting them to make arrangements. They have someone that can run an obituary in the paper down there, so I told them to do that. The woman I spoke with, Louise, actually knew Penny and was sad to hear of her death. She said that Penny was well known and well liked by the entire town."

"Good. I was worried about having a funeral up here because she's only lived here a short time. I wonder if there's someone that would like to speak and give a life sketch. I don't think I know enough about her to do that." Kate took a deep breath. "Did she leave a list of people to contact?"

"No. I'm afraid not. Maybe you can find an address book or something in her home. That's where I would start," Ron suggested.

"And who is the executor of the estate, Ron?" Jay asked.

"Why, Kate is. I thought Penny had told you," Ron turned a page in the folder. "She has left everything to you and asked that you sell anything you don't want. She also requested that all proceeds from the sale of any items go to Primary Children's Hospital." Ron looked up at the couple. "Any questions?"

Kate shrugged. "Well, yeah. What do I do first?"

Ron smiled. "You need to decide on a day for the memorial and let Louise down in Ephraim know. Then you need to put together the memorial program. It doesn't have to be long. Louise, I'm sure, will have some ideas for that."

She looked at her husband. "Maybe I could put a slide show together or something. It's going to be tricky since I really don't know anything about her life before she moved here."

Jay nodded. "We'll all help."

Ron stood up and shook the couple's hands. "Sounds good. Don't hesitate to call me with any other questions you have." Ron walked with the couple to the office door. "I'll talk to you soon. Thanks for coming in."

Jay held the car door as his wife climbed into her seat. "Should we run over to Penny's house now and see what we can find?" Kate asked.

"I have a meeting in an hour, but we can stop for a minute."

Jay headed south on the freeway and drove across town to Penny's home. They stepped into the empty house and turned on the lights.

"Should we look for an address book? She must have extended family, right?" She frowned and looked around the room. "I wonder where she would keep things like that?"

"Where do we keep ours?" Jay asked opening a drawer in a side table near the couch.

Kate smiled. "I keep mine in a drawer in the kitchen," she said heading to the other room.

They opened several drawers and rummaged through collections of recipe books and other assorted papers. At the back of a drawer full of office supplies was a worn book full of names and addresses. "I guess I'll start with this."

They locked the house and climbed back into the car. As they pulled onto the freeway, Jay turned to Kate who'd been sitting quietly looking through the book. "Any luck? I don't suppose the names are labeled with words like cousin or aunt." Jay chuckled softly.

"It's not going to be that easy. I'm not sure where to start. There isn't anyone with the last name of Haws. I assumed Del had brothers or cousins with that same last name, but there's nothing listed." Kate flipped through the book and read a few more names. "I suppose he could have had sisters and their names changed when they married. I don't know much about Penny and her husband. I might have to search her things to figure out whom to call. It's going to take me days to go through everything." Kate sighed as she thought about the task ahead of her. She hadn't slept very well last night, thinking about her sweet friend and how she was going to miss her bright smiling face.

"I'm sorry about this, Kate. I wish I could help you, but I have to get back to work," Jay said as he exited toward home. "I think you might want to write a short letter and send it to everyone in the address book letting them know Penny has died. Especially those that don't live near enough to hear about it in the newspaper."

"I guess you're right. I'll do that tomorrow." Kate closed her eyes and leaned her head against the seat. "I'm sure Janae will want to help, but first I need to tell the kids that Penny died. I don't even know how to do that." She shook her head. "They're going to be so . . ." Kate sniffed, "heartbroken."

Jay reached across and held her hand as a several tears trickled down her cheeks. "They'll be fine. They're strong."

"I know. They have suffered more than I ever have. Losing their mother had to be so difficult." Kate heaved a sigh and looked across at her husband. "Should I wait for you to come home to tell them?"

"Sure." Jay put the car in park and leaned across to kiss his wife. "I'll be home for dinner."

Kate climbed from the car and waved as her husband pulled away from the curb. She found Janae sitting in front of the television with Megan on her lap. "Hi honey. How'd it go?"

"Fine. We just had a piece of peanut butter toast and some milk. I was about to put her in bed."

Kate reached for Megan and snuggled her against her chest. The baby babbled hello before popping two fingers into her mouth. "Are you ready for a nap?" Kate asked, patting her daughter's back as she wandered down the hall. "I could use a nap myself."

"Can I go to Marianne's now?" Janae stood and followed Kate down the hall. "We're going to walk down to get a snow cone."

"Yes. Do you have money?"

"Uh huh." Janae stepped into the bedroom she shared with Megan and opened a drawer. She stuffed a couple dollars into her pocket. "Mitch said to tell you he would be at Tyson's shooting hoops." Kate was glad that Mitch was more careful about letting someone know where he was after the incident last week.

"Alright. Thanks for watching Megan. Try to be home by four o'clock okay?" Janae nodded as Kate pulled the door shut on the room. "What should we have for dinner?" she asked Janae.

"Tacos."

Janae always asked for tacos or enchiladas, but Kate didn't mind. Those were two things she'd become quite good at making. Cooking still wasn't on the top of her list of favorite things to do, but she found great satisfaction in providing a meal for her family.

"Sounds good. We'll see you in a few hours then. Have fun and be safe." Kate smiled as the girl left through the front door and ran down the block toward her friend's house.

Kate stepped to the freezer and pulled a package of hamburger from inside and placed it in the microwave to defrost. The little dog scratched at the door seeming to know that Kate was starting to fix dinner.

"Hello, Rudi." She scratched the dog's head and filled his water dish. He lapped at the water and gazed expectantly up at Kate. "It's not time for dinner yet."

She picked up her phone and dialed Connie's number. She would see her friend at work tomorrow, but she wanted to tell her about Penny's death before she heard it from someone else.

"Hey, Connie. How are you? Are you busy?"

"No I have a minute. What's up?"

"I'm afraid I have some bad news." Kate paused. "Jay and I went to check on Penny last night . . . and well, she didn't answer the door. Her neighbor had a key so we let ourselves in and we found her in bed." Kate blinked back the tears that threatened. "She died, Connie. Probably a couple days ago and no one was there with her. I feel terrible about it."

She heard Connie's breath catch. "What? She died?"

"Yeah. I don't know how. Jay thinks she had a heart attack. But anyway, I just talked to her lawyer today and he says Penny named me, as the executor of her will, so I get to clear out her house. Sounds familiar doesn't it . . . and I'm supposed to plan her memorial too."

"Wow, Kate. I'm so sorry. What can I do to help?"

"Well, I have to work tomorrow for Robin, so I thought maybe tonight after Jay gets home I would go to Penny's house and start cleaning." The microwave beeped and Kate opened the door, turned the package of meat over and pushed start again. "Do you want to come help me with that? I thought maybe we could put together a slide show of her life, but I don't know much about her past. I don't even know if she has family around that could help with that." She chewed on her lip. "The police are looking for her next of kin."

"Of Course. I'd like to help. What time are you going over?"

"About six thirty, I guess," Kate said as she pulled a frying pan from the cupboard.

"I have to make sure my husband will be home by then, but I'll try to be there. Oh hey, I've got to go." Connie said goodbye and hung up the phone.

Janae and Mitch arrived home just as Megan was waking from her nap. "Do you want to grab the baby Mitch?"

The young man strolled down the hall and tossed his basketball into his bedroom. A few moments later he reappeared with the one year old in his arms. "What did you do today, Megan?" he asked as he sat on the couch and repositioned his sister in his lap.

The baby babbled happily and smiled up at the redheaded boy. "Oh yeah?" Mitch laughed and looked over his shoulder at his stepmother. "When will she start to talk?"

"She does talk. She says ball and dada," Janae said as she sat down next to Mitch and Megan. "And she says cup and uh oh."

"Yeah, but when will she really talk?" he patted the baby's head and smiled.

"Most babies can make simple sentences by the time they are two," Kate explained as she pulled the cheese from the fridge and began to grate it onto a plate. She watched as Janae and Mitch tickled and talked to the baby.

"Marianne's little sister is three and she talks constantly! But she's hard to understand sometimes. I always have to ask Marianne what she said." Janae reached for her sister. "My turn."

Mitch handed the baby to her and stood up from the couch. "What's for dinner?"

"Tacos," his sister called out.

The boy sneaked a pinch of cheese and sat on a stool at the counter.

"I'm starving."

Kate smiled at the boy and stepped to the pantry. Mitch was always hungry. She found a box of Spanish rice. "I just have to make this rice and then as soon as Dad gets here we'll eat."

Kate pulled a pot from the shelf and set it on the stove. She tore open the box of rice and poured it into the pan as Janae stepped into the kitchen with Megan on her hip.

"I had this crazy dream last night about Grandma P. She was riding a horse. She was younger, but I knew it was Penny because of the three moles on her face. Isn't that weird? I'm going to ask her if she's ever been on a horse." Janae smiled down at Megan. "Do you think Grandma P has ever ridden a horsey?" She bounced Megan making the little girl laugh.

Kate watched her daughters for a moment. She tried to collect her thoughts as she read the instructions on the back of the box. She had hoped to put this conversation off until after dinner. She removed a measuring cup from the cupboard, and measured the water for the packaged rice. She turned on the heat, placed the lid over the pan and turned back to the children.

"Come sit down for a minute." She gestured to the living room. "I was hoping to wait until your father got here to tell you something, but maybe I won't." Janae and Mitch followed her to the couch. "Is something wrong?" the girl asked setting the baby in her lap.

Looking at the three children lined up on the couch, Kate had an overwhelming feeling of love wash over her. She smiled at her stepchildren and wondered how she'd ever even existed before they were in her life. It broke her heart to have to tell them about Penny's death, but she couldn't wait any longer. "Your dad and I went to see Penny on Monday night, you know, and well . . ." Kate chewed her lip and clasped her hands together. "We couldn't get her to come to the door, but her neighbor, Kim, you've met Kim right Janae?" The girl nodded and Kate continued. "She had a key, so we went inside to see if Penny was home."

"She died, didn't she?" Mitch asked matter-of-factly.

Janae's mouth fell open. "No!" The young woman looked to her stepmother for confirmation and Kate nodded.

"Yes. I'm so sorry."

Janae's face twisted in pain and she quickly set the baby on the floor with a thump before rushing down the hall to her bedroom. Megan began to cry and Kate hurried to pick her up. She soothed the baby and looked down at Mitch. "I wasn't sure how to tell you guys. How did you know?"

"You just seemed so nervous and Grandma P was old." Mitch shrugged his shoulders and stood up. He walked into the kitchen and pulled open the fridge. "Should I make some juice?"

"Sure." Kate found a toy for Megan and set her on the floor. "Oh! I didn't set a timer for the rice." She stepped to the stove and quickly turned down the heat. She stirred the rice and replaced the lid. "It probably needs another ten minutes, I guess," she said as she pushed a button on the timer. "Will you keep an eye on it while I go talk to Janae?"

Mitch nodded as he opened the can of frozen juice and found a pitcher. "So when's the funeral?"

Kate stopped and turned back. "I don't know yet—probably next week sometime. We have to notify her family that she's passed on." Kate waited for a response from the young man.

He nodded and squeezed the contents of the can into the pitcher and started adding water. "I'll miss her, but I know she's fine where she is."

His stepmother sighed. "Yes. She's with her husband and other family now. It's always hardest on those of us that are left behind."

Kate turned and walked down the hall, not sure what she was going to say to Janae.

Chapter 8

The doorbell startled Kate as she sat on the floor surrounded by stacks of papers in the little office in Penny's house. She had been searching through files trying to find any family members to contact about the old woman's death. She set down the file in her hand and slowly stood up, stretching her legs as she made her way to the front door. Connie stood on the porch with a box of donuts in her hand.

"I thought we would need some sugar to keep us going."

"Thanks. Come in." Kate closed the door behind her friend. "I've been looking through her files, but I haven't found anything useful yet. Mostly just bank statements and utility bills. Penny kept everything it seems."

"And now you get to sort through it all. I am not looking forward to doing that when my father dies. He is the biggest pack rat I know," Connie said setting her purse and the donuts on the couch. She laughed and followed Kate into the back bedroom.

Kate nodded. "And I don't dare throw anything away yet. I have to make sure all her bills are paid and find out if she owns this home or if she was renting." She sighed. "I'm tired just thinking about it."

"Well, that's why I'm here. Tell me what to do." Connie paused at the bookshelf and lifted a framed photograph. "Is this Penny with her parents? Wow, she and her mother looked almost identical."

"Yes, it must be." Kate gazed at the picture of Penny as a teenager, standing between a man and a woman who were obviously her parents. "She's so young. Let's put that one in the box. I'm taking a few things home to use in the slideshow." Kate pointed at a box by the door. Connie set the picture in the box and returned to Kate's side.

"I need to find more pictures of her family. I only have the ones that were sitting out in frames and there weren't even very many. If I remember right she was an only child. But I have been trying to remember if her husband Del had any brothers or sisters."

"Maybe we should look for photo albums." Connie looked around the room. "Have you seen any?"

"Not yet. I was hoping to finish looking through this filing cabinet first, but I can do that later. I bet she has boxes of photographs somewhere."

Kate moved toward the closet in the room and pulled the bi-fold doors open. There were several boxes stacked on the floor and several more lined up on the shelf above. "These look promising." She lifted a box and handed it to Connie. "Let's move out into the living room where we have more room." The two women stepped over the pile of folders and moved into the larger room, each carrying a box from the closet.

Connie smiled as she opened her box. "Jackpot. There are photo albums in this one. What did you find?"

"Tax returns." Kate set her box aside and moved to the couch next to Connie.

"Old black and whites. I love these!" Connie exclaimed as she opened the first book and studied the timeworn photographs.

"Maybe we should put a sticky note on the pages we want to use. I'll see if she has any in the kitchen." Kate stepped to a desk area where a can of pens stood beside a landline phone and several phone books. She spotted a stack of colorful sticky notes and carried it back to the living room. "Have you found any good ones?"

"Yeah. This album is of her wedding. It looks like it was an extravagant affair. Her parents must have had money," Connie said looking over at Kate.

"Well, Penny was their only daughter. They probably wanted it to be special since it was her mother's one chance to throw a wedding," Kate said leaning to get a better view. "Go back to the beginning, so I can see it all."

The two women perused the photo album placing sticky notes on several pages. "I wonder if there are any names on the backs of the pictures. I still need to figure out if any of these people are still alive and let them know about the memorial service," Kate said as she tapped what looked to be a photo of the family.

Connie pulled the picture free and flipped it over, but the back was empty. "Sorry."

Kate took the picture and studied it further. "These teenagers would still be alive you'd think and this younger couple too. How am I going to get names and phone numbers?"

"Do you even know her parents' names?" Connie asked flipping back through the album to a picture of Penny's parents. "And I wonder if Del's parents came to the wedding."

"I have no idea," Kate said.

"Where did they get married?" Connie asked as Kate shrugged her shoulders. "You need a marriage license or something."

"Right and a birth certificate for both Del and Penny. They must have those here in the house somewhere." Kate reached into the box and pulled out another album. "Maybe one of these has stuff like that in it."

Kate opened to the first page and found a picture of Penny and Del smiling in front of a small house with 1978 written across the bottom of the photo. "Well, there's the first date I've seen. Maybe Penny was better about putting names and dates on pictures in this book."

Several photos were of Del sitting on the back of a horse and Kate paused on a picture of Penny standing in front of a diner. "Look at that—Penny's Diner. She told me she worked at a diner, but I didn't know it was named after her." Kate laughed. "Maybe it was just a coincidence."

Connie pointed to a photo on the next page. "Hey. This one has names. Luther and Lizzy."

The two people in the picture were standing in front of the diner. The thin blond woman was wearing an apron and squinting into the sun, her hand raised in an attempt to shield the bright sun from her eyes. Luther, the burly black man, had his arm around Lizzy and a friendly smile on his face.

"I wonder if they're still around? Maybe I can find Luther and Lizzy and get some good stories about Penny. They probably knew her pretty well." Kate put a sticky note on the page. "I should try to find out if the diner is still open. Maybe the owner could give me more information too." Kate looked up at the clock. "Hopefully I can find a number and call them tomorrow."

"It sounds like you might need to make a road trip to Ephraim," Connie said as she reached for a donut and moved into the kitchen. "Do you think there's any milk in the house?"

Kate shrugged. "You can check the fridge. I haven't even looked in there yet. It's just another thing on my to-do list. I might need to recruit more help."

Connie pulled the door to the fridge open. "It's pretty empty actually and nothing smells bad." Connie lifted the milk and read the expiration date. "July 29th. What's today? The 28th?"

Kate's breath caught. "Is it really the 28th?"

"I think so. Why?"

"Oh my goodness!" Kate looked up at Connie as she returned to the living room with a glass of milk. "Today is my anniversary! How could I forget? Jay didn't even say anything when he kissed me good-bye tonight."

"Maybe he forgot too." Connie bit into her donut and chewed thoughtfully. "You guys are pretty busy."

Kate shook her head and massaged her neck. "I suppose we wouldn't really do anything until the weekend anyway, but I should have at least said something to him."

"Don't worry. You can make it up to him." Connie giggled and Kate blushed. Reaching into the box of donuts, Kate found a donut with chocolate sprinkles and took a tiny nibble.

"Do you really think I have to make a trip to Ephraim?" Kate asked changing the subject.

"It would probably be helpful. Didn't you say there was someone at the funeral home that knew Penny? I bet there are other people in town that remember her." Connie licked her fingers and finished her glass of milk.

"You're probably right. I work tomorrow, though, and I can't really leave until the weekend anyway. I guess I'll finish going through things here and then go down on Saturday. Do you want to come?" Kate asked.

"I would, but I can't. My older brother is in town with his family from Iowa, so we're having lunch and spending the day at the park with everybody."

"That's okay. I suppose I can go on my own. I guess I'll make a list of names from these photos and see if I can track people down." Kate pulled a pen from her purse and searched for a piece of paper. "I need something bigger than these sticky notes." She walked to the desk in the kitchen and found a pad of paper. The name Guy was written across the top of the page with a phone number scrawled underneath. She pulled that page free and set it next to the phone.

She returned to the couch and wrote Luther and Lizzy on the paper. "Did you see any other names in that book?"

"Maybe." Connie skimmed through the book and found a picture of a little boy with a dog at his side. "This guy's name is Roberto. He was about eight or nine years old I would guess." She turned a few more pages and found a photo of a tall unshaven man with the name Finn written across the bottom. "And this is Finn apparently."

Kate added the names to her list. "Not much to go off of, but maybe someone will know them."

The two women searched through two more photo albums and added one more name to Kate's list, Karen. "She must have worked with Penny too. See? She has the same apron on." Connie tapped the photo of the teenage girl. "This had to be taken in the 80's. Look at Karen's hairstyle. Big bangs that stood up on end were so unflattering. I don't know why anyone thought they looked good."

"I guess you never wore your hair like that?" Kate laughed.

"I'm not that old. I was still wearing pigtails in the eighties." Connie set the book on the coffee table and stood to stretch her back. "It's getting late. I think I better get going."

Kate stood beside her friend and nodded in agreement. "I guess I can put this box back." She picked up the box of tax returns and stepped back into the office with Connie trailing behind. "Oh. I need to put away these folders that I got out earlier."

She set the box in the closet and began to retrieve the file folders from the floor. Connie reached for a folder and the contents spilled out onto the carpet. "Oops. I didn't realize it was full of newspaper clippings." Connie gathered up the papers, reading a few of the headlines as she tucked them back in the folder. "Some of these are pretty old." She held up a clipping that was marked with red ink. "This one's about a guy named Ralph Walker who was injured in a construction accident in 1983. It says he was impaled!"

"That sounds painful." Kate grimaced.

Connie skimmed a few more titles. "They're all about different kinds of accidents and other tragedies. Maybe Penny's husband was preoccupied with catastrophes." Connie shook her head as she collected more papers. "My husband, Chris, loves to watch those Emergency Room shows on TV. You know the ones about terrible car accidents or people that get stuck in farm equipment. " Connie looked up at Kate with a shiver.

"Jay loves that too. It must be a guy thing." Kate leaned closer.

"Yeah. I suppose." Connie picked up the remaining clippings and found one with a sticky note on it. "Hey this one is more recent." She glanced at the article and drew in a sharp breath. "This is about my brother, Brock, and his accident."

Chapter 9

The house was dark as Kate pulled into the garage. She climbed from the car as the automatic door closed behind her. She stretched her neck and opened the door into the kitchen. She flipped on the light and found a beautiful bouquet of flowers on the island in the kitchen with a tiny card tucked into the center. Kate pulled the card free and read the note from her husband.

"Happy Anniversary to my beautiful wife! Kate, my love for you grows more every day! Love, Jay"

Kate smiled and read the note a second time before leaning toward the roses. "I can't believe I didn't remember," she mumbled as she made her way down the hall to her bedroom. She could see the light on under the office door. Jay was still up.

She slipped off her shoes and padded across the room to the bathroom. After brushing her teeth, she crossed the hall and quietly opened the door to the office. Jay was sitting in his recliner, his reading glasses on his face, but his eyes were closed. Kate's breath caught as she watched for his chest to rise. She drew nearer and her husband startled awake, making her sigh with relief.

"I'm sorry. Did I wake you?" She stepped to the side of his chair and smiled.

"I guess I dozed off." Jay pushed the recliner into a seated position and took Kate's hand pulling her into his lap. "How did it go?"

"Fine. I found a bunch of pictures to use and lots of other junk that I will most likely just get rid of. It's going to be a big headache to go through it all."

Jay nodded. "I'll have to come help next time." He wrapped his arms around her and sighed. "I'm glad you're home."

"I love the flowers," Kate said, as she snuggled into her husband's embrace and sighed at the comfort she found there. "What an awful wife I am, though. I can't believe I forgot." Kate frowned and looked up into Jay's face.

He kissed her gently and whispered in her ear. "Don't worry. We can celebrate it later."

"I know but I still feel bad."

"How about I take you out to dinner tomorrow night."

"That's sounds like a great idea," Kate said as she covered a yawn. "I'm sorry. I'm beat."

Jay pushed Kate to her feet and followed her into the bedroom. "I think it's time to tuck you into bed."

The couple knelt beside the bed and Kate managed to stay awake as her husband prayed for continued guidance and blessings for his family. At the close of the prayer, Kate leaned toward her husband and placed a kiss on his lips. "Thanks. I love you. Happy anniversary."

"I love you too," he said as Kate climbed into bed. Jay pulled the blanket up over his wife and leaned down to kiss her once more. "I'll come to bed after I shut down my computer."

"Ok. I'll see you in a few minutes," Kate said as she rolled onto her side.

The morning sun broke through the blinds at the window and Kate was surprised to find it was already seven in the morning. She hadn't heard Jay come to bed and she hadn't heard him get up for the day. She scrambled out of bed and threw on a robe before stepping into the hall. She could hear a few noises coming from the kitchen and was pleasantly surprised to find both of her daughters at the table with a bowl of cereal in front of them.

"You should have gotten me up." Kate slid into the seat next to Janae and smiled at Megan who was seated in the antique high chair. Two years ago, Kate had rescued the old chair from her grandmother's things when the family home had been put up for sale.

"That's okay. I know you were tired from working at Grandma P's." Janae shrugged and gave a tiny smile.

Kate was glad to see a smile on the girl's face. Janae had been so troubled about Penny's death. With time, she hoped her stepdaughter would return to the happy girl she was.

"Yes. It's going to be a big job to get everything taken care of." She rested her hand on Janae's arm. "Maybe you could come help me next time I go."

Janae nodded as Megan dropped her spoon on the floor. Kate stood and picked up the spoon and rinsed it at the sink. "I have to work today. I switched days with Robin."

"Is Grandma coming over here?" Janae asked.

"No. I am taking Megan to Aunt Anna's for a play date with Bella," Kate said as she began to feed Megan the rest of her breakfast.

Kate's sister Anna had a daughter just six months older than Megan. Bella was Anna's fourth child, but first daughter. Anna loved having Megan over to play and it worked well when Kate's mother wasn't available to babysit.

"Can I go over too? Marianne is out of town with her family and I'll just be bored here," Janae said as she took her bowl to the sink. "I could work on addressing the envelopes and getting the notes sent about Grandma P's death."

"That would be great. We need to get them sent today if we can." Kate lifted her youngest from the chair and washed her tiny hands at the sink. "Did you change her already?" Kate asked Janae. "She doesn't feel very wet this morning."

"I did, but she wouldn't let me dress her, so I just put her pajamas back on."

"Okay. I'll dress her and then jump in the shower. Thanks honey." Kate wandered down the hall and quickly dressed the baby in shorts and a top. She heard the shower start in the hall bathroom as she carried Megan into the master bedroom. "I guess you get to watch something while I shower. Let's see if Mickey is on this morning."

Kate set the baby on the floor as Mickey Mouse appeared on the screen singing a silly song. Megan would be distracted for at least ten minutes, which would be long enough for Kate to quickly shower.

Janae chattered with the baby in the back as Kate drove the short distance to her sister's home. "I'll pick you up at about three thirty," Kate explained as she pulled up to the curb. She unbuckled her seatbelt and hurried to remove Megan from the back of the car.

Janae approached the house and rang the bell, waiting as they heard a commotion on the other side of the door. Her cousins, ten-year-old Robbie and eight-year-old Calvin pulled the door open and stared through the screen at them.

"Let them in," Kate heard her sister call in an exasperated voice. Anna sounded a bit stressed already for being so early in the day. The boys pushed the storm door open and Kate followed Janae into the house. Megan wiggled to get down when she saw Bella sitting on the floor with a doll in her hand.

"How are you this morning, Bella?" Janae asked as she squatted in front of the eighteen-month-old girl. Bella smiled shyly at Janae and popped her thumb into her mouth. Kate set Megan next to her young cousin and grinned as the two little girls smiled happily at each other.

"Thanks for doing this, Anna." Kate stood up and looked at her sister who was still in her robe, her hair pulled back in a messy bun and her face bare of any makeup—a very uncharacteristic look for Anna. "Is everything okay?"

Anna sighed deeply. "Yeah." She tugged at the belt of her housecoat and stepped into the living room. "I was up late working on the dresser I'm refinishing. The sprayer was clogged and the paint went on unevenly. A lady is coming to look at it tonight, so I wanted to redo the whole thing before I went to bed." She pushed a stray hair out of her eyes. "It turned out pretty nice, but I didn't get to bed until after midnight."

Kate nodded. "I'll have to see it when I get back." She motioned to her stepdaughter. "Janae wants to stay today, so she can help with the kids."

Anna smiled brightly at Janae. "That will definitely help." Anna stepped to the front door, hiding behind it as she opened it for her sister. "We'll be fine. You go to work. We'll see you after three, right?"

"Yes. Thanks."

Kate went to her car and drove to the hair salon in Spanish Fork. Connie was washing a woman's hair and smiled as Kate put her purse in the back room.

"How did you sleep? I kept waking up. I had some crazy dreams about Penny and some guy named Roger." Connie shut off the water and helped her client sit up. "I don't even know any Rogers," she said as she dried the lady's hair with a towel.

Kate tied on her apron and stepped to the front desk. "Not me. I was wiped out. I didn't wake up even once and I don't remember any dreams." She flipped through the appointment book and found Penny's next appointment and took a steadying breath before erasing it. The bell on the front door chimed and her day began.

She was busy with clients all day, which kept her mind off the fact that Penny was gone, but her mind wandered a few times to the monumental task of clearing out the woman's house.

"Are you going back over to Penny's again tonight?" Connie asked as she ate lunch in the back with Kate.

"Jay is taking me to dinner for our anniversary, so I don't think I'll go tonight."

"Oh right. Had he forgotten about it too?" Connie asked sipping her drink.

"No. There was a bouquet of flowers waiting for me when I got home. I felt so bad." Kate stood and tossed her trash in the wastebasket.

Connie nodded and followed Kate to the front of the salon as Connie's sister-in-law walked in the door. "Hi Emily," Connie said as she tied her apron. "Come on over." The woman set her purse on the floor and sat heavily into the chair.

Kate stepped to her own station and smiled at Emily. "Hi. How are you?"

"Fine. How's your baby girl?" the woman asked leaning forward to see the picture taped to Kate's mirror.

"She's walking and thinks she doesn't need a second nap." Kate sighed.

"Oh no. That's always tough." Emily answered as Connie snapped the protective cover around her.

Connie began mixing the color for her sister-in-law as Kate straightened her bottles of hair products. "And how's your husband?" Kate asked. "Is he in a walking cast yet?"

Brock, Connie's brother, had been in a serious car accident a few weeks earlier. Connie said that they were really struggling financially trying to care for their three growing kids. Emily didn't work outside the home, so Brock was the only source of income and he hadn't been able to work since the accident.

"Yes, he's off the crutches, but has to wear the boot for another month. It's not the best situation, but at least he can work . . . sort of."

"Did Brock find a truck?" Connie asked as she started to apply the hair dye to her sister-in-law's hair.

Emily's face suddenly lit up. "It's funny you should ask. You're never going to believe what happened last night!"

Chapter 10

"You know Brock had been searching the classifieds to find a truck we could afford, but that's been nearly impossible," Emily said with a pout. "We weren't even sure how we were going to pay off the medical bills let alone buy a new truck." The woman frowned, but suddenly her face brightened as she continued the story. "But last night just as we were putting the kids to bed this guy knocks on our door and asks to speak with Brock. He says he has some good news . . ." The bell chimed and a new customer came through the door interrupting the conversation.

Kate jumped up from her chair. "Oh! That's my next client." She pointed at Emily. "Let me get started with Kristen, but then I want to hear what happened." She beckoned for her newest patron to take a seat in the swivel chair.

Kate draped the woman and pumped the seat a bit higher. "Hi, Kristen. What are we doing today?"

"Just a trim. I don't even have time for a wash," Kristen said with a grimace. The hairdresser nodded and spritzed Kristen's hair with water.

"But I do have good news. I finally have a job interview in an hour." Kate knew that Kristen had been looking for work for several months now.

"That's great. Is it something you'll enjoy?"

"Yes! I'll be doing web design which is what I studied in school."

Kate began combing through her hair. "I'm so happy for you." The hairdresser paused and lifted a lock of hair. "How much should I take off?"

"An inch maybe?" Kristen scrunched up her face. "And if you can style it for me that would be fantastic."

"Are you doing anything fun this weekend?" Kate asked as she pulled her scissors from her pocket.

"Well, I guess so . . . if you think babysitting a bunch of kids is fun." Kristen laughed at the hairdresser's look of surprise. "I'm watching my sister's kids for a few days while she goes on a cruise."

"Wow. You're a good sister to do that."

The two women chatted for the remainder of the haircut until Kate began to dry and style Kristen's hair.

Connie finished applying the color to Emily's hair and set a timer. "Do you want something to read?"

"Sure."

Connie handed her sister-in-law a magazine and stepped to the counter to answer the phone. When she returned, Kate had finished with Kristen and was handing the younger woman a mirror.

"Looks great. Hopefully it will help me get the job," Kristen said as she stood up and pulled out her wallet. "Babysitting is fine, but it doesn't quite pay the bills."

As Kristen left the salon, Kate began sweeping up the hair on the floor. "Okay. So who was this guy at the door? An insurance agent or something?"

Emily set the magazine in her lap and shook her head. "No. He was a young kid—maybe early twenties—and he seemed kind of nervous. He said he had something for us and asked us to come outside with him. I was worried at first since we didn't know him. I mean he seemed nice, but it was late at night . . . ." Emily laughed nervously and Connie raised an eyebrow in her direction. "But you know Brock—nothing fazes him, so he just followed the man out the door. I grabbed my phone, ready to call the cops, in case this guy tried anything funny."

Kate collected the hair in the dustpan and put the broom away as Emily continued her story. "But it turns out he was a good guy and you'll never guess what he had for us." Emily paused dramatically.

Connie shrugged.

Kate sat in her chair and asked, "What?"

"A new truck!" Emily reached up and scratched her nose. "Well it's not brand new, but better than the one we had. I thought Brock was going to cry when the kid told him it was his . . . with no strings attached."

"He just gave it to your husband? He doesn't have to pay for it?" Kate asked.

"Yeah. This guy . . . he never really told us his name, but he said all we needed to know was that someone had heard of Brock's accident and wanted to help."

"You mean he wasn't the one giving Brock the truck?" Kate asked.

"No, he said he was just the deliveryman . . . and he wouldn't tell us who it was."

Emily turned toward Connie, her excitement filling the room. "But that's not all. As we were admiring the truck, Brock said something about taking out a loan to replace the tools he'd lost, but the man shook his head and jumped up into the back. Brock leaned over the side of the bed and we watched in amazement as the man opened the built in tool box and stood back with a big grin on his face." Emily licked her lips and swung her gaze back to Kate. "The box was full of tools."

Kate blinked and looked across the room at Connie. "Cool!"

Emily continued, "Brock won't admit it, but I know he had tears in his eyes at that point. He kept saying 'wow' as this guy showed him the different tools in the box."

The timer began to ring announcing the end of the color treatment and another customer came through the door. Kate moved to the counter and Connie began to rinse her sister-in-law's hair.

Fifteen minutes later, Kate had given the male customer a haircut and Connie was trimming Emily's hair.

"So anyway. Before the man left us last night, he handed Brock the keys and the title to the truck." Emily took a deep breath and wiped at her eyes. "It couldn't have come at a better time. We thought about it all night trying to figure out who would have done this for us, but we can't even imagine who had the money to do that sort of thing."

Kate could see more tears collecting in Emily's eyes. Connie reached for a tissue and handed it to her.

"I'm so happy for you guys." Connie agreed with a smile. "But you know Chris is going to be so jealous. He's wanted a new truck for years. Will Brock be home tonight? Maybe we'll stop by to see it."

"He went to work today, but I don't know how he'll feel when he gets home. I told him not to overdo it, but he's been so bored lately I'm sure he's working harder than he should," Emily said as she adjusted the cape on her lap. "But just come over after dinner if you want to. We'll be home."

Kate checked the clock and realized it was time to leave. Her sister was probably past her breaking point. "I'm so happy for you, Emily. What a wonderful blessing. I have to get going though. It was so good to see you."

As Kate climbed into her car she decided to run over to Penny's house while she was in town and pick up a few boxes to look through before her date with Jay. Pulling up to the curb, Kate shut off the engine and stared up at the little house. How quickly life had changed. One day Penny was laughing and playing with her kids and the next day she was gone. Kate wondered if anyone in Penny's family was aware of her death. The police hadn't contacted her, so as far as she knew there was no immediate family in the picture. There had to be someone that checked in on the older lady occasionally.

She hurried up the stairs and pulled out the house key. She unlocked the door and slipped inside the muggy house. Her eyes roamed over the furniture in the room and her gaze rested on the organ in the corner.

"What am I going to do with all this stuff, Penny?" Kate sighed and moved through the house into the back bedroom. She picked up the boxes of photo albums and carried them to her car. She propped the front door open and went back in for another box. She decided to fill a box with file folders hoping that her husband would be able to decide if they were trash or not. She emptied the top drawer of the filing cabinet and carried it out to the car.

"Hello there?" a voice called from behind her. "Do you need any help?"

Kate spun around to find a woman dressed in shorts and a tank top standing on the sidewalk beside the car. "Oh hi. I think I've got it, but thanks."

The woman nodded and looked back up at the house. "I heard she died. So sad. I'm gonna miss her."

Corky, the little dog that liked to visit Penny came bounding up to the women.

Kate smiled. "Hey little dog. How are you?"

"Get down, Corky," Gigi commanded.

"Oh is he yours? I don't mind. I have a schnauzer too."

Kate stepped closer and extended her hand to the woman. "Hi. My name is Kate. I was Penny's hairdresser . . . and friend. You must live around here."

The woman looked down at Kate's hand and gripped it lightly. "Yeah. I'm Gigi. I live in the gray house." Gigi released Kate's hand and pointed down the block.

"Good to meet you. I've been asked to take care of her house. I also have to plan the funeral since she doesn't seem to have any family around. Did you know Penny well? Maybe you could say a few words about her at the funeral?"

The woman paled and shook her head. "I couldn't do that. I'm no good at talking in front of people." Gigi pushed a lock of hair behind an ear and looked across the yard at the dog. "When's the funeral? I would like to come pay my respects . . . but only if you don't make me say anything."

"Of course. That's fine." Kate waved off the worry. "It will be next Wednesday in Ephraim."

"Okay. Well . . . you let me know if you need anything. Penny was a good soul. She helped me get out of some pretty tight scrapes in the past." The woman turned away quickly and called to the dog. "Let's go Cork!"

Kate returned to the house and found another box of photo albums in the closet. She carried it to the porch, locked the door and stepped to the curb. She stowed the last box in the backseat and climbed behind the wheel.

As she drove past Gigi's home she wondered what Penny had done to help the woman. Those were the type of stories she was hoping to share at the memorial, but first she had to find people who had stories to tell. She would start with the list of names she'd made the other night. Hopefully some of them were still around.

Chapter 11

Jay rolled over and hugged Kate as dawn broke through the bedroom window. "Good morning sweetheart. Did you sleep well?"

"Yes. Much better. That wonderful dinner last night put me in a coma." Kate laughed as she remembered going to bed on a full stomach. Jay had taken Kate to her favorite restaurant and spoiled her rotten. They'd dined on lobster and salmon, topping the meal off with a chocolate mousse.

"I know, but it was worth every bite, wasn't it?" Jay snuggled her tighter and kissed the top of her head. "I especially enjoyed the company though." They lay in silence for a few moments before Jay spoke again. "What are your plans for today? Are you working at Penny's?"

"I have a few phone calls to make and a bunch of boxes to sort through. I suppose I'll shred those old documents you said were trash. Then I'll see if I can reach the owner of the diner."

"It sounds like you're going to be about as busy as I am today." He kissed her one last time and threw the covers back. As he headed for the shower he turned back. "Will you make sure Mitch mows the lawn today. He said he would do it yesterday, but it didn't get done."

"I know. I was gone all day and I guess he ended up getting called into work." Kate sat up and stretched her back.

Mitch had begun working at the local grocery store as a bagger and Kate had hardly seen him much in the last couple of days. They needed to have a family day soon and take the kids hiking or on a picnic. Maybe once the funeral was over they'd have time for that.

Kate dressed in a pair of sweats and an old t-shirt and wandered to the kitchen. If she hurried she'd be able to make breakfast for Jay and the kids before he headed off to work. She fed the dog and put him out. She began frying the bacon and scrambled six eggs in a bowl. She popped two pieces of bread into the toaster.

As she set four plates on the table, she heard Megan beginning to stir. She pulled glasses from the cupboard and hoped Janae would bring her sister out. After setting the glasses on the table, she turned to find Jay standing in the kitchen with Megan in his arms and her favorite blanket clutched in her tiny hands.

"Look who woke up in time to see daddy before he left." Jay kissed the baby's fuzzy head and Megan nestled her face into Jay's chest, a smile spreading across her tiny face. The little girl adored her father and from the look on Jay's face, the feelings were mutual.

Kate turned the bacon and pushed the lever down on the toaster. "I'm sorry. It will be another few minutes. Do you have time to eat?" she asked as she wiped her hands on a towel.

"Yes, I can wait." Jay patted the child's diaper. "Should I change her?"

Kate nodded. "If you wouldn't mind."

Jay spoke softly to Megan as he walked back down the hallway, pausing as the blanket slipped to the floor. He bent to pick it up and a memory surfaced in Kate's mind.

"What a lovely blanket, Penny. Did you make it?" Kate asked as she pulled the soft yellow coverlet from the gift bag.

"Oh no. I never learned to do that. My aunt made it a long time ago for . . ." Penny stopped abruptly, her lips pressed together tightly. She looked down at Megan who slept soundly in her arms before glancing back at Kate with a feeble smile. *"I want Megan to have it."*

Kate studied the woman's face briefly as she fingered the knitted afghan. "It's lovely. Thank you, Penny." She leaned forward to kiss Penny's wrinkled cheek and placed the blanket over her two-month-old daughter. *"We'll cherish it always."*

Kate's family walked into the dining room as she set the syrup and ketchup on the table. She glanced at the baby in her husband's arms and noticed that Jay had put the child in a dress—her nicest church dress.

Oh well, Kate thought with a smile.

"Don't you look pretty this morning," Kate said as she lifted the baby and put her in the high chair. "Mitch can you grab her a bib. We don't want to spoil her nice dress."

The family ate a quick meal before Jay hurried out the door. Mitch returned to his room and Kate heard the shower start a few minutes later. Janae helped clean the baby's face and hands before taking her out of the chair.

"You can set her on the floor with a few toys and go get ready for your class."

Kate cleaned up the kitchen and carried Megan back to the master bedroom. She changed into a clean shirt and a pair of jeans and quickly ran a brush through her shoulder length hair. "I guess I'll shower later," she said looking into the mirror as she pulled her hair into a messy bun.

A knock sounded at the bedroom door as she scooped up the baby. She opened the door and found Mitch on the other side. "I have to work in a couple of hours, but I thought I'd go see Tyson first."

"Well, actually your dad asked me to remind you to mow the lawn today. It might rain later, so I think you'd better do that this morning." Kate wished Jay had mentioned it to his son before he'd left for work. She hated being the nag.

Mitch took a deep breath and turned away. "Fine, but I don't see why it has to be mowed. It looks fine."

Kate shrugged and followed the boy down the hall. "Well, Dad thinks it needs it." She set the baby on the floor in the living room. "Thanks Mitch. I know you're busy now that you're working, but we still need help around the house."

Mitch mumbled something and grabbed his iPod from the charger in the kitchen before heading to the garage. Kate tore off her shopping list from the pad and put it in her purse. After dropping off Janae, she hoped to run to the store for a few things. Janae came into the kitchen and sat on the stool at the counter.

"When is Grandma P's funeral?" she asked as she picked up a pen and tapped it on the counter.

"Oh. I need to call the funeral home and set that up. I forgot to do that." Kate looked at the clock. "I wonder if anyone is there yet." It was only eight thirty. "The funeral will be next week for sure, but I will call and make arrangements today. Would you like me to braid your hair? I think we have time?"

Janae bobbed her head and Kate went to find a comb and a hair tie. She put a French braid down the back of the girl's head and spritzed it with a bit of water.

"There you go. It's getting so long. We might want to trim it again." Kate remembered the first time she had ever cut Janae's hair. Jay had brought the kids into the salon for haircuts and she had ended up cutting Jay's hair as well. She hadn't known he was a widower at that time, but soon found out when he asked her out on a date. It was only a short time later that they were engaged and a few weeks more that they were married. Some days it seemed like ages ago, and at other times it felt as if it was just yesterday.

Kate's phone began to ring, shaking her from her thoughts. She rushed to grab it. She didn't recognize the number.

"Hello?" she said as she moved to sit down at the table.

"Is this Kate Lundquist?" a woman's voice asked on the other end.

"Yes."

"Hello Kate. This is Louise from the Olsen Funeral Home in Ephraim. I was given your number in order to make arrangements for Penny's funeral. I'm not disturbing you, am I?"

"Oh Louise. I'm sorry I didn't call you. I meant to, but I have been so busy." Kate stood to find a pencil and paper and motioned for Janae to follow Megan who was wandering away from her toys.

"Don't you worry about that now, honey, I'm sure you're busy. We do need to settle on a day for the funeral, though. I am going to run the announcement in the paper and need a date. Would next Wednesday work? Say about one in the afternoon?" Louise asked.

Kate stood in front of the calendar on the wall. "Yes. Of course that would be just fine." Kate jotted the time on the calendar. "Now do I remember right that you will make up the program?"

Louise answered quickly. "Yes, honey. You just tell me who will do the speaking and what songs you'd like and I'll have it printed up."

Kate chewed on the pencil in thought. "Well, that's my problem. I don't know who should speak and I wish I knew Penny's favorite songs. You don't happen to have any suggestions?"

Louise began to rattle off names of people that knew Penny and Kate scribbled them on the paper in her hand. The woman suggested a few hymns that she might choose from as well.

"Now Kate, you don't have to figure it all out right now. I can print the program the night before. You take your time and get back to me when you can."

Kate took a breath and looked back at the paper. "I will. Thanks for all of your help Louise. I appreciate it."

"Oh I love to help. It gives me such pleasure." Louise paused. "We sure do miss Penny. She was like sunshine to this town and when she left we almost didn't know what to do with ourselves. I'm sure she's bringing light and joy to the souls in heaven even as we speak."

"I'm sure you're right. Thanks again." Kate began to say goodbye, but caught herself. "Louise? I wondered if the diner where Penny worked is still open."

"Why it sure is. I ate there just the other day. They have the best cobb salad in town."

Kate smiled. "That's good. You don't happen to have the phone number for the diner handy do you?"

"I can get it for you in a jiffy. I have it written down in my purse. For a small charge they'll bring you your lunch, which I've only done once, but I know I have the number here. Let's see."

Kate heard Louise set the phone down. The woman came back on the line a moment later. "Ok, honey. Have you got a pen?"

"Yes. Go ahead."

Louise gave Kate the number and had her repeat it back.

"Thank you, Louise. You have a nice day. I'll call you soon with that information for the program."

Kate hung up the phone and set it on the counter. She read through the names that Louise had suggested, trying to decipher what she'd scrawled on the note.

"Nora Walker, Clyde Morgan, and . . ." Kate squinted at the last name on the list, "and Ernie somebody." She wished she had phone numbers to go with the names, but at least she had the number for the diner now.

Chapter 12

"Penny's Diner. This is Sandy. How can I help you today?"

Kate sat straighter in the chair and looked across her living room. "Uh hello. This is Kate Lundquist. I was wondering . . . I know this may sound weird, but well . . . could I speak to the owner?"

"Why sure. I hope everything is okay. You didn't find a hair in your food last time you were in now did ya?"

"No, no . . . nothing like that. I just want to ask him, uh . . . a few questions."

"Well, let me see if he's around today. I think I saw him earlier. Can you hold on a sec?"

Kate could hear the bustle of the noisy restaurant, as Sandy apparently walked through the building with the phone. Kate stood and wandered down the hall to listen at Megan's door. The baby had just gone down for a nap, but hadn't been very happy about the idea. No noise came from the bedroom, and Kate hoped the baby would sleep for at least an hour. Janae was at her art class and Mitch had gone to a friend's. Kate wanted to get a few things done while she had some time to herself.

"This is Tom."

Kate stepped back into the living room.

"Hello. This is Kate Lundquist. I'm trying to find someone that may have known a woman named Penny Haws. I heard that she worked at the diner for many years. Do you know her?"

"No. I can't say that I do? I could ask Sandy, but I'm pretty sure we don't have anybody named Penny working here. That would be something though, huh? Since that's the name of this place." The man laughed loudly into the phone.

Kate nodded and took a deep breath. "Well, she doesn't work there now. Actually, she died recently."

"Sorry to hear that," Tom said apologetically.

Kate nodded her head and tapped the pencil on the tabletop. "The reason I called, Tom, was because I was hoping to talk to someone that knew her, so I could get some information about her life."

Tom didn't speak immediately making Kate wonder if she had the right owner or even the right diner. "I'm sorry. Are you the owner?"

"I am. But I don't know anyone called Penny. I bought this place last year, so if she worked here before that I wouldn't know her." Tom spoke in his booming voice. "You might want to call Clyde. He's the one that sold me the diner. He would most likely know this Penny woman since he's older than dirt." Tom laughed again into the phone.

"Would you happen to have his phone number?" Kate asked cutting the man's loud laughter off.

"I bet I do. Let me take a look."

Tom groaned into the phone and Kate heard him take few deep breaths as he searched for Clyde's number. "It's got to be here. I spoke to him just the other day. Oh, wait. He called me."

Kate began to speak. "That's okay . . ."

"No hang on. I'll ask Sandy. She runs the show here. I'm sure she'll know where to find it. Don't go anywhere."

More noise came through the phone as Tom made his way back to wherever Sandy was. Kate could hear Tom explaining to Sandy that he was looking for Clyde's phone number. A moment later Sandy was back on the line.

"Hello? Are you still there? I have Clyde's number right here. Are you ready?"

"Yes. Go ahead," Kate said as she wrote down the number and put Clyde's name beside it. "And what is Clyde's last name?"

"Morgan. Clyde Morgan. Hopefully he's at home. He spends a lot of time fishing these days." Sandy laughed. "Now that he's retired, I think Dotty, sends him fishing just to get him out of the house."

Kate laughed. "Thank you."

"Oh you're welcome. You have a nice day now."

Kate hung up with Sandy and dialed Clyde's number. It rang several times before a gravelly voice came on the line.

"This is Clyde."

"Hello. Mr. Morgan. This is Kate Lundquist. I live about an hour north of you in Springville. I am a friend of Penny's. Penny Haws. Do you remember her?"

There was a pause as Clyde cleared his throat and Kate glanced up at the clock.

"Do I remember Penny? She was my partner for years—practically ran the diner. Even named it after her. She objected of course, but I went and did it anyway. She and Del were like family." The man coughed and cleared his throat again. "What did you say your name was?"

Kate shifted in her chair. "This is Kate Lundquist. Penny used to come into my shop to get her hair done. I wanted to make sure you had heard that she . . ." Kate felt her throat close up as tears began to collect in her eyes. She sniffed loudly into the phone. She really hated to be the bearer of bad news.

"Hey now. Penny wouldn't want you fussin' over her. I mean I feel terrible about her passin', but she had a good life. She really did."

Kate swallowed and wiped at her eyes. "It sounds like you've already heard she died."

"Yep. Word gets around pretty fast down here."

"Well, I guess so. And it sounds like you knew Penny pretty well, then. Would you mind saying a few words about her at the service?"

"Who me? Naw. You don't want me ramblin' away in front of a crowd," he said with a laugh.

"Well, I guess that just leaves me then," Kate chuckled, "but I don't know much about her life before she moved up here. Can you tell me about her?"

"That's a tall order. Let's see . . ." Kate waited as the old man muttered to himself. "I'm not sure where to begin . . . Penny and Del were the salt of the earth. Yes sir. They were the best people you could ever hope to meet." Clyde paused for half a minute.

Kate decided to prompt him, hoping he would tell her more. "You mentioned the diner was named after her," she said as she tapped her pencil. "How did that happen?"

The old man cleared his throat. "Well now. That was probably forty years ago that I bought that diner. Penny was waitin' tables for Don, the previous owner, and had been for years. She was like a mother hen, took care of ever'body just like we was her family. Yes sir she was a real favorite with customers and employees alike." The man chortled. "I was a lowly dishwasher at the time . . . workin' in the back."

Kate glanced down the hall, trying to listen for the baby.

"So by and by, Don, the owner of the diner talked about sellin' and well I was tired of washin' dishes and decided this might be my big break. I scraped together enough money for a small down payment and then Don let me make monthly payments. It was a huge undertaking. I was young and didn't really have a clue what I was doin'." Clyde took a ragged breath. "After a year of tryin' to make the payments, and keep the diner open, Penny came to me with a plan. She knew I was on the verge of throwin' in the towel and closing up shop . . . literally. But she wouldn't hear of it. She told me she had some money that she'd like to invest in the diner." The old man stopped in this story. "Now listen, I knew what Penny made as a waitress and it weren't much. I asked her flat out how she could come up with that kind of money." He cackled into the phone. "She told me to stop bein' impertinent and just take the money."

Clyde sighed and continued his dialog. "Although I was desperate, I worried about takin' her money. I wasn't sure the diner would ever turn a profit, but she insisted. She hounded me for a good while, and I finally gave in. But I told her that we had to make it legal-like and that she would have a say in how things were done. She balked at that idea. She said she just wanted to help and that she planned on still waitin' tables. Made me promise that no one would ever know she was a co-owner. A few weeks later we went to see Ernie to have papers drawn up and Penny became my partner. Of course when I sold it last year, she got her money back plus a nice profit."

Kate jotted down some notes as Clyde talked. She wondered if that was where Penny had gotten the money for the scholarship funds she had given to Kate's kids. "When did you change the name of the diner?"

"Well, that's another long story, but I'll see if I can tell you the condensed version." His raspy laugh came through the phone again. "The diner was called Wendy's when I bought it from Don and if I'm rememberin' correctly it had been in his family since the 1940's. He had inherited the restaurant from his uncle that just happened to be married to a woman named Wendy."

Kate nodded as she wrote Wendy on the paper.

"I was content to keep the name. I didn't have the cash to make any changes to the signs anyway. But several years after Penny and I became partners, a new restaurant became quite popular—one with a pretty young red headed girl on it's logo."

Kate smiled to herself as he continued. "At first that didn't bother me none, but eventually with Penny's encouragement, I decided to "distinguish myself from the other place" as Penny put it. I needed folks to recommend a good place to eat and not have them sendin' people to the wrong Wendy's." Clyde laughed until he was gasping for air. He gained control and coughed several times as Kate waited.

"I'm sorry. Anyhow, I thought maybe I should do like Don's uncle had, you know name it after my wife. I went to Margie, my wife at the time, and told her we was looking for a new name for the place. I asked her if she'd ever imagined havin' her name in lights."

Kate laughed softly.

"She wasn't thrilled with that idea, threatened to divorce me if I put her name on the building." Clyde paused and cleared his throat. "She divorced me a few years later anyway, but that's another story yet."

He drew a breath and continued. "So I decided to make a contest of it. I asked my workers and customers to submit ideas and promised a free lunch for the winning name. I was surprised and downright pleased that several people suggested we name it after Penny. Once word got out that I was considerin' the name, people began callin' it Penny's place even before the new sign was hung."

Kate smiled. "That's a wonderful story. Can I share that at the memorial?"

"Be my guest. She was a great lady. I sure missed her and Del when they was gone." He cleared his throat. "I couldn't make it up to Del's funeral. Still regret that. I was stuck in the hospital fightin' an infection in my lungs, but you don't want to hear 'bout that."

Kate frowned. "I'm so sorry. Will you be able to come to the service next week?"

"Oh yes. My wife, Dotty, and I wouldn't miss it."

"Well thanks again, Clyde I really do appreciate you talking to me."

"No bother. You need anythin' else?" Clyde asked.

"Actually," Kate looked down at her page. "I was looking through pictures of Penny and came across one of her standing in front of the diner with two other people—Lizzy and Luther. They must have been employees, I guess. Do you know if they're still living in Ephraim?"

"Luther? Ah right. Luther Glover. He's still around. Lives with his daughter in the middle of town."

"Do you happen to have his phone number? I'd like to talk to him." Kate said.

"I don't have a number for him. But I've been to his house a time or two. It's easy to find. If you head north on Main and take a right on 200 North, you'll find him in the third house on the left."

Kate jotted down Clyde's directions wondering if he realized she wasn't in Ephraim. "And do you remember Lizzy?"

"Lizzy. Little blond lady; had a couple of kids. Let me think. What was her last name?" Clyde paused. "Dotty? What was Lizzy's last name? The one that worked at the diner?"

Kate heard a muffled female voice on Clyde's end. Apparently, his wife had a better memory. "Right. Lizzy Jacobs. I don't think Lizzy's livin' here anymore, but her daughter, Laurie, worked down at the salon on Main for a spell. I think Dotty had her hair done there. Hey Dot?" Clyde called to his wife again. "Do you know if Laurie is still doin' hair at that place you went to?" There was a pause and then Clyde pulled the phone away. Kate heard him explain, "You know, Lizzy Jacob's daughter, Laurie."

Kate wrote down the name Lizzy Jacobs as she waited to hear if Dotty had any more information.

Clyde coughed and came back on the line. "Dotty says she hasn't been back to that salon, but she's pretty sure Laurie is still in town. Her married name is Barber, she thinks," Clyde said.

"Okay thanks. I'll see if I can hunt her down." Kate took a breath and looked over her notes. "I guess that's all then."

"Hey hold on a minute," Clyde said as Kate heard Dotty talking again. "My wife is wonderin' if you'd like her to play the organ at the service. She's mighty talented on the organ."

"Oh yes that would be wonderful. I'll add her name to the program." Kate said.

"When will the service be?"

"Next Wednesday at one o'clock at Olsen's," Kate answered. "Thank you, Clyde. I look forward to meeting you and Dotty next week. You take care." Kate told the old man goodbye and hung up the phone.

Chapter 13

The smell of French fries filled the car as Kate pulled into Penny's driveway. She looked up at the house and saw that several notices had been stuck to the front door and two newspapers were sitting on the porch. She needed to get the newspaper stopped and have the mail forwarded to her own home. There were a thousand things left to do and Kate was feeling overwhelmed. With a sigh she turned off the ignition and looked at Janae.

"Can you get the food and the drinks and I'll unbuckle Megan."

Janae nodded and gathered the fast food in her hands and climbed from the car.

After her phone call with Clyde, Kate had found the baby standing up in her crib jabbering. She'd quickly changed the baby and headed out to pick up Janae from her art class. The three of them would be spending the afternoon going through boxes and cleaning out Penny's house.

"What are we going to do with all of Penny's clothes?" Janae asked as Kate pushed the key into the lock. The door swung open and the girl stepped into the dark living room and her mother switched on the light. "And what about all her furniture?"

Kate set the baby on the floor and laid her bag on the couch. "I guess we will donate her clothes—unless someone wants them. Penny wanted us to have a yard sale and give the money to charity. We'll keep a few things though, so let me know if you find something you'd like to keep."

Janae looked around the room and nodded. She moved into the kitchen and set the food on the table. "It's really weird being in her house like this." She stepped across the living room to the piano and lifted the lid. "Remember when she taught me this song."

Kate smiled as Janae slid onto the seat and began to play a simple tune. A warm feeling rushed over her as she thought about the gentle woman that had touched all of their lives. It had been Penny who had insisted that Janae had a good ear and needed to take lessons. Kate's mother had been thrilled to teach piano to her new granddaughter. There'd been plenty of mini recitals in Penny's home as Janae continued to learn to play.

The baby waddled to the piano and began to plunk at the keys as Janae finished. Kate smiled and lifted Megan into her arms. "Let's have some lunch." She set the toddler on a chair in the kitchen and started to remove food items from the bag.

"Should I get some plates out? Grandma P wouldn't mind if we used her dishes right?" Janae stepped to the cupboard and opened the door. Inside was a stack of cream-colored plates with tiny roses around the edges. Janae carefully removed two plates and set them on the table. "These are so nice. Do you think she has some other ones instead?"

Kate smiled.

"Just be careful. Those are what she used every day. I remember eating on them a few times in the past. She told me they were a wedding gift from her mother."

A memory flashed through Kate's mind of the first time she had eaten at this table. She'd come to see Penny after Del's death and the new widow had given her a thick slice of homemade bread. That visit had been the beginning of their friendship outside the salon and was a memory that would always stay with Kate.

Janae squirted the contents of a ketchup packet onto the plate and dumped her fries next to it. Megan reached for a fry and babbled happily as she popped it in her mouth. Kate laughed and unwrapped her sandwich.

"I think we'll keep the dishes and her glassware. We need to bring in the boxes from the trunk, so we can pack them. I've always wanted some china to put in the hutch," Kate said as she wiped her mouth with the napkin. They ate in silence except for the baby's occasional prattling. Kate glanced around the small kitchen.

"I thought you could clean out the fridge and pack up the dishes. I need to go through a few more files and pack up the office."

"Sure. Did you bring newspaper to wrap the dishes in?" Janae asked as she put her trash in the can under the sink.

"Yes. Take the keys and bring in the boxes and newspaper from the trunk of the car."

Kate wiped the baby's hands and set her on the floor with a few toys. Then she walked through the house picking up knickknacks and framed photos that were low enough for the baby to break. She paused as she admired the picture of Penny and Del on their wedding day. She set it on the kitchen counter beside the tiny glass hummingbird that seemed to be hovering over a bright pink flower.

Janae came into the house and dropped the boxes on the linoleum. "The neighbor, Kim, saw me and asked if we needed help. I told her I didn't think so."

"That's fine. I know she wants to help, so maybe I can have her help with the yard sale next week." Kate nodded and pointed at the baby. "I am going to work in the office. Can you keep an eye on her?"

"Yep. Meggie and I will clean out the fridge. Won't we?" Janae laughed as the little girl clapped her hands in agreement. "Should I just put all the salad dressings and stuff like that in a box?"

"Yes. I would check the expiration dates and throw out anything that's old including any leftovers that you find."

Janae nodded and pulled open the fridge door.

Kate stepped into the back room and flipped on the light. The closet door was slightly ajar. She pulled it open wide and lifted the boxes from the shelves. She peeked inside several and set them by the door to take home with her. She reached to the top shelf and hefted the heavy box to the floor. She pulled off the lid and discovered that it was full of old ledgers. She removed one from the top of the pile and turned to the first page. Neat handwriting covered the page with a column of numbers running down the right side.

"Penny and Del were much better records keepers than I am," Kate mumbled to herself. Even with her computer program, she hated to keep track of her receipts and record them. Penny had accounted for everything it seemed. Kate skimmed through the pages in the book and noticed that it was mostly full of household items or farm supplies for the ranch. She set the ledger aside and flipped through another one. This ledger wasn't as detailed and had what appeared to be initials in the descriptions. Many of them had just the name Ernie written beside the dollar amount.

"I wonder if Ernie was a ranch hand?" she said out loud. "That seems like a very lucrative job if that's how much they make," she added as she lifted another ledger out of the box. She perused the third book, which contained more of the same except that a new name, Fred, started to appear at regular intervals on each page. Fred was getting paid weekly and his was a more modest yet consistent paycheck. Kate set the books back into the box and pushed it near the door. Jay would have to decide what to do with them. She had no idea if they were important now that Penny was gone.

Her husband had asked her to gather any financial information she could find, so they'd know what Penny owed on the house and what money she had in the bank. Kate agreed with Janae that it felt funny going through Penny's private documents, but she knew it had to be done.

Kate sat beside the filing cabinet and removed several files marked bank statements and one full of mortgage information. She also found a file marked medical and pulled it from the drawer. As she glanced through the stack of medical bills, she was surprised to find a large bill from a doctor Bentley for a broken wrist requiring pins. She wondered if Del had been injured while working with his cattle.

"Megan needs a new diaper." Janae interrupted Kate's thoughts as she spoke from the doorway, her baby sister in her arms. "And I finished cleaning out the fridge. Should I start on the dishes?"

"Yes. Let me change her and then I'll help you with the dishes." Kate set the file folders on top of the boxes by the door and lifted Megan into her arms.

"Are you stinky?" Kate asked as Janae plugged her nose and nodded. The tiny girl giggled and struggled to get free from her mother's grasp. "No you don't. You have to be changed. Janae, can you bring me a diaper and wipes? I'll change her in the bathroom."

The girl did Kate's bidding and returned a moment later. She set the wipes beside Kate who was kneeling on the tile floor fighting to hold the toddler still. "We'll be quick, sweetie. Stop moving. The last thing we need is a bigger mess to clean up."

"Meggie. Look up here." Janae called to the baby and made a silly face distracting Megan long enough for Kate to change her diaper.

"Thanks. Let's get some packing done and then we'll need to hurry home to get dinner started." Kate carried the diaper to the trash bin outside and wondered when it would be picked up. She decided to lug it to the curb now so she wouldn't miss the garbage pick up day.

As she turned to walk back to the house, Corky came bounding up to her. "Hello, little dog. What are you up to?" Kate looked toward Gigi's house. "Does your mama know you're out here?"

The dog barked and sat down. Kate knew he probably missed Penny and the treats she used to give him. "Maybe I have something in the house for you. Let me go see," she said to the dog.

As if he could understand her, Corky followed her to the porch and waited outside the door.

Kate walked into the kitchen and opened the pantry door. "The neighbor's dog is outside and I promised him a treat. Have you seen any doggy biscuits in here?" Kate paused. "Aha. I knew she'd have something."

Janae grinned. "Really? Let me take it to him." Kate dropped several dog treats in her daughter's hand and smiled. "See if he will do a trick for it. Penny said he knew a few."

Kate picked up Megan and followed Janae out the door. They watched as Corky danced, shook hands and caught the treats. Janae patted the dog's head and laughed. "What a smarty. You're almost as good as Rudi." The dog barked and watched Janae intently.

"Corky? What are you doing over here?"

Kate turned to see Gigi coming up the walk.

"Is he bugging you?"

"No. Janae was just giving him a doggy treat. I hope that's okay."

"Sure. Penny did that. I think he misses Penny." Gigi frowned and looked away.

"We all do," Kate said softly.

They all stood in silence for a moment.

The neighbor turned to Kate. "Hey. Do you know someone that drives a black jeep? There was one parked here the other night with a guy sitting inside. I don't know if he tried knocking on her door or not. I watched him as he sat there for about five minutes and then he just drove off. It was kind of weird," Gigi said as she rubbed at a spot on her arm.

Kate shook her head. "No. That doesn't seem familiar. I wonder if he knew Penny?"

The woman shrugged. "Yeah maybe."

"Did you get a good look at him?" Kate asked.

"Well, sort of." Gigi replied as Corky took off down the block, barking madly. The dog's owner shook her head and continued. "From what I could tell he wasn't a very big guy. I think he had dark hair, cut pretty short, but that's about all I could see. It was getting dark." The woman stopped talking and looked down the block after her dog. "I've been keeping an eye on the place, you know, since she's gone now. If he shows up again I might call the cops."

Megan fussed to get down and Janae took her from Kate and walked up the pathway toward the house. "I've heard that sometimes thieves will read obituaries and rob the home while everyone is away or in this case they might realize the house is vacant. Thanks for watching it. I hope you don't have any trouble."

Gigi took a big breath and nodded. "Well, I've got to run to work." She turned and headed for her house calling again for her dog.

Kate walked back into Penny's house and found Janae and the baby, sitting at the piano. Megan looked up with a grin on her face as she pounded on the keys. "Be careful. Play it softly."

"Could we keep this piano? I like the keyboard we have, but I would love to have a real piano instead," Janae explained over the noisy tune the baby was playing.

"I think that would be a good idea. We'll have to talk to your dad about it."

Janae nodded and let Megan play a few more notes before setting her on the floor.

"Let's pack up the dishes we want to keep and maybe go through the pantry. The things we plan to sell can stay here in the house since we'll have the yard sale right here in her neighborhood."

An hour later the car was packed with several boxes and Kate was locking up the house. She glanced out at the street and saw a black jeep slow and then accelerate past the house. A shiver ran down her spine as she wondered if it was the same jeep that Gigi had seen.

Chapter 14

"This is going to be fun," Jay said as he pulled onto the freeway heading toward Highway 6 as the sun peeked over the tops of the mountains. "I haven't been to Ephraim in years. Renee and I took the kids to see the pageant in Manti when they were younger, but they don't even remember the trip. We'll have to bring them down again next year when Megan is older."

Kate smiled. "Yeah. I don't remember it much myself. I think the pageant runs through the month of June, right?"

Jay nodded. "I think so."

Silence filled the car as they entered the canyon and the landscape changed. Kate glanced at her husband, glad that he had decided to come with her. She had planned to go to Ephraim by herself until her mother suggested that Jay and Kate take an anniversary trip and let her keep the kids.

"Thanks for coming with me," Kate said as she clutched her husband's arm and leaned in to kiss his cheek. "I know it's not the perfect anniversary trip, but at least we'll have some time alone . . . maybe." Kate sighed and dropped her hands in her lap. "Well, for part of the time . . . when we're not talking to Penny's friends."

"I'm happy to go. It's nice to get away. I don't mind visiting a few people as long as we can go to dinner this evening and not have to rush home to the kids." Jay smiled. "And besides, I reserved a room at a bed and breakfast in town. That should be fun."

Jay laughed as a pretty blush rose up on his wife's cheeks. She giggled in spite of herself and couldn't stop the smile that spread across her face. It *would* be nice to not worry about the kids for a couple of days.

"So you were able to get out of your meetings for tomorrow?" Her husband was usually very busy on Sundays.

"I asked my counselor to cover for me. I hardly ever take any time off. He was fine with it." Jay reached out to take his wife's hands. "I'm all yours for the next thirty-six hours."

Kate squeezed his hand and took a cleansing breath. "I wish we could go to the temple while we are down there, but I guess we won't have enough time."

"Not if you want to see everyone on your list," Jay said with a quick glance at Kate.

She pulled the list from her purse and read through the names of people she hoped to talk with. "Clyde told me how to find Luther Glover, so I think we should try him first. He's living with his daughter and I think Clyde said he was retired."

Jay slowed as he caught up to a semitrailer.

"I want to find Lizzy or her daughter, Laurie, at least. Clyde said she's a hairdresser—smart woman if I do say so myself." Kate laughed. "I should try to find out who Ernie is too. I saw his name in Penny's ledgers and Louise mentioned him as well." She looked up as Jay zipped around the slower vehicle. "That should be enough to keep us busy for a few hours."

Kate put the paper away and turned on the radio finding an oldies station that they enjoyed listening to. Jay sang along, making up lyrics when he didn't know them. As the rolling landscape flew past, Kate leaned against the seat back and drifted off.

What seemed like only moments later, Jay was touching her knee.

"We're here Kate," Jay said, breaking into Kate's nap. "I need the directions to Larry's house?"

Kate sat up and tried to clear her head. "Huh?"

"You know the man that worked at the diner? Linus? Lex? What's his name?"

Kate laughed. "His name is Luther."

"Right. Where do I go?" Jay pulled into Ephraim and slowed to a crawl.

"Are we on Main Street?" she asked as she pulled out the paper.

He nodded.

"Okay. Turn onto 200 North and it's the third house on the left," she read from her notes.

Jay turned down the street and stopped in front of a white clapboard home. Grass clippings blew across the path to the front door. Two plastic lawn chairs sat empty on the porch beside the bright blue door.

"I wonder if anyone's home. I wish I had a phone number to call. Do you think they'll mind us just dropping in?" Kate asked as she stared at the little home.

"Only one way to find out," Jay said as he climbed from the car.

She took a breath and grabbed her purse. "Yeah, I guess so." Once again she realized she was glad she'd brought her husband along. She may not have been brave enough to knock on this stranger's door if she'd been alone. Jay came around to her side of the car as she opened the door. She stepped onto the sidewalk and shielded her eyes as two little dogs came around the corner of the house, barking.

Jay took his wife's hand and spoke calmly to the dogs. "Hey doggies. Are you coming to say hello? I know we look tasty, but we just came to visit. My wife really won't like it if you bite her ankles."

Kate smiled and gripped his hand as the dogs continued to yip at them as they made their way up the path. "Sugar! Beans! You leave them alone. Come on. Get in the house."

Kate looked up to find a dark haired woman with a dark complexion standing on the porch. Sugar and Beans gave a final high-pitched woof and turned toward the house. "They work even better than a doorbell," the woman's cheeks turned up in a smile as the dogs ran inside. "What can I do for you folks?"

"Hi. We're looking for Luther Glover. Clyde Morgan told us he might be here. I'm sorry I couldn't call first, but I didn't have a phone number." Kate paused and extended her hand. "I'm Kate Lundquist and this is my husband Jay."

"I'm Asia, Luther's daughter," she said as she shook first Kate's hand and then Jay's. "I'll tell him you're here. Is he expecting you?"

"Well, no. We're friends of Penny's and—." Kate paused at the stunned look on Asia's face.

"Is everything okay with Penny?" The woman frowned, her eyebrows lowering over her coal black eyes. "I just got the prickles slinking down my back as you said her name. That happens to me sometimes." She looked at Kate with concern in her eyes. "Something's wrong."

Kate pursed her lips and nodded her head. "She passed away earlier this week. That's why we're here. We wanted to talk to anyone that knew her and put together a life sketch."

"My father will be heartbroken to hear that she's gone. He loved that woman near to death." Asia threw a hand up to cover her mouth. "Oh my, what a terrible thing to say." She turned and stepped into the house, waving them forward. "Come on in. I know he'll want to talk to you."

Kate and Jay followed the woman into the house and stood for a moment inside the door as their eyes adjusted to the dim interior. The wood floor creaked as they were led to a faded couch tucked beneath a large window. Soft light green drapes framed the window that looked out to the side yard.

"If you'll wait here, I'll find my father." Asia motioned to the couch and hurried from the room.

Jay took a seat on the couch, but Kate stood admiring the antique furnishing of the home.

"I love the feel of this old house. It reminds me of my grandma's place in Idaho."

Jay agreed from his position on the couch. Kate tipped her head to study a painting that hung on the wall. "I love how the gold hues catch the light from the window," she said pointing at the artwork.

"Mmhmm," Jay said. "The stalks of wheat actually look like they're swaying in the wind."

Kate leaned toward a watering can of fresh daisies resting on a sideboard beneath the painting. "So pretty."

She stepped toward the front hall and peered through the arched doorway. In the opposite room, she could see four sturdy chairs surrounding a wooden table. She moved to get a better view of the white porcelain pitcher that rested on a doily in the middle of the tabletop.

"I love old pitchers with basins and that doily looks like it's hand made," Kate commented as she turned back toward Jay. She was startled to find Asia standing behind her.

"It is. My mama made that when she and Pop first got married," Asia smiled and nodded toward the dining room. "Memaw insisted that my mama learn to crochet." Asia sighed. "Mama tried to teach me, but I would have nothing of it. Wish I'd been more willing, since Mama's gone now."

Kate nodded and walked back into the living room. "Your home is lovely," she said as she sat beside her husband.

"Thank you. We're comfortable here," Asia sat on a chair. "Pop is just getting his slippers on. He'll be here shortly."

"We were admiring that lovely painting. Do you happen to know who the artist is?" Jay asked.

Asia nodded. "Pop painted that a few years back. It's my favorite. He's got a real knack for painting." Asia said with pride as her father came into the room.

"My ears are burning. You talking about me?" Luther asked as he moved to greet his guests.

Jay stood to shake the black man's hand and Kate did the same.

"Nice to meet you Mr. Glover. We hope we aren't interrupting anything," Kate said.

Luther gestured for them to sit and he deposited himself in an easy chair in the corner of the room. "Call me Luther. I was just finishing up my morning grits. My knee's been bothering me of late, so I'm moving a bit slower than usual." The old man popped the footrest up on the recliner and adjusted himself in the chair. "What's this I hear about Penny? She can't be gone already." Luther looked across the room at Kate who was nodding. "Well, I guess you just never know when the Lord's going to call you home." He drew in a deep breath. "He took my sweet Winnie before I was ready, that's for sure."

"I hate to bring sad news, but it's true, Penny died about a week ago. They say she had a heart attack and died in her sleep," Kate said as she glanced between Asia and Luther. Jay took Kate's hand and squeezed it as she continued. "I've been asked to be the executor of the will and I'm planning the memorial service for this Wednesday at one o'clock here in town. But the thing is, I've only known Penny for a few years . . . you know since she moved up to Utah County. I was hoping to find a few people to tell me about her life."

Luther nodded and scratched at his chin.

"What would be even better is if one of you would like to speak at the service?" Kate looked at Asia then settled her gaze on the elderly gentleman in the corner.

Luther grunted and shook his head. "Never was good at public speaking . . . unless Penny wanted me to . . . then I might reconsider," Luther looked at Kate expectantly.

She smiled at the old man's willingness and shook her head. "No. She didn't mention you specifically. In fact she never told me much about her previous life at all. It's been a real challenge to figure out where to start." She reached into her purse and pulled out the pictures she'd brought. "I found this picture of you with Lizzy and Penny." Kate stood and handed the old photograph to Luther. Asia moved to stand beside her father's chair. "These photos led me to you. I'm hoping you can tell me about Penny."

Luther studied the picture and handed it to his daughter. "That was taken a few days after we got the new sign hung." The man shook his head and studied the picture closer. "Clyde was determined to put it up by ourselves and save some money, but it wasn't as easy as he thought. We ended up hiring someone to do it proper, which was a relief to me since like I said, I have a bum knee."

Asia handed the picture back to Kate and returned to her chair. "Pop played football in college. He was a star linebacker until someone landed on his knee," Asia said, a look of pride in her eyes despite the shake of her head.

Luther scratched at his chin. "I suppose I could tell you a story or two about Penny. How much time do you got?"

Chapter 15

Ephraim, July 1986

Luther slid open the back door of his delivery truck. "Did you get those tomatoes?" Clyde asked as he came out the back door of the diner.

"Oh course I did. I was tired of you breathing down my neck about it," the young black man laughed as he lifted a box of tomatoes and handed them to Clyde. "I got everything you asked for."

They worked quickly to unload the truck, carrying the food in through the diner's rear door. The small restaurant wouldn't be open for two hours yet, but the kitchen staff was busy preparing for the day.

Luther stood at the kitchen door with a dolly loaded with a dozen large trays of eggs. "Hey, Billy. Can you get the door?"

The young man stepped to the walk-in refrigerator door and pulled it open wide.

"How's it going, Luth?" Billy asked as he unloaded the egg cartons onto the shelves. "Did you see the game?"

Luther had caught a few innings of the All Star Game the day before, but he was sure Billy had watched every minute of it. The guy was a huge major league baseball fan.

"I only saw a bit of it, but I read the write up in the paper this morning. Sounded like a real nail biter," Luther said as he wheeled the dolly out of the cold storeroom.

"Yeah. I still can't believe the American League pulled it off," Billy said excitedly. "I was kind of worried there in the eighth inning, but I knew they could do it. Clemens was amazing. Three perfect innings, and of course, he was named the Most Valuable Player."

Luther smiled at the kid's enthusiasm.

"Billy? Billy! Are you still jawing about that game?" Clint, the head cook, leaned his head around the corner and called to the young man. "How about you let Luther get back to work and you start cutting up these onions."

The young man shrugged and pointed in the deliveryman's direction. "I'll talk to you later, Luth. Say hello to your family." Billy hurried back into the kitchen and Luther rolled the dolly out to the parking lot. He closed the back of his truck, and returned to Clyde's office to pick up his paycheck. He was met in the hallway by one of the waitresses as she stepped out of the break room.

"Why hello, Luther. How are you?" Penny smiled as she tucked a pencil behind her ear and tied on her apron.

"Doing fine," he said. "Did Del get that tractor fixed? I would have offered my help, but I am not the guy you want trying to fix anything mechanical." Luther chuckled.

"He did. Things are always needing repair, but my husband can fix anything, thank goodness." Penny smiled. "How's your mother? Did you say she was about to have her last treatment of chemo?"

"Yes ma'am. The chemotherapy leaves her weak, but she's getting used to the routine and claims she's fine. Sure wish I could be there for her." The big man shrugged. "But at least my sister, Trina, is in Texas to check on her." Luther shook his head and smiled weakly at the petite woman nodding in front of him. "Trina has her hands full with those terrors she calls kids, so I'm not sure how much help she is to my mother."

Penny nodded. "You tell your momma I'm praying for her speedy recovery. I wish there was something more I could do." Penny sighed and patted the man's arm. "You keep up the faith. It's sure good to see you Luther."

"You too, Miss Penny." Luther nodded and stepped past her and into the office where Clyde was seated behind the desk.

The man at the desk looked up from his paperwork. "I guess you're wantin' to get paid?" Clyde asked as Luther stood just inside the door of his office.

"I was hopin'," Luther said with a laugh. "Gotta buy my babies some new shoes."

Clyde pulled an envelope from inside his desk and held it out to the Luther. "How's the wife and kids?"

Luther stepped closer to the desk. "Fine. Winnie is looking forward to school starting soon, but Tony and Asia are happy to have a few more weeks of summer left." The deliveryman took the envelope and tucked it into his pocket.

"Are they both in school now?" Clyde asked as he set his pen down and leaned back in his chair.

"Much to Winnie's relief, yes. Asia is in the second grade and Tony will be starting kindergarten." Luther shoved his hands into his pockets. "It's hard to believe how fast they're growing up."

Clyde nodded vigorously. "Just wait 'til they start drivin'. My boy got his license last week and his momma hasn't slept since." Clyde chuckled as the phone began to ring. The chair squealed as Clyde leaned forward to grab the phone. "You have a good day Luther."

Luther nodded and headed out the back door. He had a few more deliveries to make this morning. The truck door gave out a loud screech as he pulled it open and climbed inside. He reached to fasten his seatbelt and felt something crunch under his weight.

"What the—," he pulled an envelope free from beneath his leg, his name printed neatly across the front. Inside he found three crisp one hundred dollar bills. His jaw dropped as he read the neatly typed note included with the bills. "Go see your mother."

***

A smile spread across Kate's face as Luther ended his story. "Cool, but who gave you the money?"

"The note wasn't signed, but I had a sneaky suspicion. Only a few people knew that my mother was sick and most of them didn't have the means to pay for a plane ticket. I wasn't even sure Penny could afford it, but I'm darn certain she was the one that left the money in my truck."

"Did you ask her about it?" Jay wanted to know.

"No. I didn't want to embarrass her, but she was like that—very generous. I heard stories from other people about her buying their meals or not charging them for extra drinks and such." Luther rubbed his chin. "It meant a lot to people."

Kate nodded. "I know first hand that she had a generous heart," she said thinking of the many times Penny had given them gifts—just because.

"Have you heard about a guy named Finn?" Luther asked.

Kate shook her head. "No. That doesn't sound familiar. Who's Finn?"

The man raised his eyebrows and began a new tale.

***

"Clyde, he's still here this morning. You want me to run him off?" Luther asked as he stepped into the back office of the diner.

"What?" Clyde asked as he looked up from a pile of paperwork.

"That bum. The one camping out by the dumpster? Should I scare him away or are you going to call the cops?"

"No. I don't think we need to do that. I told the girls not to go out there alone. I've been havin' Billy take the trash out. The guy seems to be keepin' to himself," Clyde resumed his work. "Most likely he'll move on in a few days."

Luther glanced over his shoulder. "I hope you're right. Not sure it's good for business having him hanging around." Luther scratched at the stubble on his chin. "I got the fruit and fish you wanted. Anything new to add to the list before I head out?"

The owner of the diner glanced up at the deliveryman. "I think Penny had a list going. Will you find her and see what she says? I've gotta finish up with this bugger and get it sent off before I leave today. Dang taxes are gettin' so complicated." Clyde mumbled under his breath as the big man turned back out into the hallway.

Luther walked through the door of the diner's busy kitchen and called to the young cook who was standing beside a large mixer.

"Hey Billy. How are you this fine day?"

"Morning, Luth," The young man said with a shrug. "Fine, I guess. Just mixing up this batch of bread."

Luther stopped beside the mixer. "Doesn't Penny usually take care of the bread?"

"Yep. But she asked me to pull it out and form it into loaves." Billy shut off the machine and shook his head. "I hope she don't expect it to be as pretty she does it."

Luther laughed. "I'm sure you can handle it. So where is Penny? She's the one I need to talk to."

"I don't know. She said she'd be right back. She couldn't have gone too far." Billy grabbed a large trowel and began unloading the dough onto a pastry board.

Luther made his way to the front of the restaurant and peeked into the empty dining area. Lizzy stood at the hostess desk wiping down the menus. "Hey Liz. Have you seen Penny?" he asked.

The petite blonde paused in her work and gestured to the back. "I saw her earlier. Isn't she in the kitchen?"

"Nope."

Lizzy shrugged. "Then I don't know. Sorry."

The man pushed back through the swinging doors and passed Billy who had already made two loaves and was working on a third.

"Nice job."

Billy grunted and threw the dough into a waiting pan.

Luther continued to the back hallway and glanced into the boss's office. Clyde still sat at the desk with his head bent over his work. Luther stepped to the other side of the hall and poked his head into the break room, but found it empty as well. "Where is that woman?" He pushed open the door to the parking lot and stood with his hands on his hips as he surveyed the area behind the diner. The man he'd seen loitering earlier was nowhere to be seen.

"Hopefully he's gone for good," he mumbled to himself before another thought crossed his mind.

"Oh no. What if Penny came out here with that guy hanging around."

Luther's heart raced as he jogged across the pavement toward the large dumpster that stood in the corner.

"Penny?" he called as he rounded the corner.

He stopped abruptly— almost running into the drifter. The disheveled man turned in surprise and took a step away from the larger man. Luther frowned and scanned the area for Penny before turning his attention back to the homeless fellow.

The stranger stood completely still, his hands hanging at his sides. Luther took a deep breath and studied the man, noticing that the guy was no longer wearing the dirty t-shirt he'd had on earlier. In fact the man appeared to be in the middle of buttoning a clean blue shirt. The deliveryman shifted his weight and realized that there was a plastic bag under his right foot. He lifted the bag and found a pair of pants inside with the tag still on them.

"Got some new duds?" Luther asked as he tossed the bag to the man. "Where'd you get those?"

The man caught the bag and lifted his chin defiantly. "What's it to ya?"

Luther scowled and stepped toward the man. "Maybe you'd like me to call the cops. Is that what I should do?"

The unshaven man looked repentant and shook his head. "Nah. I'll be leaving. Just needed a place to rest up and get some food." The man dropped the bag and finished buttoning his shirt. He smoothed his new shirt and asked, "You wouldn't know if there's anyone hiring here in town?"

Luther scratched his chin and looked the man over again. "What are you good at?"

"I like fixing things. Cars mostly."

Luther tried to recall if he'd heard of anyone hiring. "You could check down at Mick's mechanic shop. He might have something for you."

Luther watched as the man pulled the pants from the bag and ripped the tags free. "I don't want to see you here tomorrow, you hear? You go on and find some place else to sleep.

The drifter nodded as Luther turned back toward the diner. He stopped abruptly as Penny rounded the corner.

"Oh Luther. There you are. Billy said you were looking for me?" Penny smiled at Finn and nodded. "I see you've met Finn."

Chapter 16

"Finn hung around town for a few more days and Penny gave him odd jobs to do for food. He never found work in Ephraim, but I heard he had a lead on some work in Mount Pleasant," Luther said from his recliner.

Kate stretched her neck and glanced at the clock on the wall. "So Finn's not around anymore? It would be interesting to hear what happened to him."

Luther shook his head. "Nope. I haven't seen him at least."

Asia's cell phone rang and she pulled it free from her pocket.

"The kids." She said as she pushed the button to answer. "Hello?" She walked into the kitchen.

Luther pointed at his daughter's retreating back. "Asia's kids are with their dad today. He lives in Fairview."

"Well, we should be going anyway," Kate said, as she stood up from the couch.

"It was so nice to meet you, Luther," Jay said as he reached to shake the man's hand.

"My pleasure," Luther said as he pushed the button to release his leg rest.

"Oh don't get up. We can see ourselves out," Kate said as she shook Luther's hand. "Oh I meant to ask, we're trying to see a few more people while we're down here. Do you know someone named Ernie?"

"Ernie Hollingsworth? He works at the bank," Luther said. "But he won't be there today of course. You'll want to stop by his house. He's on the other side of town. Have you got a pen handy?"

Kate reached into her purse and pulled out a pen and paper. She jotted down the directions to Ernie's home and smiled.

"Thanks. That will help tremendously." Kate tucked the paper away and made her way to the front door as Jay held it open. "You have a good day, Luther. We hope you'll come to the funeral service on Wednesday."

"I'll be there. You take care now."

As Jay opened the car door for Kate, Asia stepped onto the porch. "Goodbye folks. Good to meet you." She waved as they drove away.

"Nice people," Jay commented as he pulled up to a stop sign. "Are you getting hungry for lunch yet? Or should we go find Eddie first."

Kate snickered.

"No, I'm not hungry . . . and it's Ernie not Eddie." She tapped her temple. "We seem to be having a few senior moments today."

Jay raised his eyebrows and feigned innocence. "Who me? I knew it was Ernie. I was just testing you."

"Right." Kate smiled.

Jay turned serious. "It's not really that funny. I will most likely actually lose my mind in the next couple of years—something you should have thought of when you agreed to marry this old man." He pulled onto Main Street. "Where do we go from here?" he asked, changing the subject.

Penny's Diner

"Forty-seven is not old." Kate just shook her head. "I'll tell you when to turn." She peered through the windshield at the shops in the small town. "Hey, there's Sunny's Hair Salon. I think that's where Lizzy's daughter works. Let's stop there first."

Jay slowed and parked beside the curb.

Kate touched her husband's arm as he shut off the ignition. "Now her name is Laurie. Don't go calling her Lucy or Lisa."

She laughed at her husband's offended expression.

"Hey now, if you're going to be mean, maybe I should go into that pawn shop next door while you're visiting with *Laurie*." Jay opened his car door and came around to his wife's side. He opened the passenger door and led her to the salon without saying a word.

Kate couldn't tell if he was seriously annoyed or not. "So you don't really want to come in with me? I like having you along."

"Of course I'm coming. I was only kidding." Jay pulled Kate closer and kissed her soundly. She was embarrassed to hear a horn blaring followed by a catcall from the street. Her husband released her with a grin on his face.

"Better?" he asked.

She smiled.

"Me too. Let's go see Lexie."

Kate rolled her eyes as Jay opened the door to the salon.

"Welcome to Sunny's. Do you need a haircut today?" the woman at the desk asked.

Kate shook her head. "No, actually I was looking for a woman named Laurie Barber. Does she work here?"

"Yep. She's finishing up with that guy's cut. Do you want to wait for her?" She motioned to a woman who appeared to be a few years older than Kate. The hairdresser was talking animatedly to the man in her chair; the woman wore a colorful flowing skirt above a pair of green converse sneakers.

"Yes, we'll wait. Thanks." Kate and Jay sat on a pair of orange plastic chairs. Jay reached for a magazine and Kate pulled out her phone.

She checked for text messages from her mother and then checked her email. She quickly read through several messages and came across one from Facebook from someone she didn't recognize.

"Do you know anyone named Justina Brown Hardy?" she asked her husband. "She wants to be friends on Facebook. I hate it when I get requests and I don't know the person."

"I don't know. I hardly ever get on there. Mitch set me up with an account and I haven't looked at it much since." Jay closed his magazine and tossed it back on the table. "It looks like Laurie is done."

Kate put her phone away as the flamboyant hairdresser approached.

"Hello. Candy says you're looking for me." Laurie smiled and pushed a lock of red hair behind her ear causing the dangling earring to dance. "What can I do for you?"

Jay turned to his wife allowing her to speak. "Hi Laurie. I'm Kate and this is my husband Jay. We came down to Ephraim today to talk to a few people who knew Penny Haws."

130

"Oh really? Are you reporters or something?" Laurie looked at the couple with a squint of her eye.

"No. We're just her friends." Kate shifted her weight and pursed her lips and asked softly, "Did you hear that Penny died?"

Laurie nodded and tucked her hands into her apron pockets. "Yes."

"Well, the thing is I'm the executor of her will and . . . maybe this is kind of weird, but I am trying to get some ideas for what to say at her memorial service next week." Kate took a breath and adjusted her purse on her shoulder.

"Oh, of course." The woman nodded and looked around at the almost empty salon. "I can take a quick break now." She turned abruptly and walked to the back of the shop, removing her apron as she went. Laurie called to her coworker. "I'll be back for my appointment at eleven." She breezed through the salon and motioned for Jay and Kate to follow her. "Let's go down the block to the coffee shop. They have some tables outside where we can chat."

Jay followed the two women out the door and grabbed his wife's hand. Laurie walked swiftly down the block, greeting a couple that passed her on the sidewalk. She turned and waited as Jay and Kate caught up.

"I just heard about Penny this morning. I did Jen Beaumont's hair and she gave me the news. So sad. Penny wasn't that old was she? I'd guess somewhere in her seventies. My mother just turned sixty this year. She moved to St. George, but we all went down for her birthday. Here we are," Laurie paused in her explanation and moved toward an empty table, a large umbrella giving it shade. "Mel owns the place. He bought it from my brother-in-law a few years ago," Laurie said as she took a seat on a plastic chair. "Do you want a soda or a coffee?"

Kate shook her head and looked at her husband. "I think we're fine thanks."

Laurie leaned back in her chair, and adjusted her skirt over her crossed her knees. "So where do you live? Up north where Penny was living? I used to do Penny's hair before she moved. She and I go way back," Laurie stopped and turned to get the waiter's attention. "Hey, Austin? I could use a Dr. Pepper," the hairdresser said to the man in the black trousers and white polo. "And can you bring some ice water for my friends."

"We live up in Springville," Kate said before Laurie started up again. "I am a hairdresser myself. That's how I met Penny."

Laurie bobbed her head, her copper earrings jiggling beneath her red locks. "Awesome. Hairdressers unite!" she made a fist and pumped it in the air with a laugh. "I loved Penny. She took care of my brother and me when we were younger. Sometimes Mom had to work late and Penny would bring us dinner and check on us. We had a little apartment south of town. It only had one bedroom that Mom and I shared. Josh slept on the couch." Laurie looked up at Jay with a shrug. "Mom was divorced, doing the best she could."

Jay rested his arm across the back of his wife's chair as she began to speak.

"We talked to Luther this morning, and Clyde the other day, but it sounds like you might have a few stories about Penny that we haven't heard. I know you have to get back to work—" Kate paused as Austin set three glasses on the table.

Laurie winked at the waiter and took a long sip of her drink. "I have time. I'm just trying to think of which story to tell you." She stirred her drink and took another sip. "I remember this one time Mom was working at the diner and we were home alone. I must've been about ten and Josh was eight." She stopped her story and looked up at Kate. "That sounds sort of bad, but the neighbor was supposed to be checking on us—we never really saw the lady much, but that was the plan. Anyway Josh decided he was going to play with his friends and I couldn't stop him."

***

"You aren't supposed to leave the house until Mom gets back, Josh," Laurie yelled from the balcony of the apartment building. Her brother walked the bike to the end of the sidewalk and looked up at her.

"I'm just going down to the ball field. I'll be back before Mom gets home," he called as he jumped on his bike and took off.

Laurie grumbled and stomped back into the apartment. She sat on the lumpy couch with the denim cover and picked up the book she'd been reading. "Who cares if he gets in trouble? I don't care. Why should I care," she said staring at the page.

After a few minutes of not reading, she tossed the book on the couch and walked into the bedroom. She turned on the radio, opened a magazine and thumbed through the pages as she sat on the bed.

She checked the clock. Her mother's shift ended at three o'clock. It was only two. She dropped the magazine and wandered back into the living room. She stopped in front of the television. They only had four channels and there was never anything on that she liked. She stepped into the kitchen and pulled a piece of white bread from the bag and began to eat it.

A noise out front caught her attention. She moved to the front window and pulled down the metal blinds. It was hard to see much from the second story apartment, but she thought she heard someone calling her name. Maybe Josh had come back. She went to the door and opened it wide.

"Laurie!"

She leaned over the balcony and scanned the parking lot. To her left she noticed that two bikes lay on the ground, the tires still spinning from having been recently abandoned.

"Oww. It hurts so bad," she heard her brother's voice behind her. "Laurie, help me."

Josh was clutching his arm and his best friend Benny was standing beside him, a look of panic on his face.

"What happened?" Laurie rushed to his side and grabbed his shoulder.

"Ow. Don't touch me." Josh complained.

She looked at Benny. "Somebody better tell me what happened."

The other boy looked at his shoes and said quietly, "He fell. We were just riding our bikes and he crashed."

Her little brother had been riding his bike like a pro since before he could make full sentences. It was very unlikely that he just crashed. Laurie had seen a ramp set up at the park and she knew Josh had helped build it. "You were jumping off that stupid ramp weren't you," she scowled at her brother. "Mom told you to stay off it." Laurie shook her head. "Great. This is just great."

Benny sighed and mumbled as he turned to go. "I'll...uh... see ya, Josh." He ran down the stairs and hopped back on his bike.

Laurie stared at her younger brother, his face pale and twisted in pain. She gently put her arm around his shoulders and led him into the apartment. "Maybe if we put ice on it. Sit down," she motioned to the couch and ran into the kitchen. She pulled out a tray of ice and banged it on the counter. She twisted the plastic mold and ice popped out all over the tiled surface. She grabbed an old bread bag and threw the ice inside and hurried back to Josh who had gone even paler. She laid the ice pack on his arm and he yelled.

"Well, you do it then." She handed him the ice and sat beside him. "Mom will be here soon," she looked at the clock. They still had at least forty-five minutes before she would get home, maybe less if she took the bus. Some days her mother just walked the three miles instead of spending money for bus fare.

"Laurie, it hurts. Can't you call Mom? I think it's broke." Josh started to cry, something her little brother hardly ever did.

"Mom said not to call her unless it's an emergency. Don't you think you can just wait until she gets here?"

"This is an emergency!" Josh cried harder and wiped his nose on his shirt with his good hand.

Laurie sighed and walked to the phone that was hanging on the wall in the kitchen and lifted the receiver. She punched in the number for the diner and waited.

"Penny's, how can I help you?"

"Hello. This is Laurie Jacobs, Lizzy's daughter. I need to talk to my mom." Laurie paused. "Can she come to the phone?"

"Hey Laurie. Let me check. Hold on okay, hon?" the hostess said in a sugary voice.

Laurie stretched the phone cord as far as it could reach and peeked into the living room. Her brother was lying on his back, his arm still held firmly against his striped shirt. He'd stopped crying, but she could see a trail running down his dirty cheek. She stepped back into the kitchen and leaned against the counter, listening to the noise of the diner coming through the phone.

"Laurie? Is everything okay?" Lizzy spoke into the phone startling her daughter.

"Mom! Josh went to the park on his bike. I told him not to go, but he did anyway," Laurie began to cry. "He hurt his arm Mom. I put some ice on it, but he's crying."

"Hey now. Laurie. Stop crying. It'll be okay," her mother took a deep breath that even Laurie could hear. "What time is it? Two-thirty?"

Laurie nodded as she looked at the clock on the stove. She wiped her eyes on a kitchen towel and waited for her mother to tell her what to do next.

"I'll see if I can leave a bit early. Maybe someone can give me a ride home." Laurie heard her mother sigh again. "I don't know how I'm going to pay for this," Lizzy mumbled into the phone. "Does it look like it's broken?"

"I don't know, but he says it really hurts."

"What was he doing? Oh never mind. I have to go. I'll be there as fast as I can Laurie."

Chapter 17

The hairdresser shook her glass of ice and set in on the table. "He needed two pins in his wrist." Laurie bobbed her head, her earrings swaying with the motion.

"Ow. Poor kid," Kate crossed her arms and rested them on the table.

"Did the diner offer insurance to help with the cost?" Jay asked, ever thinking about the financial end of things.

"No, that's why Mom was so upset. I mean she hated to see Josh in pain, but she could barely put food on the table. How was she going to pay for my brother's surgery?" Laurie looked at Jay with a smile. "That's where our friend Penny came into the picture."

***

"Penny, thanks for the ride home," Lizzy said as she climbed from the car. "I'll see you tomorrow." She closed the door and hurried toward the stairs that led to her apartment, passing her son's bike on the way. She stopped on the bottom step as she heard Penny speak from close behind her.

"Is this Josh's bike," Penny asked as she righted the bike and rolled it out of the way.

Lizzy turned surprised that Penny was still there. "Uh . . . yeah it is." The woman watched as Penny leaned the bike against the side of the building and began to climb up the stairs. "I think we'll be fine Penny. You don't have to come up."

Penny smiled and said kindly, "Now Lizzy. Are you planning to carry your boy to the hospital? I am not leaving until we get him to a doctor and taken care of."

Lizzy released a breath. "I guess you're right. Thank you, Penny."

They hurried up the stairs and into the small apartment where they found Josh lying on the couch and Laurie sitting on the floor with a book in her hand. Lizzy knelt by the couch and touched her son's shaggy brown hair. "Hey baby. I heard you got hurt," she said softly.

Her son opened his eyes and frowned.

"I think I broke my arm. It really hurts." He cradled his left arm as a tear slipped from the corner of his eye.

"Hey now. Don't cry we'll take you to the doctor and get it fixed up." Lizzy helped her son sit up and then stand. "Do I need to carry you?"

The boy shook his head and leaned against his mother as they passed by Penny.

"Laurie grab your mom's purse," Penny said, pointing at the bag her mother had dropped beside the couch. The girl picked up the purse and put it over her shoulder as she joined Penny on the landing outside the apartment. "Have you eaten today?" Penny asked as the redheaded girl pushed the button in on the doorknob and pulled the apartment door shut.

"Yeah . . . a little."

"Well maybe we'll get an ice cream after we see the doctor. How does that sound Josh?" she called to the boy in front of her.

The boy nodded still clutching his injured arm as they made their way back to Penny's car. Lizzy climbed into the back seat with Josh and Laurie took the passenger seat next to Penny.

"There's a clinic over on Third South. I've taken the kids there before," Lizzy said from the backseat.

"I think we need to take him to the ER, Lizzy," Penny said as she turned onto the street. "He's going to need x-rays most likely. I'm going to run you down to the hospital in Gunnison." Penny looked in the rearview mirror and saw the pout that had formed on Lizzy's face.

"I can't afford a trip to the ER," Lizzy said in a frustrated tone. She looked down at the boy whose head was lying in her lap. She wondered if she should call the kids' father. She hadn't seen Dan in over six months and the child support checks were barely enough to pay the rent.

"He has to get the arm fixed. Don't you worry about it, Lizzy; Del and I will take care of it."

Lizzy shook her head. "That's too much to ask, really Penny. I couldn't let you pay for it. I'll call their father . . ."

Penny glanced over her shoulder as she stopped at a red light. "I don't want to hear another word about it. I am going to pay for it."

"Fine. But I will pay you back."

The car grew quiet and Penny turned on the radio. Singing along as the car sped south toward the hospital.

***

"Penny took care of us just like she always did." Laurie checked her bright green watch. "Oh my. I have a client coming. Sorry, but I have to run. Thanks for stopping by to see me. Maybe we can talk more at the memorial service. I've already arranged to take the day off. See you then." Laurie pushed her chair under the table and strode away, her red hair flowing around her shoulders as she hurried down the block.

Jay stood and pulled Kate up beside him. "Another great story. I'm starting to think the woman was a saint," he said with a laugh.

"It sounds that way doesn't it?" Kate paused. "I do remember seeing a bill for a surgery as I was digging through boxes. I assumed it was for her husband, but I guess not."

"I bet that was a huge bill. It probably took a while to pay that off." Jay took Kate's hand as they walked back to their car.

Jay started the engine and put it into drive. "I'm getting hungry. Where would you like to eat?"

Kate shrugged, and then laughed when Jay and she both suggested, "The diner?"

"Of course," Kate said as she snapped her seatbelt and Jay headed down Main Street. "We should go and see where Penny spent her days."

"Do you have an address?"

"No. I hope we can just find it." Kate leaned forward as they drove several blocks through town. As they rounded a curve in the road Kate called out, "There it is. Wow. That's so cool to see Penny's name on the sign."

Jay pulled into the lot and parked the car. "It looks busy."

They walked up to the door, stepping under the red and white awning as a couple exited the diner. Jay caught the door and held it open as Kate went inside.

"Hello. Welcome to Penny's." The hostess smiled. "Two today?"

Jay nodded and placed a hand on his wife's back.

The woman checked her board and grabbed two menus. "This way, please," she said, moving through the restaurant toward a booth near the window. "How's this?"

Kate smiled and slid onto the seat. "Fine," she said reaching for the offered menu.

Jay took his menu, pulled out his reading glasses and slipped them onto his nose.

"Corrie will be your server. Have a good lunch," the hostess said before returning to her post at the door.

The couple scanned the items on the menu as the lunch crowd buzzed around them.

"Do you think the menu is still the same as it was when she worked here?" Kate asked.

Jay looked over his glasses at her. "I'm sure it changes over the years, don't you think?" He pointed at his menu and added, "Did you see the Clyde burger? Wasn't that the name of the old owner?"

"Uh huh." Kate leaned back. "But it has mushrooms on it so I don't think I'll try that. Do you think they have one called The Penny?" She ran her finger along the list of burgers.

"I didn't see one," Jay said closing his menu.

"I guess not." Kate closed the menu and set it on the table. "Well, I think I'll have soup and a salad. The sign at the front said the soup of the day was minestrone. What are you getting?"

"The Clyde." He set his menu on top of Kate's. "And a strawberry shake."

The waitress arrived at the table a few moments later and took their orders. "I'll grab your drinks and get that going for you." Corrie smiled and left the table in a hurry.

"I feel like we've stepped back in time," Kate said as her eye roved over the diner's decor. "I love the chrome stools and the black and white checkered floor." Kate ran her hand over the red vinyl seat. "I wish we had a picture of the interior to know if it's changed much."

"I bet they've had to update the kitchen, and I'm sure the cushions have had to be reupholstered. Things wear out." Jay crossed his arms and leaned against the back of the bench. "I'm sure they tried to keep things close to the original."

"Yeah. I hope so. The exterior looks almost the same as the old picture I have." Kate pulled out the picture of Lizzy and Luther standing in front of the diner with Penny. "See?" She held up the photo as the waitress returned with two glasses of water and set them on the table.

"Is that this place?" she asked, catching sight of the picture in Kate's hands.

Kate turned the photograph toward the woman and nodded. "Yes it is. How long have you worked here? Did you ever know a waitress named Penny?"

"I've only been here about a year, but I love this place." Corrie said as she set a couple of straws on the table. "So there really was a lady named Penny?"

"Yes, Penny was a waitress here for years. She even became an owner at one point," Kate said as she put the picture away. "She just passed away and we came to Ephraim to prepare for her funeral."

"Ah. Sorry to hear that, but that's pretty cool." The young woman smiled at Kate. "I bet she's glad you're here."

A lump formed in Kate's throat and all she could do was bob her head. Jay reached across the table and squeezed his wife's hand as the waitress scurried away.

"She's right," Jay said fiddling with his glasses and leaning forward in his seat. "I think Penny would be happy we've come to this place she loved."

They sat in silence watching the customers as they ate and visited with each other. Kate tried to envision her friend bustling around the diner, serving lunch. It wasn't that hard to imagine.

Jay broke into her thoughts. "I keep wondering how Penny had the money to invest in the diner. I doubt she made much money here. Have you come across any paperwork about a loan?" Jay asked. "It could be that she and Del had to take out a second mortgage on the ranch to do it."

Kate took a sip of her water and set it back down gently. "I found those ledgers and bank statements that you've been looking at, but that's all."

"Yeah. I brought those ledgers with me, but I can't remember seeing anything about a loan." Jay wiped the condensation from his drinking glass and swirled his ice.

Corrie arrived with their food and asked if they needed anything else.

"No. This should keep me busy for a while," Jay said as he adjusted the top bun on his four-inch high burger.

"Enjoy." Corrie grinned and stepped away to another table.

"Is there an egg on that burger?" Kate asked in amazement.

"Yep. And mushrooms and fried onions." He licked his lips and lifted the burger to his mouth, struggling to take a bite.

Kate sipped at her soup, blowing on each spoonful. "I wonder how the kids are doing? Do you think I should call?"

Jay shook his head and continued to work on his burger. "They're fine," he mumbled between bites.

Corrie passed by their table. "How's everything?"

"Good. Thanks," Kate replied as she pulled a piece from her roll and dipped it in the cooling soup.

As she ate, Kate watched the hostess seat an older couple at a nearby table. As the couple took their seats, Corrie emerged from the kitchen and set two glasses of soda on the table in front of them. The waitress laughed at something the man said and the wife frowned and shook her head. Kate decided they must be regulars at the diner.

After another moment, the server gestured in Kate's direction and the man turned in his seat and looked directly at her. Kate looked down at her salad, speared a piece of lettuce and popped it in her mouth.

Chancing another glance in the couple's direction, Kate realized that Corrie was crossing the diner toward her. The waitress smiled and stopped beside Jay and Kate's table.

"I'm sorry to interrupt your lunch, but Mr. Walker over there says he knew Penny." Kate glanced across the room at the gentleman who was still looking her way. "He said to give you this." The waitress handed Kate a business card. "He'd like to talk to you after you have lunch."

Kate read the name on the card. *Ralph Walker, Property Management.* She nodded at the man and smiled. He returned the smile and twisted back around to face his wife.

"What does the card say?" Jay asked as he wiped his mouth on a napkin.

"Ralph Walker. Does that sound familiar?" Kate asked.

Jay took a drink of his shake and turned to look at the couple across the way. "I don't know. Not really."

"I know I've heard that name before."

Kate set the card aside, trying to recall where she'd heard of Ralph Walker. She finished her lunch and placed the dishes on the edge of the table. She pulled out her list of names and read through it.

"Louise mentioned a Nora Walker. Probably his wife, but I thought I'd heard his name before as well." Kate removed the packet of pictures in her purse and fished through it. "Nothing."

"You'll just have to wait and see what he says," Jay said.

Corrie stopped at the table and reached for Kate's dishes. "How was everything?"

"Very good."

"Did you save room for dessert?" the server asked as she looked at Jay.

"Uh . . . no. That was delicious, but I am stuffed," Jay answered with a grin.

"Well then, I'll get your check, but there's no hurry. You're welcome to wait here for Ralph and Nora to finish."

Corrie removed the dirty dishes and hurried to the kitchen. Jay patted his stomach and said, "That shake was good."

Kate laughed and studied her list, ticking off the people she'd talked to. "Besides the Walkers," she gestured across the room, "Ernie is the only one left on my list. Do you think we'll have time to stop by his house?"

Jay nodded. "I think so, but then I would like to drive to Manti and see the sights down there before we check into the bed and breakfast."

"That would be nice," Kate agreed.

Corrie set the bill on the table. "Thanks so much for coming in today. Good luck with the funeral," the young woman paled. "I mean . . . have a good day."

Jay placed a credit card with the bill and returned it to the edge of the table.

"I'm going to find a rest room." Kate said as she stood and looked around. Corrie breezed by with a tray of food. "Which way is the restroom?" Kate asked, catching the server's attention.

"Straight back," Corrie nodded to the rear of the diner.

"Thanks."

Kate passed through the restaurant and found the tiny bathroom. When she came back to the booth, Jay had a piece of pie and two forks in front of him. He chuckled at her wary expression.

"Corrie brought it. She said it was on the house. I couldn't turn her down."

They ate in silence enjoying the creamy pie. Jay scooped up the last bite and Kate ran her finger through the leftover whip cream. "Mmm. That was yummy."

Chapter 18

"Was that the banana cream pie?" Ralph asked as he approached the table. "They still use Penny's recipe you know."

"You're kidding?" Kate smiled broadly. "Do you think they'll let me have the recipe?"

"I have it," Nora said. "I'll get you a copy. Hi, I'm Nora and this is my husband Ralph by the way."

"Mind if we join you?" Ralph asked as he stood beside the booth with his wife. "We heard you were asking about Penny."

"Yes, of course. I'm Jay Lundquist and this is my wife Kate," Jay said as he stood to shake Ralph's hand and motioned toward Kate. The couples shook hands all around and Jay slid in next to Kate. He pointed at the empty bench across the table. "Have a seat."

"Thank you," Nora said as she scooted onto the vinyl cushion. "Have you been to our diner before? It's a real gem isn't it?"

"This was our first time," Kate answered. "I do love it. We'll have to come back down another time and bring the kids."

"Oh so you have children. How old?" Nora asked as she adjusted her skirt.

"We have three. A boy, fifteen, a girl, thirteen and a baby girl that just turned one." Kate looked at Jay who'd taken her hand under the table.

"You're too young to have teenagers," Nora said with a smile at Kate.

Jay laughed. "Notice she wasn't talking to me."

Kate squeezed Jay's hand and Nora laughed.

"My first wife died a few years ago. Kate is my second wife, and yes, I robbed the cradle," Jay explained as he always did when meeting new people.

The group nodded in understanding and Ralph rested his clasped hands on the table. "Nora and I have four children," he said, "and eleven grandchildren."

"With one on the way," Nora added with a grin that lit her entire face.

"Wow. That's fantastic." Kate smiled at the couple. "Do you get to see them very often?"

Nora shook her head. "Not as often as we'd like. Our oldest son moved to Phoenix and took four of the grandkids with him. But our two daughters live in American Fork and Lehi and they each have three children, so we see them a little more often. Matt, our youngest, lives in Cedar City and they are expecting a second boy in November."

"How nice." Kate released Jay's hand as she reached for her purse. "As I guess you know, Penny died this week." Kate took a cleansing breath and wondered how many times she'd said that in the last week.

Nora sighed and Ralph put his arm around his wife's shoulders and said, "Yes, word gets around pretty quickly."

Kate opened the envelope and removed the pictures. "I have been asked to take care of Penny's estate and also to speak at the funeral, so I have been going through her belongings." She set four pictures on the table. "I brought a few old pictures with me, hoping someone could tell me about them. Do you recognize any of these people?"

"Well, this of course is Del on his horse and that's Penny there beside him," Nora commented on one photo. "My they were young then."

"And this is Luther and Lizzy as it clearly says," Ralph said with a laugh. "Have you had a chance to talk to Luther? He's still here in town."

"Yes we talked to Luther this morning," Jay said. "And we just saw Laurie, Lizzy's daughter, at the hair salon."

Kate looked up at Nora. "Did you know Lizzy?"

"Yes. We did." Nora smiled. "We've lived here forever."

Kate laughed. "I guess you have." She looked back at the old photo. "They both told us some very interesting stories."

Ralph nodded. "I bet you could stop just about anyone on the street and get a story about Penny or Del." Ralph paused. "Well, at least from those over the age of fifty," he said as Corrie passed by with a tray of drinks.

Nora picked up one of the other photos. "This looks like Karen Moore and her mother Jessica. Doesn't it Ralph?"

Ralph inspected the photo and nodded. "Could be."

"Karen is all grown up now. She used to visit her mother every month until she passed away about two years ago. I haven't seen her lately. Last I heard she lived in the Salt Lake area." Nora set Karen's photo back on the table and lifted the second one. She peered at it for a moment and turned it toward her husband. "Is that Clyde and . . . what's her name? You know his first wife?"

"I know who you mean, but I can't think of her name." Ralph shrugged and arranged the pictures in a neat row. He looked up at Jay. "Clyde remarried after his first wife ran off with some guy she knew from college."

Nora nudged her husband. "She didn't run off. She and Clyde were having trouble anyway. They got a divorce and yes, eventually she married that other man." Nora added the picture of Clyde to the row on the table. "I don't know her name either. It's going to bug me all day."

"That's alright," Kate said. "I just thought I'd see if you knew who they were."

Ralph cleared his throat. "Seeing those old photographs brings back so many memories." He tapped the picture that had been taken in front of the diner. "We were coming to this diner way back then."

"Is this where you first met Penny?" Kate asked, glancing around the diner.

"Yes. We came in at least once a week and Penny was usually the one to take care of us," Nora said a melancholy expression crossing her face.

"We preferred Penny over Lizzy, but we couldn't always get her table." Ralph grunted as Nora elbowed him.

He frowned at his wife. "Well it's true. Lizzy was always forgetting things and sometimes mixed up the order completely."

Nora nodded, but did not comment.

"We loved Penny . . . still do. She was one of our favorite people in the world, but not because she was the best waitress in town." Ralph's voice caught and he tapped the table in front of Penny's picture unable to finish.

Nora touched her husband's hand. "I'll tell them, dear." She looked at Jay and then Kate. "We heard you were asking about Penny so we wanted to tell you about an accident Ralph had some years ago and the impact it had on our lives."

***

Nora felt her legs buckle as she collapsed onto a kitchen chair. She gripped the phone and asked into the receiver, "Which hospital are they taking him to?"

"Gunnison," the man said on the other end. "I'm really sorry, Mrs. Walker."

Nora nodded slowly and dropped the phone back into its cradle. She took a ragged breath and glanced across the room at seven-year-old Ethan who was sitting in front of the television watching his favorite show. She could hear Allison and Erica in their bedroom playing with dolls. The baby was sleeping, but should be waking soon.

"What am I supposed to do? Pack everyone up and head to Gunnison?" She felt tears collecting in her eyes as she recalled the conversation she'd just had with Ralph's boss. Somehow her husband had been impaled by a piece of rebar at the construction sight where he was working.

Nora shuddered. The image of her husband being carried off with a piece of rebar still sticking out of his chest made her feel light headed. His boss, John, said that Ralph was alert and talking, but they were rushing him to the nearest hospital. She stood up and turned off the stove. The dinner would have to wait until she got back.

"Ethan? Mommy has to . . ." Nora paused, not sure what to tell the boy. She didn't want to frighten the children. Ethan didn't budge from his position in front of the TV. Maybe it was easier to just find a babysitter and not tell them anything. Who knew how late she would be at the hospital. She reached for the phone and scanned the directory for a babysitter's number. It was Friday afternoon and she worried about finding someone on such short notice.

She dialed The Smith's number and waited.

"Hello?" a young woman's voice answered. "This is Pam."

Nora was glad that the Smith children made it a habit of giving their names. With six daughters, Nora always hated to guess.

"Hello, Pam. This is Nora Walker. I know this is last minute, but I'm looking for a sitter for tonight. You wouldn't happen to be available would you?" Nora asked trying to keep her voice even.

"Hi Mrs. Walker. No. I can't do it tonight. I have a date, but maybe Brenda can. Should I go find her?"

"Yes please."

"Okay. Just a moment," Pam said as she set the phone down.

Nora could hear Pam calling through the house for her sister. After a full minute, another young woman picked up the phone and spoke into it.

"Hello?"

"Is this Brenda?" Nora asked.

"Yes."

"Hi Brenda. This is Mrs. Walker. I'm looking for a sitter for tonight. Can you watch the kids for me?"

"Tonight? Well, I think so. Let me check with my mother."

"I'm really in a—" Nora began to say as the phone clunked against a hard surface, "hurry." She shook her head and took a deep breath. "Please hurry," she mumbled under her breath.

The girl came back on the line.

"Mrs. Walker? Mom says that's fine. What time do you need me?"

"Right now if you can. I have to run to the hospital. My husband had an accident," Nora bit her lip and steadied her breath. "Do you think your mother could bring you over?"

"Sure. I'll be there in a jiffy."

Nora hurried through the house collecting toys and scattered belongings, tossing them onto her unmade bed. She hated to leave the house in such a huge mess, but she had very little choice at this point. She poked her head into the girls' bedroom.

"Girls? Mommy has to go out for a little while. Brenda is coming to watch you. Will you listen for Matthew and show Brenda where his diapers are?"

The two little blond girls bobbed their heads.

"And I can help her feed him if he gets hungry," three-year-old Erica said with a grin.

"Kiss!" Allison cried as her mother began to back out of the room. The five year old had begun needing a kiss every time her mother left the house.

Nora hugged her daughter tightly and kissed her head. "You be good and help the babysitter." She stepped into her bedroom and changed into a clean outfit. She ran a brush through her hair and hurried into the hallway as the doorbell rang.

Ethan jumped up to answer the door and turned to call to his mother. "Mom, somebody's . . ." He paused as his mother touched his shoulder.

Nora opened the door to find Brenda standing on the porch. "Hello Mrs. Walker. How are you Ethan?" Brenda asked as she hurried into the house.

"Good." Ethan nodded and returned to his cartoon.

Nora smiled feebly at Brenda. "I have chili on the stove that we were going to eat. It's should be ready soon, but if you don't want that there's macaroni in the cupboard."

The young woman smiled confidently. "I got it. Don't worry about us."

"Thank you so much Brenda." Nora felt her eyes blur. "The baby is in bed, but he should be getting up soon and the girls are in their room. Thank you for coming so quickly."

Nora grabbed her purse and rushed out the door. She stopped on the driveway as she realized Brenda's mother, Linda, was waiting at the curb inside her running vehicle. The girl's mother opened her car door and called to Nora.

"Nora. What happened? Brenda said something about the hospital. Is everything okay?"

Nora's eyes filled with tears. "Ralph had an accident. He fell on a piece of rebar. They're taking him to the hospital."

"Oh my goodness. Here jump in. What hospital is he going to?" Linda asked as she ran around to open the passenger side door.

"Gunnison. But I can drive myself," Nora said. "You probably need to get back home."

"Don't be silly. I'll go with you. Dave and the kids will be fine. I told them to eat without me."

Nora only hesitated another moment. "Okay. Thank you, Linda. I'm a nervous wreck. I'm not even sure where the hospital is."

"I had to take Christina to the emergency room about three months ago, so just relax, I'll have you there in no time."

Linda sped down the block, the tires squealing as she took the corner too fast. Nora clutched the door handle, praying for her husband and hoping that she herself would arrive at the hospital in one piece.

Chapter 19

"You were impaled?" Kate asked, interrupting Ralph's story. "That's horrible."

Ralph raised his eyebrows and bobbed his head. "Yes. It was."

Jay sat forward. "Where did it go in?" he asked clearly interested in the details of Ralph's story.

"Back here," Ralph turned and touched the right side of his back, almost to his armpit. "It broke my shoulder blade, but thankfully it missed the major arteries."

"Did it go all the way through?" Jay asked.

Kate frowned in Jay's direction.

"Yes." Ralph hesitated, glancing at Kate.

"How did it happen?" Jay prodded.

"We were building a home out in Fairview and the foundation was done, so we were backfilling around it. John was running the backhoe and I was wetting the dirt down with a hose. I had been keeping my distance, but I noticed a water jug that had been left in the dirt and I stepped forward to retrieve it." Ralph shook his head. "That was my mistake. John swung the bucket around and didn't see me. I jumped out of the way, but the back hoe still grazed me and I fell backward, landing on an exposed piece of rebar." Ralph shook his head. "It was just one of those freak accidents."

Jay sat back. "Wow. I've heard of people being impaled while they're driving down the road and something flies through the windshield—"

Kate grabbed her husband's arm. "I know this fascinates you, but I am feeling sick."

"Sorry." Jay looked apologetic, but only momentarily. "Did they have to cut the rebar to get you into the ambulance. I've heard it's better to leave the object in until you get to the hospital."

"Yeah. John realized what he'd done and went ballistic when he saw the rebar poking out of my chest. I don't remember much after that because I was in and out of consciousness, but they decided not to remove the rebar. They cut the bar below me and left it in." Ralph stopped as Kate shuddered.

"I think that's enough about that," Nora said interrupting her husband. "Are you okay Kate?"

Kate took a deep breath and closed her eyes. "Yeah."

The woman picked up her tale. "So as I was saying, my neighbor Linda drove me to the hospital, but I didn't even get to see Ralph for several hours. He had already been taken into surgery. Eventually the doctor came out and told me the details of the injury. He said Ralph was stable and would heal fine. I didn't realize "fine" meant he wouldn't be able to use his arm for several months."

Ralph nodded and cleared his throat. "The physical therapy was torture and I felt useless after lying around the house for a few weeks." Ralph rubbed at his shoulder. "I got workman's compensation eventually, but that didn't cover everything," he complained as he looked over at his wife. "We had four kids to feed and Nora couldn't go to work, so things were really tight."

"I tried to do daycare and took on a few extra kids, but we were seriously struggling to keep our head above water."

Kate let out a breath with a sigh. "I'm so sorry."

Nora continued her story. "What happened next was the real reason we wanted to talk to you today."

***

"Ralph?" Nora called as she stepped into the backyard where her husband was sitting in a lounge chair watching the kids play in an inflatable pool. "I just got off the phone with the mortgage company." He looked up as she took the chair next to him. "There's no way we're going to make the full payment again this month, but I was hoping they would take a partial payment."

Ralph nodded and sighed deeply.

"Angie just paid me for tending her kids last week, so I thought I'd use that." Nora turned her seat to face her husband. "Anyway, I gave the lady on the phone our account number and she was looking up our account . . ."

Allison squealed as Erica dumped water over her head with a cup. The girl sputtered, but laughed as she returned the favor to her younger sister.

Ralph returned his gaze to his wife and said, "I bet the fees will be astronomical. Maybe we can ask my dad if he can loan us some money to live on for a while. He might have some savings."

"No. Listen. The woman said that according to her records we have no payments due. None." Nora grasped her husband's hand. "She said our mortgage has been paid through February."

"February? That's like six months away." Ralph scratched at his head and replaced his ball cap. "And besides, we are at least two months behind. She must have been looking at the wrong account."

Nora shook her head and corrected her husband. "Three months. We haven't made a full payment in three months. And that's exactly what I told her." Nora jumped up to rescue Matthew who had tipped sideways in the pool. "I explained that she must be mistaken, and had her double check." Nora righted the child and sat back down beside her husband. "She assured me that we were all caught up on our payments and I didn't need to make any more for the next six months."

"Did she say how this had happened? Somebody had to have paid them. Mortgage companies aren't in the charity business," Ralph rubbed at his injured shoulder. His physical therapist expected him to stretch the shoulder every day and work at lifting his hand higher. Raising his arm still caused tremendous pain, but at least he had some mobility.

"She couldn't tell me anything. Only that it was paid. I don't think she knew any details. She just answers the phone." Nora turned her attention back to the kids in the pool. Ethan had left the water and was digging in the sandbox. His feet and legs were covered in sand as it clung to his wet body.

"Do you think your family paid it? They know we're struggling."

Nora frowned. "I'm sure they'd like to, but who in my family could really do that?"

The couple sat in silence.

"Everyone knows you haven't worked for several months," his wife said softly. "They all read the article about your accident in the paper." Nora wrinkled her nose. "I wasn't going to tell you, but Penny saw me in the grocery store this morning and asked how things were going. I almost broke down in front of her." Nora shook her head. "She could see I only had a few things in my shopping cart. When I got out to the car there was a bag of food sitting in the back seat."

"Do you think Penny put it there?"

"I don't know. It could have been anyone, I guess."

"It's hard to keep a secret in this town," Ralph said as he continued to stretch his right arm. "People just want to help."

"I appreciate the help, but it's embarrassing. I really hate being a charity case." Nora picked up a towel and grabbed her youngest child. "Time for lunch and a nap, little boy."

***

"That's where I've heard your name," Kate exclaimed. "My friend Connie was helping me clean out Penny's house and she spilled a file full of newspaper clippings. As we were cleaning them up, she read the article to me about your accident. We thought maybe Del was just interested in those kind of stories."

"You read the article about my accident?" Ralph looked baffled. "Why would Penny still be holding on to that?"

"I am starting to realize that Penny had a lot of secrets." Kate looked around the diner. "Good secrets, but a whole side of her that I never imagined."

Jay was nodding. "She was constantly helping people . . . and sometimes in really big ways. Laurie told us that Penny paid for her little brother's surgery when he broke his arm."

Nora's mouth dropped open and she quickly clamped it shut. "Well I'll be. Then it really might have been her." She looked over at Ralph. "I had my suspicions, didn't I?"

Ralph agreed. "We knew she went out of her way to help people, but when Nora suggested Penny might be paying our mortgage I couldn't believe it was true." Ralph wrinkled his forehead. "Where would she get the money? Were they mortgaging the ranch up to their eyeballs?"

"It could be. I've been looking through her documents, but haven't found anything about a second mortgage. We did find a few ledgers." Jay motioned to the car. "I actually brought some. Maybe we can take a look at them before we head out."

"Well, sure. We're done here right?" Ralph checked his watch and looked at his wife.

The foursome stood and walked to the parking lot. Jay opened the backseat and lifted two ledgers from a box. "What year were you injured?" Jay asked.

"It was the summer of 1983."

Jay checked the spine of the book where Penny had neatly printed the years. "This might have what we're looking for in it." He flipped through the pages and ran his finger down the page.

"Hey! There we are," Ralph said pointing at an entry for Walkers with the amount of $648 in the column beside the name. Jay turned the pages and found several more payments for the same amount.

"I guess there's your answer." He smiled up at Ralph and Nora.

Nora had tears in her eyes. "She was too good."

Ralph placed his arm on Nora's shoulders and nodded. The group stood in silence for a moment before Jay set the ledgers back in the car.

"It was so nice to meet you folks," Ralph said as he reached for Jay's hand. "Are you heading home today?"

"No. We're staying until tomorrow," Jay said as he closed the car door.

"Well, have a good afternoon," Ralph nodded in Kate's direction. "You let us know if we can do anything to help with the funeral."

"Thank you. I will."

The two couples retreated to their cars, and Jay backed out of his spot and stopped before turning onto Main.

"Where to? Ernie's?"

"Yes. Head north and then take a left at the light." She looked at the notes on her paper. "I'm glad we came down here. It helps me feel connected to her—knowing that

Penny lived in this town and passed through all these same places."

"Mmhmm." Jay stopped at a red light. An older couple crossed the street hand in hand. "That could have been Penny and Del a few years ago. That couple has probably lived here their whole lives."

Kate watched as the couple stepped onto the sidewalk and the man said something to his wife. "Maybe. I don't even know where Penny and Del were born?"

Jay stepped on the gas and continued on his way. "You haven't come across a birth certificate yet?"

"No. I haven't been through all the boxes yet, I guess. Take a left at the next street." Kate pointed in Jay's direction.

"It's possible that those documents are in a strongbox somewhere or even in a safety deposit box."

"Could be. Did Ron mention her having a safety deposit box?" Kate asked as she pointed again. "Take a right."

"I don't know. My memory is failing, remember?" Jay laughed as he drove through a quiet neighborhood. "I'll try to remember to ask him."

"Here it is." Kate gestured toward an older two-story home with green shutters. "Nice house. I love the wrap around porch."

Jay parked at the curb and peered through the windshield at the home. "I like the big tree. We need to get one of those."

"Yeah. It's probably been here for a hundred years or more. I don't think we're going to find anything like that in our neighborhood."

"Well, maybe we should move down here," Jay said as he opened the car door and climbed out.

Kate opened her own door and took Jay's offered hand. "It looks like we've been noticed. Someone's standing at the window."

Chapter 20

The couple walked up the front path, pausing at the bottom of the steps as the front door swung open. An older man stepped out of the house and met them with a tentative smile.

"Good day. How can I help you?" he asked.

Jay released Kate's hand and climbed the two steps to shake the man's hand. "Hello. I'm Jay Lundquist and this is my wife Kate. Are you Ernie?"

"It depends who's asking. You aren't from the IRS now are you?" the man chuckled.

Kate moved up to stand beside her husband and smiled. "We're friends of Penny's. We came down from Springville to meet a few people that knew her." She hesitated, wondering if he had heard about their friend's death.

The man looked surprised, but grinned at the mention of Penny's name. "Oh for heaven's sake yes. Come have a seat." He motioned to the row of chairs on the porch and waited until Jay and Kate were seated on the cushioned loveseat. "Ernie Hollingsworth. Good to meet you." He nodded as he took his own chair. "It's still so hard to believe that Del and Penny are truly gone. They were such wonderful people. Touched a lot of lives those two did."

"That's what we keep hearing," Kate said as she removed her purse and set it at her feet. "I'm not sure why Penny asked me to handle her memorial since I have only known her for a few years. I know there are people more qualified." Kate shook her head. "But that's what we're here for—to gather a few stories to tell at the service."

"You've come to the right place. I have a few stories about Penny, so many in fact, I wouldn't even know where to start," Ernie said lifting his chair and turning it to face the couple more directly.

"We've talked to a few people already. We saw Laurie Barber and she mentioned the doctor's bill, and Ralph and Nora Walker told us about the mortgage payments Penny made on their behalf."

Ernie was tapping his chin and nodding.

Kate took a ragged breath. "I also talked to Clyde on the phone. He couldn't say enough good things about Penny and Del. He told me how Penny helped keep the diner open."

The man's eyes sparkled and a grin split his face. "That she did. What a wonderful blessing that was—for Clyde and for the whole town. We needed that diner just as much as we needed Penny. That diner was the command post, if you will, for Penny's life long work. And I don't mean the work she did as a waitress. No sir-ree. I mean the loving acts of kindness she performed every single day. She went out of her way to help everyone—strangers and townsfolk alike."

"That's what we've learned." Kate swiped at a tear that threatened. "She was always so good to our family. It was extremely hard to tell the kids about her death. They loved her like a grandmother."

Jay put his arm around his wife and said, "We also talked to Luther and he told us how someone gave him money to buy a plane ticket so he could visit his sick mother. He was certain the money came from Penny."

"I wouldn't put it past her, and I'm sure that's only the tip of the iceberg." Ernie seemed lost in thought for a moment, staring off into the distance. "I don't know everything Penny did because of course—she wanted to keep her secrets under wraps. But there were a few times when she needed my help. I was sworn to secrecy, but at some point I think she deserves to be recognized." Ernie tugged at his ear and frowned. "Hopefully she won't be turning over in her grave if I tell you that I took care of the mortgage payments for Ralph," Ernie said softly as he gazed out toward the street. "And the doctor bills for Lizzy." He turned back toward the couple on his porch. "I'm glad you're hearing about the incredible good she accomplished in this town."

Kate nodded. "Would you mind telling us how you met Penny?"

"It was at the diner of course!" Ernie laughed as he began his tale. "I was in my late twenties and Penny was a few years older. I had just moved to town."

***

"Turkey club on white, light on the mayo," Penny repeated as she stood beside the table of the younger man. "Did you want fries or fruit with that? The melon is fresh and perfectly ripe if you'd care to try it."

"Fruit it is." Ernie looked at the blond woman's nametag and smiled. "Thanks Penny." He handed her his menu and watched the petite waitress move to another table. She hadn't written down his order, so he hoped she wouldn't forget to go easy on the mayo. Nothing bothered him more than being heavy handed with the mayo. He took a swig of his drink and scanned the room—not that he knew anyone in this town yet.

He had only arrived in Ephraim last week. He was one of the newest graduates of Southern Utah University. He and his wife Gloria had both found work in Ephraim confirming the decision to settle in this small town. Ernie had accepted the teller position at the bank and Gloria had found a job at a dental office.

As he studied the room, Ernie found his gaze returning continually to a woman and her three children at a nearby booth. The dark haired mother seemed to be at her wits end with the youngest child. The young boy was not cooperating in the least with his mother. He stood on the bench and sang at the top of his voice, then shook his head vigorously from side to side as his mother tried to coax him to sit down and eat his lunch.

A moment later, Penny came through the swinging doors with a small cup in her hand. She spoke quietly to the little boy and placed a cup in front of him. As he slipped down to his seat and reached for the drink, a flash of relief crossed the mother's face.

Ernie heard Penny say, "Chocolate milk works every time." The waitress smiled at the boy's mother and moved to a table at Ernie's left.

She began to remove the dirty plates. "Can I get you anything else today?"

The couple shook their heads. "Just the check, thanks Penny." As the waitress stacked the dishes on top of each other a fork slipped from the pile. The man caught it in mid air.

"Nice catch, Ralph," Penny said with a laugh. "I bet you played baseball in High School."

"As a matter of fact I did. Short stop. MVP my senior year." The man glanced at his wife. "I haven't seen my old glove for years though. I hope we kept it."

Ralph's wife shrugged. "Don't ask me."

"I'll be right back with your check," Penny said before glancing in Ernie's direction. "Your lunch should be ready as well."

She hurried to the kitchen with the dirty dishes and returned a moment later with Ernie's sandwich. She set the plate of food on the table and reached for his empty cup. "Root beer right?" she asked, taking the glass before he could even answer.

"Thanks," Ernie said to himself as he watched the pint-sized waitress stop at Ralph's table with the check.

"Thanks for coming in today," she said as Ralph pulled out his wallet.

Penny hurried away, pausing momentarily to greet a new customer before making her way back to the kitchen. The energetic little woman appeared to know everyone and nothing seemed to slip her attention. She was definitely in her element as she smiled and moved through the diner.

Ernie stabbed a piece of melon and popped it into his mouth. Perfect—just as she had promised.

"Now for the real test," he said softly as he lifted the top slice of bread from his sandwich and eyed the perfect amount of mayo. "She's good."

***

Kate pushed a lock of hair behind her ear as the wind picked up and ruffled it. "She was always good with details."

"That's what made her a great waitress," Ernie said as he sat straighter in his chair. "So like most people in town, I became a regular at the diner. The food was good, but it was mostly Penny's friendly manner and the way she took care of the customers that brought people back."

"I bet it was," Kate said. "The service is the biggest factor in whether I'll go back to a restaurant or not."

The man nodded and shifted in his seat. "And it wasn't just the customers that loved Penny. The employees that worked with her every day were often blessed by her kindness as well." Ernie ran a hand over his stubbly chin. "You know how she helped Lizzy out."

Jay nodded.

"I remember when she asked me to pay those doctor bills. I told her several times to find herself a good accountant and let him take care of her finances," Ernie said with a chuckle. "She'd say, 'Why do I need an accountant when I have you?'"

Jay laughed. "Are you still a teller?"

"No. I moved up to the position of loan officer, but even before that happened I was helping her with these extra "services". I really didn't mind. It was always gratifying to see the joy she brought to so many people." A smile lingered on the old man's face. "Let me tell you another quick story about Lizzy and Penny."

***

"You have food waiting Lizzy," Karen called. "Better get it out."

Lizzy mumbled under her breath at the younger waitress. "Been here a month and she thinks she knows everything."

The diner was bustling with customers and Lizzy's tables weren't getting the attention they deserved. It wasn't entirely all her fault. The kitchen had put the wrong dressing on a salad and one plate was missing its fries.

"I'm coming," Lizzy hurried to drop off a drink refill at one of her tables, and rushed back to the kitchen. She filled her tray with plates of food and carefully balanced them on her shoulder as she crossed the diner to the booth at the back. She rested the tray on the edge of the table and set a grilled cheese sandwich in front of the little girl at the table.

"Here you go."

The girl squinted at the plate and scooted it across to her brother. "I had the chicken strips not the cheese sandwich."

"Oh right." Lizzy placed the chicken strips on the table and smiled at the pouting child. "Sorry."

"The chicken salad for you," Lizzy said placing a plate in front of the mother before handing the last dish to the father, "and the barbecue special for you, sir."

The father looked at the plate and back at Lizzy. "This looks really good, miss, but I actually ordered a burger," the man said returning the plate to the waitress.

"You did? Oh gosh. I'm sorry. What kind of burger was it?"

"The bacon cheeseburger with extra onions," he said with a sigh, "and onion rings."

Lizzy drew in a deep breath. "I'll have that out to you as quickly as I can. I am so sorry sir."

The man nodded, clasped his hands under his chin and frowned as his family began to eat without him.

Lizzy set the plate of food on her tray, balancing the whole thing on her hip. She quickly pulled a pad from her pocket with one hand and tried to look through the orders.

"Hey Liz. I think that's mine," Ernie spoke from behind her.

"Oh Ernie. Yes. I'm sorry. Can I get you a refill?" she asked as she placed the food on the table.

"No. Penny grabbed me one," the banker said with a tiny smile. "I could see you were frazzled so I asked Penny."

Lizzy frowned. "I could have done it . . . but you're right. Things are a bit nuts today. Anything else you need?"

"No. I'm fine. Go get that guy's burger ordered."

Lizzy shot him a grateful smile and ran back to the kitchen.

***

"That was a typical day for Lizzy, but she worked hard to take care of her family." Ernie gazed out over the lawn, his mouth turned down in a frown. "That family left just before I did," Ernie said, "and I knew they weren't happy. From what I could tell they didn't leave much of a tip."

The older man returned his gaze to Kate and Jay. "As I stood up to leave, I saw Penny drop something on the table. I was curious as to what she was doing, so I stepped closer and realized there was a ten dollar bill on top of the tip the family had left." Ernie lowered his eyebrows and let his words sink in.

"Penny was such a generous woman." Jay commented. "But Kate and I never met her husband. Del? He was a rancher, right?"

"Yes. They had land a few miles west of town where Del raised cattle. He even raised pigs occasionally. Have you ever had a fresh ham? Penny brought me one for Christmas one year," Ernie said as he licked his lips and rubbed his hands together. "That was the tastiest meat I ever had."

A car drove past and tooted its horn. Ernie waved.

"Who owns Del's land now? Maybe we should take a drive out to see the old homestead." Jay looked at his wife. "Would you like to do that?"

"Sure that's a great idea." Kate folded the paper in her hands and returned it to her purse.

"Roberto bought it," Ernie explained as he stretched his legs out in front of himself and crossed his arms over his chest. "He lived there as a child when his grandfather worked for Del. He came back to town some years ago and ended up buying the place. I'm sure he wouldn't mind if you stopped by."

Jay stood and extended his hand to Ernie. "It's been a pleasure talking to you."

Ernie pushed to his feet and took Jay's hand. "Same to you."

Kate smiled and raised her purse onto her shoulder. "We'll see you at the Memorial Service on Wednesday."

"Yes. Thanks for taking care of that. Expect a big crowd." He shook his head and sighed. "That woman left a real mark on this town."

Kate stepped down the steps with Jay following close behind.

"Have a good day, folks," the man called as they climbed into the car.

Chapter 21

Kate clicked her seatbelt as Jay started the car and left the neighborhood, heading south toward Manti. "I can't wait to see the temple. Can we stop there first?"

Jay smiled. "I need to pick up something, but I think you will see the temple on the way."

"What are you picking up?"

"Patience Kate. It's a surprise."

Kate furrowed her brow and studied her husband. "What kind of surprise?"

"If I told you then it . . . "

" . . . wouldn't be a surprise," Kate finished. "I know, but when did you have time to plan a surprise?" She touched his arm. "Amber, your secretary, must be in on it. Maybe I should call her."

"Just stop it. You'll like this surprise and yes, maybe Amber helped a little. You know I need help for stuff like this and I couldn't very well ask you." Jay squeezed his wife's hand. "Manti is only fifteen minutes away. You can wait fifteen minutes can't you?"

"I guess." Kate gazed at the farmland for several miles, but then she reached into her purse and found her phone.

"Hey. Who are you calling?" Jay asked as he spied the phone.

"My mother. I thought I'd check on the kids."

Jay nodded. "Just making sure."

Kate dialed her mother's number and let it ring until it went to voicemail. She left a message and disconnected. "I guess they went out somewhere. She did say they might drive up to Thanksgiving Point."

"I'm sure they're fine."

"I could try her cell, but she never hears that." Kate set the phone back in her purse. "So are we going to dinner in Manti? Do they have any nice restaurants even?"

"I'm not that hungry. Are you?"

"Of course you aren't. You had a mammoth sized burger plus a shake . . . which you didn't even offer a bite of to me." Kate pouted and looked back out the window with a laugh. "I'm not hungry yet, but I'll need some food in a few hours."

"I have plans for dinner. You don't need to worry so much." Jay grabbed her hand and kissed her knuckles.

"You and your surprises." She leaned over and kissed her husband on the cheek. They sat in silence for the remainder of the drive until the temple came into view. "Oh. There it is. I love to see the temple."

Jay broke into song, "I'm going there someday."

Kate laughed and sang along as they passed the majestic building on the hill.

"So where are we staying?" Kate questioned, as her husband slowed the car and took a turn down a quiet street. "I know it's a bed and breakfast, but what's it called."

Jay rolled his eyes and took a cleansing breath. "You're worse than the kids. It's called Amelia's Bed and Breakfast. Have you heard of it?"

Kate shook her head.

"Well, me neither but Amber claims it was highly rated. She's never steered us wrong before."

Kate sat quietly as her husband pulled a note from his pocket. "Here tell me where to turn."

Several turns later, Jay stopped in front of a charming Victorian style home and put the car in park. "Stay here. I'll get us checked in and be right back."

"I want to come in . . . " Kate bit her tongue as her husband gave her the evil eye.

"I'm just checking in for now." He left the car running. "I'll leave the keys in case it gets too hot."

Jay removed the suitcase from the trunk and walked up the path to the large porch. Kate saw him disappear through a bright red door. She rolled down the window for some fresh air and shut off the engine. A cat ran across the lawn and hopped over the wooden fence as Kate craned her neck to see if Jay was coming yet.

A few minutes later, Jay exited the home without the suitcase, carrying a cooler in his hand instead. He set the cooler in the back seat and climbed behind the wheel. He started the car and headed toward the center of town and turned south.

"I thought we were going back to the temple."

"We are . . . later." Jay drove toward the opposite side of town.

Kate chewed on her lip as they left the small town and sped through more farmland. "How do you even know where you're going?"

"The map said to just stay on this road until we get where we're going," Jay answered cryptically.

She frowned and tapped her fingers on her leg. "Right."

"Let's play twenty questions," Jay said. "You can go first."

Kate chose an object in her mind and Jay began asking questions.

"Is it bigger than a breadbox?"

"Yes," she said and smiled as he continued to ask questions to narrow it down.

After several rounds of the game, Jay pulled off the road and stopped at a brown ranger pay booth.

"Welcome to Palisade State Park. Are you camping or here for day use?"

"Just for a couple of hours," Jay answered as he handed the woman cash. She nodded and handed him the receipt instructing him to stick it to the inside of his windshield.

"Have a nice evening."

Jay rolled up his window and smiled across at his wife. "Does this remind you of anything? Dinner in the back seat, a wooded area near water?"

"Are we going to skip rocks?" Kate asked, thinking of their first date two years ago in the canyon near their home.

"We might. I remember you seemed to like how I wrapped my arms around you to help you throw the rock last time we tried."

Kate felt her face grow warm. "And yet we've never been out skipping rocks since."

"Really? Are you sure? Well, we'll have to remedy that today."

Jay shut off the car and hurried around to open Kate's door. "I do remember how nervous you made me," he said, pulling her into an embrace. "I felt so awkward, but you fell for me anyway." He kissed her quickly and took her hand. "Let's walk down by the lake and then we'll come back for the picnic dinner."

They stepped onto the path that led to the water as a breeze tugged at their clothes. It was a perfect day to be at the lake as was evident by the amount of families spread out along the water's edge. Kate gazed across the lake to the low hills that served as a backdrop.

"It's not the biggest lake, but it does seem popular," Jay said as they maneuvered closer to the water.

The lake's edge was filled with bright colored tubes and paddleboats. A father and son stood in the shallow water, watching minnows flit around their ankles. Further out, two canoes were heading back to shore, the frantic paddlers obviously in a race.

"Have you ever been in a canoe?" she asked her husband as they paused under a tree.

"When I was a kid at scout camp we used some. I remember my best friend trying to tip it over."

Kate squinted up at Jay. "Sounds typical."

"He couldn't do it, thankfully. I wasn't the best swimmer and the water was really cold," Jay explained with a laugh. "But we splashed each other enough that we ended up drenched anyway."

The couple continued their leisurely walk along the shore. "Did you bring a fishing pole?" Kate asked as they came upon an older man and a young girl casting their lines into the water. The gentleman in the fishing vest inclined his head and muttered, "Good afternoon."

Kate and Jay nodded back, pausing as the girl swung her baited hook back into the water.

"I seriously considered bringing it, but then I wondered where we would cook a fish. I didn't think you'd want to keep it overnight and have to drive home with it." They walked further until Jay squeezed Kate's hand and released it. He scanned the shore, and bent to pick up a flat rock. "This should work." He side armed the rock out across the water away from the fishers and watched as it skipped three times. "Not bad." He reached down and found several more stones. "You remember how I taught you to throw it?" He handed Kate a rock and challenged, "Let's see you beat three."

She moved closer to the water and gripped the rock as Jay had done. She flicked her wrist and was amazed to see the pebble bounce across the water four times. "Wow. It worked."

"Of course. You were taught by the best." He tossed another rock, but was disappointed when it only skipped two times. "That one was too light." He collected a few more and tried again.

"Whoa. I counted six," Kate said in awe.

"Here try again." Jay handed her another rock and Kate took a few steps toward the water and let it go. The rock skipped across the water four times and sank. "Four's not bad," he said wrapping his arm around her waist. "Your form is looking good." He nuzzled her neck and whispered softly. "I like watching you toss rocks into the lake."

A flush rose on Kate's cheeks and a grin sprang to her lips. "Oh yeah?" She turned her face up to his and kissed him softly. "And I like having you all to myself. We should do this more often."

Jay kept his arm around her waist as they turned and walked back in the direction they had come. A long necked bird landed gracefully on the water just beyond the swimmers.

"The water is so blue, it's almost enticing enough to wade in. Should we take off our shoes and see how cold it is?"

Kate shook her head. "I don't really want to . . . unless you do."

"I guess not."

They passed a dock jutting into the water where three teenage girls stood holding hands preparing to jump.

"Ready? Go!" As one, the girls splashed down into the water, sputtering as they came up for air. "Cold, cold!" they cried.

"Now we know. It's cold," Jay said leading Kate away from the rocky beach. "What should we do now?"

"I don't know. What else do you have planned?" Kate asked as Jay led her up the path.

"I thought we'd have dinner here and go back up to the temple to walk around. How does that sound?"

"I could eat now. Are you hungry yet?" she asked with a sly grin.

"Sure. I'll go get the food if you want to grab that table," Jay motioned to a picnic table under a tree.

The two went their separate ways and Kate took a seat on the cool metal bench at the table. A family at a nearby table was preparing to eat as well. The mother was unloading a cooler and handing out premade sandwiches to her three children and husband.

"This one is peanut butter," she said handing it to the youngest boy. "Cami did you have tomatoes on yours?" she asked the older of the two girls. Her daughter nodded and took the offered sandwich. The father began handing out cans of soda and the middle child opened a bag of chips.

Kate's phone chimed and she pulled it from her pocket. There was a text message from her mother.

"Saw that you called. Doing fine. Have fun."

Kate sent a reply and set the phone on the table. She looked around for Jay wondering what was taking so long. As she waited, another message appeared on her phone, but this time in email. She touched the screen and waited for it to load. The message had come through Facebook and read:

"Hello. My name is Justina. We got your note about Penny's death. My mother would like to talk to you. She is Penny's cousin. Please call me." A phone number was attached to the message and was signed Justina Brown Hardy.

"That name sounds familiar." Kate went to her Facebook app and opened the friend request she had received earlier in the day. "So Justina is related to Penny."

Kate clicked on the request and accepted Justina as a friend. She was directed to her new friend's homepage and found several pictures of a small blond woman. One picture in particular caught Kate's attention. The caption read: Mom and me. The gray haired woman with the bright blue eyes was definitely related to Penny.

Chapter 22

Jay arrived with the cooler and set it on the table as Kate tucked her phone back into her pocket. "What took you so long?" she asked as she took the small bag he held out to her.

"I went into the little shop by the ranger station to get something. Open it," he instructed, pointing at the bag.

Kate unfolded the top of the paper sack and reached inside. She withdrew a small hand painted plaque adorned with interlocking hearts. *"Friendship is reaching for someone's hand and touching their heart."*

She looked up at her husband, a smile touching her lips. "That is such a nice saying."

Jay nodded. "I was glad I found it. I was trying to find you a gift to remember this trip by and for our anniversary." He opened the lid of the cooler and began setting covered dishes on the table. "I almost bought a set of coasters with the Manti temple on them, but then I found this instead. It made me think of Penny."

Kate read the sentimental message again. "Yes. It's perfect. Thank you." She returned the gift to the bag and stood up to kiss her husband on the cheek. "You are so sweet, but I didn't need a gift—the flowers you gave me were enough." Kate started opening the containers of food. "I didn't get you anything. I haven't had a chance to even go shopping."

Jay set two plates and silverware on the table. "I don't expect a gift. Every day I get to spend with you is a gift," he wrapped his arms around Kate from behind and kissed her hair. "Sit. Let's eat." Jay sat on the bench and began to fill her plate. "I doubt this will be as good as the chicken Sister Sorensen made for us on our first date, but it will have to do."

"I'm sure it'll be fine." She slid onto the seat beside her husband. "I guess the cook at the bed and breakfast made it?" Kate asked as she took a bite of her fruit salad.

"Yes. Pierre does the cooking and his wife Amelia handles everything else."

Kate swallowed the sweet bite of salad and picked up the beef sandwich. "What's on this? It smells really yummy."

"I'm not sure. Amber took care of it." Jay admitted. "I told her to get whatever sounded good."

"It's different, but really good," Kate said, as she tasted the sandwich a second time. "Well, except for the mushrooms." She opened the bun and removed two large mushrooms and set them on Jay's plate.

"More for me." Jay popped the mushrooms into his mouth and smiled. The couple grew quiet as they concentrated on their meal and watched the family at the nearest table pack up and head to the parking lot. A bird swooped down onto the newly vacated table in search of crumbs.

Jay wiped his mouth with a napkin and sighed. "That was excellent. Pierre knows what he's doing. I bet the dessert will be fantastic."

"There's dessert?" Kate crumpled her napkin and tossed it onto her plate.

"Back at the house. Pierre said they have dessert each night between seven and eight o'clock in the parlor. We'll get some later."

Kate checked her phone for the time. "Then we'll have a little time to stop by the temple." They started putting lids back on containers and returned the dishes to the cooler.

"Yes. That's where we're headed next." Jay lifted the cooler and turned toward the car.

"Good. Thanks for dinner," Kate said putting her hand into the crook of her husband's arm as he carried the small blue and white cooler to the car.

"You're welcome. I hope you aren't disappointed that we didn't eat at a fancy place." He stopped by the car and found his keys.

"No. This has been a great day," Kate said as she climbed into the passenger seat. Jay closed her door and put the container in the backseat. He got in beside her and started the engine. "While I was waiting for you, I got a message from a cousin of Penny's." She checked her phone as they pulled out of the state park and read the message again. "The message was from Justina, Penny's cousin's daughter. She left a number to call her."

"So she must have gotten the letter you sent out to everyone. Her mother's name had to be in the address book."

"Right. I guess so."

"Well that's good. She can probably tell you about Penny's early life before she came to Ephraim." Jay eased onto the highway and headed toward Manti. "Didn't someone say Penny grew up in California?"

"I think so." Kate returned to Justina's Facebook page and looked at her information. "I guess the daughter lives in Thousand Oaks, California. Wherever that is."

Jay turned on the cruise control and looked across at Kate. "I've heard of that. It's down by Los Angeles, sort of. Maybe closer to the ocean."

"You think I should call her right now?" Kate asked.

"No. I'm sure it will be a long conversation. Call her tomorrow when we get home." Jay took his wife's hand. "The rest of the night belongs to us."

Kate smiled and held his hand in her lap as the miles zipped by. She began to doze off and was startled awake some time later as the car slowed to a stop. She opened her eyes and realized they were stopped in front of the temple. Jay put the car in park and smiled across at his sleepy wife.

"Did you have a nice nap?"

"Yeah. Sorry. All that good food made me drowsy."

"That's alright. I like watching you sleep." Jay leaned forward and whispered. "Are you still tired? We could head over to the room."

A pleasant sensation zipped through her at Jay's suggestion. She bit her lip and snickered as he wiggled his eyebrows in her direction.

"Let's take a walk first. Then, yes, I want to go see this fabulous place you've reserved for us." She shook her head and reached for her door handle.

Jay hurried around to her side of the car and grasped her hand as they crossed the lawn toward the temple grounds. "I've never been inside this temple. Have you?"

"No, but I've heard there's an amazing spiral staircase inside. We'll have to come back when we have more time."

The couple climbed up the steep hill toward the beautiful stone building. Kate stopped to catch her breath and scanned the sky above the temple. "I'd forgotten that there's no angel on top of this one."

"That's right. The St. George and Logan temples don't have an angel on top either." They continued up the hill and turned to look out over the valley. "Wow. You can see forever from up here."

Kate gulped for air and slowed her breathing. She pointed across the street to a large graveyard. "I've never walked through that cemetery. I think I may have ancestors buried there. Should we check it out before the sun goes down completely?"

"Sure."

The couple stood for another few minutes as people passed them on their way in and out of the temple. Kate felt out of place in her jeans and t-shirt, but smiled at the friendly faces that greeted her. "I guess we better head back," she said looking down the hill.

"Wait. Let me take your picture in front of the temple." Jay pulled out his phone and stepped away from his wife. "Ready?" He snapped the photo and began to put the phone away.

"Should I take one of you?" Kate asked as she stepped to his side.

"No. I don't need one of me." Jay took her hand and began his descent.

"Maybe we could get someone to take one of us together." She looked around at the few people on the path and was surprised to see a familiar face coming up the hill. She bent closer to her husband and asked, "Isn't that lady from the stake?"

"Yes, I think so," Jay slowed his step. "I can't come up with her name though. Maybe she won't—"

"President Lundquist! How are you? What are you doing down here?" the woman laughed and shook Jay's extended hand.

"We're fine thanks. We just came down for the weekend." He hesitated a moment, still unable to recall the woman's name. "Have you met my wife Kate?"

"No we haven't met officially." The woman smiled and extended her hand. "It's nice to meet you. How's that new baby?"

Kate tugged at the hem of her shirt nervously and shook the woman's hand. "She's growing too fast. She turned one this month."

"One already? You know what that means. It's time to start thinking about having another one." The woman cackled at her own comment. "I'm sure she wants a little brother to keep her company."

"Excuse us," a man interrupted with a nod as he and his wife stepped around Jay and Kate.

The woman with no name continued talking as if she hadn't been interrupted. "I know you have the older children, but they'll be grown and gone before you know it. I would have at least one more baby if I were you."

Kate nodded, unsure how to answer the bold woman.

Jay grasped Kate's hand and began to lead her away. "Well, it was nice to see you again. Have a good evening."

"You too." The woman smiled, oblivious.

They walked in silence until they reached the sidewalk. "Can you believe her nerve?" Jay said as he squeezed Kate's hand and leaned closer. "I was tempted to tell her that was exactly what we were doing down here . . . trying to make another baby."

Kate's breath caught and she swatted his arm. "You wouldn't!"

Jay shrugged with a twinkle in his eye. "I might."

Chapter 23

"I hope you slept well," Amelia said as she set a glass of ice water on the beautiful lace tablecloth.

"We did. Thanks." Kate smiled up at the proprietor.

Amelia reached for Jay's glass and filled it with water as he unfolded his napkin. "Kate especially enjoyed the large jetted tub." Jay chuckled. "I could barely get her to come down for breakfast."

The woman laughed. "Soaking in a tub is one of my favorite past times as well." She rested the towel wrapped pitcher on her hip and gestured toward the table. "If you'd like to get started with the fruit cup, we'll have the main course out in a few moments." Amelia hurried back to the kitchen.

Kate lifted the linen napkin from the cream-colored china and draped it across her lap. She speared a piece of pineapple from the small crystal bowl and pointed it at Jay. "I did love the tub. I think we should get one." She popped the fruit into her mouth and glanced around at the cozy dining room. "This is so fun. What a beautiful place. I love all the natural light and the large deck." She motioned to a pair of double doors that led out to a garden area. "I bet they host wedding receptions out there." It had been too dark last night to see much of the yard, but now she could see it had a large grassy area surrounded by beautiful trees. The garden beds were bursting with flowers of every color. "It would be perfect."

Jay nodded and looked toward the door that Amelia had disappeared through. "Yes, but what I want to know is what they have planned for breakfast. I could go for more of that chocolate mousse from last night." He popped a grape into his mouth.

"Yeah or those key lime bars." She murmured. "Whatever is on the menu, I'm sure it won't be your typical scrambled egg breakfast."

"I hope not."

She reached for her glass and sipped at the cool water, her gaze sliding over the rest of the cozy room. "You did good, Jay. We'll have to come back here another time."

"I'm glad you like it." Jay turned in his chair and pointed at the cold fireplace. "Maybe next time we can come in the winter, so we can enjoy the fires. I wonder if all the rooms have a fireplace like ours did?"

"I guess we'll find out when we come back," Kate said with a smile.

Another couple entered the dining room and headed for a nearby table. The young man nodded and Jay said, "Good morning."

The young woman giggled as her husband took her hand and helped her into her chair. Kate smiled as the younger couple leaned across the table and gave each other a quick kiss.

Jay grasped his wife's hand, drawing her attention away from the other table.

"Remember when we were young and starry eyed like that?" he asked, kissing his wife's hand. He paused with her hand to his lips. "Oh right. You still are young. It's me that's old and forgetful."

She laughed softly. "Stop it. We're still newlyweds. Two years isn't that long to be married."

He leaned forward and whispered. "You make me feel young, that's for sure. I often think about how different my life would be if you hadn't come along. You saved me from a life of loneliness, Kate."

She closed her eyes and shook her head. When she opened them, there were tears on her cheeks. Jay squeezed her hands. "What's wrong? What did I say?"

She smiled through her tears. "I just think it's funny that you say I saved you. You are the one that has given me the life I always dreamed of. You made me a wife and mother. The two things I wanted most."

A look of pure joy spread over Jay's face. "I'm so glad you're happy." He let go of Kate's hand as Amelia approached the table and set a plate of food in front of his wife.

"This morning we have eggs benedict in a nest of hash browns," Amelia said as she set a second plate in front of Jay. "And toast with homemade jam. Would either of you like a glass of orange juice?"

"Yes. Thanks," Jay said as Kate nodded in agreement.

Amelia stepped away and greeted the younger couple before heading back to the kitchen. She emerged a few minutes later with four glasses of juice, delivering two glasses to each table.

"How are the eggs?" she asked Kate as she set the juice in front of the couple.

"Fabulous." Kate wiped her mouth with the napkin.

"Can I get you anything else?"

"No, I think we're fine. Thank you."

"Well good. You let me know if you need anything else." Amelia bustled away and Jay let a tiny moan escape.

"This is so good. I wonder how hard this would be to make at home. Do you think Pierre would give us his recipe?"

"This is beyond my cooking abilities, Jay, but if you'd like to try to make it, I'd be willing to eat it." Kate bobbed her head and took another bite.

They finished the meal in silence, relishing the delicious food. Kate ran her fork through the remaining yellow hollandaise sauce and licked it with satisfaction. "So good."

Jay drained his glass of juice and set his napkin on the table. "Well, I guess we better get going if we're going to stop by Penny's old house."

Kate agreed and scooted her chair back. Jay jumped up and held the chair as she stood up with a giggle. "Thank you, kind sir." She bobbed her head and put her arm through his. She smiled at the young couple as she and Jay left the room.

Amelia rushed into the dining room with a small package in her hand. "Pierre wrapped up a few of last night's bars for your trip home."

Jay reached for the treats and smiled. "Tell him thanks. I'm surprised there were even any left over from last night. They were so good."

Kate nodded and added, "Everything we ate this weekend was just delicious and the rooms were so nice. Thank you. We had a wonderful time." Kate gave Amelia a hug.

"You're very welcome. Thanks for choosing to stay with us. We hope you will come again." The woman waved as the couple headed into the front foyer.

Jay opened the front door and let his wife step through ahead of him. He pulled his keys from his pocket and pushed the button to unlock the car. The day was beginning to warm already as they climbed into their seats and pulled away from the curb.

"Did you write down the instructions for where Penny lived?" Jay glanced at his wife as he paused at the intersection.

"Yes. It's right here," she pulled the paper covered in notes from her purse. "Ernie said to head south of town and then go east on Christensen Lane."

They found their way to Main Street and turned south. A few minutes later they were heading out into a rural area following the banker's directions. Jay slowed the car as Kate pointed down a small gravel road. "Not much out here. I would guess this must be it." He turned up the road and found a long driveway leading toward a brick home. He parked in front and shut off the engine. Kate gazed through her window at the house with two dormer windows with dark blue shutters. White and pink pansies lined the path leading to the front porch where two sturdy rocking chairs waited in the shade.

"It looks like someone is taking good care of it," Kate said as she climbed from the car. She started toward the house, but paused as she noticed a man standing in the garden at the side of the house. He wore a straw hat and was bent over at the waist. Kate could see he was picking tomatoes from the overgrown vines and placing them in a big yellow bowl.

Jay stepped up beside her and called out to the man. "Good morning."

The man straightened his back and adjusted his hat over his suntanned face. The couple stepped onto a narrow path that led into the garden area and stopped a few feet short of the bowl of tomatoes.

"What a beautiful garden!" Jay smiled and extended his hand in greeting.

"Keeps me busy." The man beamed and clasped Jay's hand. "How can I help you?" he asked, his accent confirming his Hispanic heritage.

"Ernie thought you wouldn't mind if we stopped by for a quick visit." Jay explained. "I'm Jay Lundquist and this is my wife Kate. We were friends of Penny's. We understand she and Del used to own this home."

The man's expression changed immediately, his gaze softening. "Oh yes. This is their home—always will be. I've taken over its upkeep, but their spirits are still here." Kate could see him swallow back his emotions. He looked up at Kate. "It is true then. They are both gone?"

Kate nodded. "Yes. I'm sorry."

"Del and Penny were always so good to me and my family." He took a deep breath and turned toward a line of trees to the north. "My grandfather worked this land for many years." He motioned toward a tiny shack that stood beneath the trees. "I lived there with my grandparents as a child." The man seemed lost in thought for several moments. "Oh forgive me." He reached for Jay's hand again. "I'm Roberto, so nice to meet you. Please come inside where we can talk." He picked up the bowl of tomatoes and stepped toward the house.

The couple followed Roberto to the side door of the house and waited as he hung his hat on a hook inside the door. Jay and Kate wiped their feet on the bristly mat before stepping into the entryway where Roberto stood beside a second door into the house. The mudroom was lined with shelves of canning jars full of fruits and vegetables. The man set the bowl on a workbench and reached for one of the jars before continuing into the house.

"Marguerite," he called as he stepped into the kitchen. "Come meet our visitors."

A short dark haired woman appeared in the doorway of the kitchen leading a sleepy eyed child by the hand. "This is my wife Marguerite and our daughter, Penelope." The little girl turned away, hiding in her mother's skirt. "We call her Penny."

Chapter 24

After quick introductions to Roberto's family, Jay and Kate followed the family into a small living room. Kate wondered if Marguerite had changed the room much from when Penny had lived in the home. The walls were painted with a soft yellow and there were lace curtains at the windows. A single wingback chair sat in the corner and a well-worn sofa was the only other seating in the room.

"Would you like a drink?" Marguerite asked as she stood with her daughter still tugging at her skirt. "We have fresh grape juice."

"Is that what your husband set on the counter?" Jay asked with a grin. "I would love a glass. Thank you."

Marguerite smiled and looked at Kate. "Señora?"

"Yes. That sounds delicious."

Marguerite gently nudged the girl toward her father and hurried back to the kitchen as Roberto gestured toward the couch.

"Have a seat."

He stepped into the adjoining room and returned with a dining chair. The girl stood shyly beside her father, not meeting Kate's gaze. The man sat on the chair and lifted his daughter onto his lap.

"I am so happy you have stopped by to see us. We have not seen Penny for a while." He rubbed the little girl's back as she snuggled against his chest. "Had she been ill?"

"No. It was quite a surprise that she died really. She had a heart attack." Kate glanced at the little girl wondering how much the preschooler understood. "She went to sleep and never woke up."

The man nodded. "We will miss her." He shook his head and smoothed the girl's nightgown around her legs. "How did you know her? Are you a neighbor?"

"No, I was her hairdresser, but she had become part of our family." Kate's voice caught with emotion. The man waited patiently for her to continue. "We have three kids and Penny treated them like they were her own grandchildren." Kate adjusted a pillow behind her and looked at Roberto with a brave smile.

"Yes. She was always like that. She also treated me as a grandson. When I was a little boy I would call her "Blanca" because of her white hair."

The group laughed as Marguerite returned with two glasses of juice. She handed them to her guests and took a seat in the remaining chair.

"Let me tell you about mi abuela with the white hair." Roberto smiled at the couple as he began his story. "Like I said we lived in that little house under the trees." He turned his gaze on his wife. "My grandparents were raising me because my mother had been killed in a car accident when I was very young. I never knew my father."

***

"How can the clothes even dry in this weather? It's only going to get worse once winter sets in." Penny motioned toward a clothesline where clean towels flapped in the wind, a frown on her face. "She refuses to use my dryer even though I have offered more than once."

Roberto looked up at Penny with concern. The eight-year-old boy knocked the dirt from the carrots that Del had just unearthed and set them in the wheelbarrow.

"We can't force them to take our help, Penny," Del said as he dug up another shovelful of dirt and carrots. "I doubt they want to be treated as a charity case. It's true they don't have all the conveniences that we do, but they seem happy. Besides, I have paid him more than I normally . . ." the man paused and noticed the boy listening.

Penny followed her husband's gaze and sighed deeply.

"Well, I am going to do something about it. You said there was enough power over there for . . ." she looked back at the boy, "more appliances right?"

Del pursed his lips and squinted at his wife. "What are you planning?" He lifted another scoop of dirt and watched Roberto deposit the carrots into the growing pile.

"I've decided that I need a new washer and dryer," she looked up at her husband with a grin.

"The ones you have work fine? Why would you . . ." A look of understanding crossed Del's face and he shook his head. "Let me know when they arrive."

***

"Del came to the house a few days later and told Abuela that he was there to replace her old washer and hook up a dryer. Abuela and I followed him out to the porch and found the set that had been in Penny's house the week before." Roberto smiled broadly as he remembered the old woman's reaction. "Abuela mumbled in Spanish about stubborn people and then showed Del where to put them."

Kate set her empty glass on the side table and laughed. "Are your grandparents still living?"

"Yes. They're both in their eighties now, and live with my cousin." Roberto turned toward his wife. "We visited with them recently and Abuela mentioned that dryer incident. My grandmother has always been a very stubborn woman, but Penny's kindness touched her deeply."

"Yes, I am starting to understand just how kind and generous Penny was . . . and that she could be quite stubborn herself."

"Besides my grandparents, Penny had the biggest influence in my life. She taught me to work hard and to treat everyone with respect." Roberto cleared his throat and nodded. His daughter squirmed and climbed down.

"Please excuse us," Marguerite said as she took little Penny's hand. "She hasn't eaten yet."

"Oh, of course. We don't want to keep you from your day." Jay began to stand up.

"No. Please stay. I want to speak with you more." Roberto motioned for Jay to stay seated. "When is the funeral?"

"It's this Wednesday at one o'clock at the Olsen Funeral Home in town," Kate answered. "I hope you will come and bring your family. Would your grandparents be able to attend?"

"I will ask them. I know they will come if they are feeling well enough. Thank you." The man looked toward the kitchen before continuing. "I wish you knew all that Penny did for us. She did so much." He ran a hand over his face. "To most people, Penny's kindness would seem like such a little thing, but to us . . ." He released a long breath. "She was an angel."

Kate took Jay's hand and squeezed it.

"I remember many times when my pants were old or my shirts were too tight—" The man struggled to speak and swallowed the lump in his throat. "Without fail there would be clothes in a box on the porch for me. Many times there would be candy or a toy with them. I didn't realize where the clothes and treats were coming from until I was older."

He sniffed and wiped at his nose. "I left home after high school and took a construction job. But once my grandparents decided to retire—something my grandfather had fought for many years—I came back to help Del."

Marguerite came back into the room with little Penny who had changed into a denim skirt and blouse. The two sat down and listened as Roberto finished his story.

"After a few years, Del started getting sick and Blanca realized they couldn't take care of the ranch much longer. She started talking about having me take over. I told her I couldn't afford such a large ranch and that I probably never would have that kind of money." Roberto's eyes shone with unshed tears. "She told me they would work something out and not to worry. They said I was the son they never had." He sniffed again and his voice grew soft. "Ernie helped set up a loan with the bank and I was shocked to find out that the sale price we agreed upon was less than half of what the house and land are worth." Roberto looked at his wife. "She was too good to us. Without her, we would not have a place to call our own."

The room fell quiet until Kate leaned forward and asked the young man, "Do you know where they lived before moving here? We heard they might have come from California."

Roberto tapped his chin. "I'm not sure. But now that you mention it, they did take a trip to California one year when I was in high school."

Kate furrowed her brow and regarded Roberto and Marguerite. Little Penny smiled shyly and rolled her skirt hem in her fingers.

"Blanca was very quiet about her early life. I do know that her parents died in an accident, but that was before my grandparents came to live here."

"Really? I didn't know that," Kate looked at Jay then returned her gaze to Roberto. "I'm not sure I even know her maiden name."

The young man shrugged and shook his head.

"Roberto," Marguerite said softly, embarrassed to see all eyes turned toward her. "What about those boxes you have in the attic? Maybe there is something important in there."

Her husband nodded. "I hadn't thought of those." He spoke to Kate. "Penny left a few boxes when she moved. I asked her what to do with them and she said to just throw them out. I didn't feel right about that. I thought someone might want the pictures. Would you like to see them? Maybe you should take them home."

Kate was eager to see more pictures from Penny's past. "Of course. That would be fantastic." She leaned forward anxiously as Roberto stood with a smile.

"I will get them."

He returned with two dusty boxes in his hands and set them in front of Kate. "Let me get a cloth to wipe them. I have not looked at them since Penny moved away."

"I'll get it." Marguerite hurried from the room and returned a moment later with a damp rag to clean the top of the box.

"Thank you." Kate smiled and carefully lifted a flap. Inside were old magazines and several recipe books. She made a stack of books on the floor until she reached the bottom. She pulled free a large manila envelope and opened the flap. "Oh." She said as she let a pile of pictures fall into her lap.

Jay picked up a photo of a much younger version of the Penny he knew. "She was so cute. Look at those pig tails."

Roberto's daughter joined her mother beside the couch and leaned forward to see the picture of the girl sitting on a pony. She pointed to the old photograph and said, "Oh, pretty pony. I want one like that Papa."

A soft melody filled the small living room, emanating from Jay's phone. He pulled out his phone and turned off the alarm. "I'm sorry. I forgot to cancel that. I usually have a meeting at this time on Sunday mornings."

Roberto glanced at the clock on the wall. "Oh! We need to be going soon, Marguerite."

The woman nodded with an apologetic smile toward the visitors.

"We should get on the road ourselves." Jay stood and shook Roberto's hand. "Thanks for letting us intrude on your day."

Kate reluctantly returned the old pictures to the envelope and tucked it back into the box. "I can't wait to look through all of these." She stood from the couch and peeked inside the other box. "Can we really take them both home?"

"Yes. I have no use for them. You take them." Roberto reached for a box and Jay picked up the other. "Let me help you get these to the car."

Marguerite held open the front door of the house and Kate followed the men outside.

"Thanks for coming. We'll see you on Wednesday," Marguerite said as Penny stepped onto the porch with her mother.

Kate walked down the steps and paused at the bottom. "Yes, It was so nice to meet you Marguerite and your beautiful daughter." She waved at the little girl. "Goodbye Penny."

Chapter 25

April 1956
Burbank, California

"I won't go Mother. You can't make me!" Sixteen-year-old Penny stomped her feet and crossed her arms over her chest. Her mother, Clarinda, was relentless when she got an idea into her head, but this one beat all.

"Penelope, dear. I'm sorry for the change in plans, but they've decided to leave a few weeks earlier than they originally thought. There's nothing we can do about it now." Penny's mother rested her freshly manicured hands on her slender hips and frowned at her daughter. "Uncle Garrett and Aunt Rhonda are expecting you at their home as soon as school is out for the year."

Penny gritted her teeth. "I never even wanted to go in the first place. This is just another one of your dumb ideas." The young woman sighed dramatically. "You know that Suanne asked me to help with Christian's party, which is *after* I am supposed to leave for this stupid trip now." Penny scowled at her mother and sat heavily on the white leather couch clutching the throw pillow to her chest. Christian was turning eighteen on the fifteenth of June and Penny had been helping his mother Suanne plan it for weeks. "How would it look for me to miss my boyfriend's birthday party? No way. It's not going to work."

"Maybe they can change the party to an earlier date, so you won't have to miss it."

"It's a birthday party, Mother. You're supposed to celebrate on the day you were born—not two weeks before." Penny rolled her eyes and took a deep breath. "Besides Suanne has already sent out the invitations and paid the caterer."

Penny had helped plan the menu and she knew that Suanne had hired a live band to provide music for the huge event. Penny and her friends were predicting that this party would be the highlight of the summer. But now her mother was ruining everything. Penny shook her blond locks and tossed the orange throw pillow at the fireplace.

"How could you do this to me?" she stood up and ran down the hall to her bedroom. "I'm not going!" she said again as she slammed the door.

Penny threw herself on the lamb's wool blanket that covered her bed, and let out a muffled cry. "This is so unbelievable. She can't make me go." She took several more steadying breaths. "I mean if she wanted me to go to that stupid equestrian camp again this year that would be fine, but two months in Mexico? With Uncle Garrett?" She turned on her back and looked up at the ceiling. Her mother believed that the summer break was a waste of precious time. She wouldn't allow her daughter to "wile away her days" as she often said. Penny was certain her mother just preferred not having anything or anyone interfere with her time at the club.

She looked up at the clock on the side table. She would talk to her father when he got home. Surely he could be reasoned with and wouldn't make her spend the summer with her hippy relatives on a Humanitarian trip to Mexico.

Frank Crawford arrived home an hour later, exhausted from a long day at work as an associate movie producer. "The director expects me to read his mind," he complained as he stabbed a piece of asparagus. "We agreed on the changes to the script last week, but now he wants to change everything again."

Penny sat sullenly at her place and nibbled at her food as her parents chatted about their respective days. So far she hadn't come up with a way to convince her father that the summer trip was a bad idea. She wondered if he even knew about the plan to ship her off to Mexico. It wouldn't surprise Penny if her mother had whipped the scheme up all on her own.

"How do you like this pork?" Clarinda asked cutting into Penny's thoughts. "Patricia served it at a luncheon at the club. I told her we had to get the recipe so Angelica could make it here at home." Penny's mother took another bite of the honey-glazed pork and closed her eyes. "It just melts in your mouth."

Frank nodded and glanced across the table at his daughter. "Why so glum, pumpkin?" Frank asked.

Penny sighed deeply and gave him a halfhearted smile. "It's nothing." She set her napkin on the plate, deciding that this wasn't the best time to bring up the trip. "I'm not really hungry and besides Christian is on his way." She went around to her father's chair and placed a kiss on his cheek. "I'll talk to you later, Daddy," she said, ignoring her mother's upturned cheek, and hurrying toward the door.

Her father called after her. "You have fun."

"Don't be too late," Clarinda added as the door slammed shut.

Chapter 26

Kate studied the pictures that were lined up on the table and smiled up at Janae. "Aren't these great? She was such a pretty girl, but it's hard to believe this is the same woman that we knew."

Janae nodded. "Yeah. Is this her sister and mother?" Janae asked as she touched a photograph.

"No. I've seen pictures of her mother and she was blond like Penny." Kate lifted the picture of the two teenage girls and the dark haired woman with the long braid. "And I think Penny was an only child. These women may be someone she met in Mexico."

Several of the pictures that Kate had found inside the second box had "Mexico" scrawled across the bottom. Penny, it seemed, had taken a trip to Mexico when she was younger.

"Was this taken in Mexico too?" Janae pointed at a photo of a larger group standing in front of a brightly colored building.

"I think so. It looks like they helped build that house . . . or maybe it was a school." Kate touched another picture of Penny standing next to the same building with a mug clasped in her hand. "See this is before they got the outside painted."

"Oh, right."

"It would be fun to know the details of why she went. I wish I could talk to someone that knew her then." Kate sighed.

"Is there anything else in the box?" Janae asked as she pulled open the box on the floor and lifted out a smaller box. "Did you look through these yet?"

"I didn't look at them individually. It's just a bunch of old birthday and Christmas cards . . . which might be helpful." Kate shrugged. "Let's see who they're from. Hand me a stack."

Janae passed Kate a stack and they began reading through the cards. "This is from Uncle Garrett and Aunt Rhonda, and so is this one. Should we sort them?" The girl asked starting a pile of the ones she'd looked at.

"Sure. This is from Garrett and Rhonda too." Kate added to the growing pile.

"Oh. This one's from Jolene." Janae said as she made a new pile.

"Here's a birthday card from Ralph and Nora." Kate paused. "I met them in Ephraim." She set it aside. "What we need, though, are last names." Kate grabbed a few more from the shoebox.

"None of them have envel—" Janae stopped and smiled. "Jackpot." She held up a smaller envelope. "Garrett and Rhonda sent her a letter."

Kate grinned. "Nice. What does the return address say?"

"Their last name is Crawford. They live in Glendale, California." Janae said, reading from the corner of the envelope. "Well they did when they sent this." The girl looked up at her mom. "Maybe we can find them on the Internet."

"Well, if they were Penny's aunt and uncle then they are probably dead. They would have to be like . . . I don't know . . . close to one hundred years old." Kate shook her head and read through a few more cards.

"Hey. Wait a minute!" Janae pulled a letter from its envelope. "There's a newspaper article in this letter." The girl unfolded the brittle paper. "It's a wedding announcement for Jolene." Janae laughed. "Guess what? Garrett and Rhonda Crawford are her parents. Jolene married Charles Lewis Brown on June 30th 1962." Janae looked up at Kate. "I wonder if they called him Charlie and if he always wore a yellow shirt."

They both laughed.

"Does it have a picture?" Kate asked reaching for the yellowed paper.

"Yep." Janae handed the old news clipping across the table.

Kate read through the announcement and studied the black and white photo. "She looks familiar."

"Isn't she the same girl that was in that picture . . ." Janae scooted the pile of cards aside and lifted the photo of the two teenagers and the dark haired woman.

"You're right." Kate examined the pictures side by side.

"Do you think they're related somehow? Maybe cousins?" Janae leaned forward to get a better view.

Kate drew in a sharp breath that startled Janae. "Oh! I was supposed to call that lady that found me on Facebook." She looked up at the clock. "I guess it's not too late." She picked up her phone and began searching for the woman's name and number. "You know those letters you sent out last week to everyone in the address book?"

The girl nodded.

"Well, apparently you sent one to Justina Hardy. She says her mother is Penny's cousin. I meant to call her."

Kate dialed the number and waited. After several rings she was about to hang up when a young voice came on the line.

"Hello? This is Michelle."

"Hello, Michelle. This is Kate Lundquist. May I talk to Justina?"

"Sure. Just a sec." Michelle set the phone down and Kate heard the girl call, "Grandma!"

A moment later, another voice spoke into the phone. "Hello? This is Justina Hardy."

"Hello, Justina. This is Kate Lundquist. You contacted me through Facebook. I was . . . am Penny's friend."

"Why yes, Kate. I'm so glad you called. Mother has been calling me every morning to see if I've heard from you." The woman chuckled, and then cleared her throat. "We were heartbroken to hear that Penny had died. She was such a sweet woman. Mother loved her like a sister. They didn't get to see each other as often as they liked, but they were on the phone together every week."

"I'm sorry. I hope your mother is doing fine." Kate glanced at Janae who was listening. "Will you and your mother be able to come to the funeral on Wednesday?" Kate asked.

"No. I'm afraid not. Mother doesn't travel anymore. She does want to talk to you though. She's here with the family today, so you called at the perfect time. Can you hold on a moment while I get her?"

"Yes. Thank you."

Kate chewed on her lip as she waited, trying to imagine Penny and her cousin as little girls growing up in California together. She thought of her own cousins and how close they'd been as children. She hadn't talked to any of them for quite some time, and thought it was time she did. She stood and moved into the kitchen for a paper and pencil and jotted *Ashley* on the paper, making a note to call her cousin once this funeral was over.

"Hello? Kate Lundquist?" an older woman's clear voice came through the phone.

"Hello." Kate sat back at the table. "Yes this is Kate."

"Thank you for calling Kate. I'm sure my cousin never told you about me, did she? She was always such a private sort. But now that she's gone, I want to make sure that somebody knows her story." The woman laughed into the phone. "Oh, where are my manners. This is Jolene Brown, but everyone calls me Jojo. Anyway, let's see. Where are my notes?"

Kate tapped the news clipping of Jolene's wedding and smiled up at Janae. She mouthed the name Jolene and pointed at the phone. Janae smiled broadly and nodded.

"I don't know how much you know about Penny, but I guess I'll just start at the beginning. Do you have a pencil, dear?" The woman paused.

"Yes, go ahead."

"Okay dear. Well first of all her full name was Penelope Clarinda Crawford Haws. She was born

January 12th, 1940 and was the only child of Frank and Clarinda Crawford." The woman stopped her account and laughed. "She was like my shadow growing up. I was two years older, but we were always best friends. We had some fights, of course, especially over boys, but that never lasted." Kate waited for the woman to continue. "She was the pretty one, so once the boys met Penny, my chances of getting a date became quite slim."

Kate smiled as the elderly woman cackled into the phone.

"I have a picture of your wedding announcement here in front of me and I think you are quite stunning," Kate said as she picked up the newspaper clipping and studied the woman's face.

"Oh, why thank you dear. What a kind thing to say. My Charlie always made me feel pretty. I sure do miss that man." Jolene cleared her throat. "He's been gone almost five years now . . ."

"I'm sorry to hear that."

"Mmhmm. Well, now let's see . . . Penny and I lived within a mile of each other as children, but when I turned twelve Penny's parents moved their family to Burbank. At that point we only saw each other on holidays and during the summer. I missed her terribly.

"About that same time my daddy started taking youth groups on service trips to Mexico. It became a family tradition that my brother and I looked forward to every year." Kate picked up a photo of Penny and Jolene in Mexico. "One summer my brother was away at college and had a good paying job, which made it impossible for him to come along. I came up with the idea to ask daddy if Penny might join us. I assumed she would love it as much as I did." The woman paused in her narration. "But as I remember, Penny wasn't too keen on going on that first trip."

Chapter 27

June 1956

Penny's first trip to Mexico

"We have to get a picture before we head out," Rhonda said placing her arms around Jolene and Penny's shoulders. "Garrett. Quick. Snap a picture of us."

Garrett reached into the front seat of the car and found the camera. He removed the lens cap and focused the camera on his dark haired wife and the two blonde teenage girls.

"Smile." He pushed the button and lowered the camera. "Nice, but we better get going. Does anyone need to use the bathroom? I told Scott we would meet him at six this morning. I hope traffic is light so we're not late."

Penny sighed and climbed into the back seat of the station wagon. The sun was barely coming up and she wondered again how she'd ended up sitting in her uncle's car on her way to Chihuahua, Mexico. Who in their right mind would do this voluntarily? She looked up as her cousin Jolene climbed in beside her.

"This is so great. You're going to love this. I can't wait to see the smiles on their faces when they see all the stuff we brought." Jolene pointed over her shoulder at the rear of the car. "We have blankets and clothes and stuff like toothbrushes and soap. You'll be shocked at how the people live down there. They are so poor." Jolene paused and touched Penny's arm. "But the children. Oh my goodness. They are the cutest with their big brown eyes and sweet little faces. They are always so happy to see us." The young woman giggled. "Last time they followed me around asking for dulces—that's sweets in Spanish. I only had gum, but this year I brought a bunch of candies to hand out."

Penny frowned. "Do they speak English? How do you know what they want?"

"Most of them know quite a few words in English, but I have been learning Spanish so I can communicate better. Don't worry, you'll pick it up pretty fast once we've been there for a few weeks."

Penny nodded and tried to smile. She was nervous about this trip and not at all sure she wanted to spend any time in a third world country, let alone two months. Her mother had argued that this trip would be a good experience and she was sad she couldn't go with them. Right! Her mother had no intention of going to Mexico unless it was to spend time at a resort on the beach.

Jolene's father and mother climbed into the front seat of the car. "Here we go girls," Rhonda said glancing over her shoulder. "I can't believe it's been a year already. I've been ready to go back since the day we got home. Can you believe we'll be there this time tomorrow, Jojo?"

Jolene grinned and practically bounced in her seat with anticipation. Penny turned away and worried her lip. From what Jolene had said, they usually didn't have any running water or flushing toilets on these trips. A hot shower every morning was probably a luxury she was going to be living without. Penny had never enjoyed camping and this "adventure" as her mother continued to call it, was bound to be worse than any camping trip she'd ever been on. She kept her fears to herself and pretended to listen as her aunt and cousin shared stories about trips they'd taken in the past and how much fun this one would be.

Penny stared out the window as the sky began to lighten and her mind turned to her boyfriend and the party she would miss. She hadn't told her cousin about the big fight she'd had with her mother over this trip. Her cousin was so excited to have her along that Penny hated to say anything to dampen Jolene's enthusiasm. She closed her eyes and pushed down the anger that had bubbled back to the surface. She would go on this stupid trip, but she wouldn't enjoy it.

***

"You're not eating lunch?" Jolene asked as she took the seat next to Penny.

The younger girl shook her head and frowned. "I'm not feeling well."

"Oh dear. I got sick the last time we came to Mexico. You have to be careful to not eat or drink anything except what Don makes."

Penny took a deep breath and squeezed her eyes shut as another wave of nausea coursed through her. "I didn't eat anything I shouldn't have. My stomach has just been upset all morning."

"Well, if you don't feel better soon we can go see the medic."

Jolene took a bite of her lunch and nodded toward a group of boys waiting in line to pick up their lunch. "George was asking about you today. He wondered if you were dating anyone. I told him you have a boyfriend at home." Jolene sipped her soda before continuing. "He acted like that was no big deal. Apparently he has a girlfriend too, but he said that wasn't going to stop him from having some fun on this trip."

Penny just nodded and rubbed her midsection. George had talked to her a few times, but she wasn't interested in him. After three weeks in Mexico, she was really missing Christian. She had written him several letters, but he had yet to respond.

"Hey Penny. Aren't you having lunch?" George sat on the opposite side of the younger girl and grinned. "I know the food isn't what you're used to, but it's really not that bad today." He waved his plate under her nose. "I have plenty if you want to share."

Penny smiled weakly. "No thanks." She glanced down at his lunch and gritted her teeth as her stomach rolled.

"Are you okay?" the young man asked leaning away. "You don't look so . . ." He pulled his food away as Penny scrambled to get her legs out from under the picnic table. She freed herself of the bench and sprinted toward a bush where she immediately heaved up the small breakfast she'd eaten earlier.

"Here use this." Jolene stood beside her with a napkin. "You should go lie down. I'll let Mom know you aren't feeling well."

Penny wiped her face and headed toward the sleeping area.

"Hope you feel better," George called after her.

Chapter 28

Kate touched the photos on the table. "I have pictures from some of your trips," she said into the phone. "This one says 1956. It looks like you were building something."

The woman cleared her throat. "Yes. That was the first trip that Penny came on. We built a school. It was a very simple building, but it gave the village a place for the children to learn and a gathering place for other events. After that was complete, we spent many weeks repairing individual homes and teaching them carpentry skills. Daddy was determined to not just fix the problems, but to give the people the knowledge to do it themselves."

Kate nodded. "How wonderful. Did Penny go with your family more than once?"

"Yes, actually. Penny spent three summers with us in Mexico. The second trip was when she met Del."

"Oh really? They met in Mexico? I didn't know that."

"Yes. Penny was assigned to help build a water system to collect rainwater. Del was the foreman." The woman chuckled softly. "He noticed her right away, but it took a lot of effort on his part to get Penny's attention."

***

July 1957
Penny's second trip to Mexico

"You don't think he's cute?" Jolene whispered. "Carla said he's from Arizona and single. She's nuts about him, but I don't think he's very interested in her."

The tall cowboy finished his meal and sauntered back to wash his plate and put it away. Penny watched his retreating back and had to agree that his Levis fit him nicely. "I guess he's cute, but he's always telling people what to do." Penny brushed a lock of hair out her face and took a swig of her water.

"That's his job, silly." Jolene smiled with a sigh. "Del's the nicest guy you'll ever meet. You're just sore that he made you pull all those nails out of the boards today. Someone had to do it."

"Well, I have more experience than most of these guys, but he gives me the simplest tasks." Penny swallowed her last bite of stew and gazed into the fire that had burned down to coals. "I don't think he trusts me either. He's constantly checking my work like I'm a little kid."

Her cousin shook her head and laughed. "Penny I think you're missing something. If Del is always checking on you it's because . . ." The cowboy in question stepped back into the fire circle and smiled across at Penny and Jolene before resuming his seat. He soon fell into conversation with Pete.

Jolene lowered her voice. "I am pretty sure he likes you."

Penny sputtered on the water she was drinking and coughed. Jolene patted her back. The conversations around them quieted and several eyes turned their way. Penny stood up with her plate and Jolene followed her to the portable sink. "Like that would ever happen. He's a cowboy, for heaven's sake. Can you imagine me bringing him home to one of my mother's parties? He'd probably wear his boots and a hat."

"Oh I don't know. I bet he cleans up real nice," Jolene said as a dreamy expression flitted across her face. She rinsed her plate and reached for her cousin's dish. "Maybe if you were a little friendlier you'd see what a great guy he is."

"What are you saying? I'm friendly." Penny frowned at her cousin and dried the dishes before setting them aside.

Jolene grabbed the towel and wiped her hands. "Yes. Sometimes, but it wouldn't hurt to smile at him once in a while. You scowl whenever he talks to you." She hung the towel on the hook and led the way back to the fire. Penny took her time returning to her seat, her mind in a whirl.

Chapter 29

"Penny was determined to keep her guard up when it came to men especially after the trouble she had with Christian." Jolene said through the phone. Kate switched the phone to her other ear as the woman went on with the story. "When we went on that second trip, Penny and Christian had only broken up six months earlier. She wasn't ready to open her heart up to someone new already."

"Christian was her boyfriend?" Kate hadn't heard that name before.

"Yes . . . " Jolene said cautiously into the phone, waiting another heartbeat before adding, "and the father of her child."

Kate drew in a sharp breath and quickly looked into the empty living room. She was glad that Janae had gone to her bedroom. It didn't sound like a story she was going to share with her daughter.

The woman continued. "I'm sorry I forgot to mention *Christian*. I try to forget him." The elderly woman said the man's name with a growl. "Christian was a few years older than Penny. They had been dating about three months before Penny came with us to Mexico that first time." Jolene took several breaths before she continued. "Penny was pretty sick for much of that first trip to Mexico. I knew she was struggling to keep food down, but she hid it from everyone else. My mother noticed that she was getting thin, but chalked it up to the fact that Penny was working so hard." Kate tapped her pencil and waited for her to resume. "I was worried about her, but by the time we were heading home she was feeling almost normal. I was almost positive I knew what was making her sick at that point, so I finally decided to confront her about it."

***

August 1956

Jolene smiled at the clerk and took the restroom key that was attached to a long stick.

"Thanks."

Penny followed her cousin out the glass door and to the locked restroom behind the building. Jolene unlocked the door and peeked inside.

"Yikes. Try not to touch anything."

The girls stepped inside and closed the door behind them. Jolene motioned to the toilet as she peered into the warped metallic mirror.

"You can go first."

"Gee, thanks."

"Yep. No problem." Jolene giggled and pulled her lipstick from her pocket and began to apply it liberally. She smacked her lips together and reached for a paper towel to dab away the excess. Penny flushed the toilet and stepped to the sink, but Jolene didn't move from her spot in front of the mirror.

"Were you ever going to tell me? You won't be able to hide it much longer," Jolene said softly, studying her cousin's face.

Penny looked up in surprise. She turned on the water and began washing her hands without answering.

Jolene continued. "I know you haven't had a period the whole time we were there. How far along are you?"

Penny's lips quivered as she dried her hands on a towel. "I still can't believe it's true." Tears welled up in Penny's eyes. "How could this happen to me?" She sobbed.

"Oh honey," Jolene said as she pulled her cousin into an embrace. "We'll get through this."

***

Kate cleared her throat and swiped at a tear. "I had no idea."

"Now Kate, I hesitated to tell you about this part of Penny's past. I don't want you to think she was a . . . loose girl. She wasn't. She just found herself in a vulnerable situation and Christian took advantage of her." The older woman sighed deeply. "I never did like him much and then when he went and broke her heart. Well, I wanted to . . . to . . . to do something to hurt him."

Kate nodded and checked the clock on the wall.

"From what Penny told me, Christian invited her to his apartment to celebrate his birthday early." Jolene paused to clarify. "She would be in Mexico when they had his actual birthday party, you see. Anyway, Penny told me they were drinking that night and she hardly had any recollection of what happened after that. I have often wondered if he put something in her drink." The woman mumbled something incoherent into the phone before continuing her story. "I remember the day we had to tell my mother about Penny's condition."

Kate nodded and stood up to pace the kitchen. "That must have been hard."

"Yes, but Mother took it in stride and said she'd guessed it already. She was immediately concerned that we needed to let Aunt Clarinda know. Penny had been quite stoic up until that point, but at the mention of her mother, she began to sob uncontrollably. She was completely terrified of telling her mother." Jolene let a breath escape. "Mother was a good woman. She dialed up Clarinda later that day and told her the news herself."

***

August 1956

Rhonda spoke calmly into the phone. "No, Clarinda. Don't come yet. Give her some time. She doesn't want to come home right now. I promised her that she could stay here until we figure it all out."

"Well I'm sure she wants to see Christian. He's the father isn't he?" Clarinda gasped. "Or did she meet someone in Mexico?"

"No! Things like that don't happen on our trips," Rhonda said, her voice rising. "Besides from what I gather, she's almost three months pregnant." The women were silent for several moments and then in a more controlled voice Rhonda continued. "We'll find out more next week. I have an appointment set up for her with my doctor."

There were several heartbeats of silence before Clarinda spoke.

"Oh . . . uh . . . I guess that's okay for the initial checkup." Clarinda stuttered. "I mean I'm sure your doctor is fine for *you*, but I have someone I would rather she sees."

Rhonda felt her anger rise again. She loved her sister-in-law, but she wouldn't be bullied. "Well as long as she's here, she might as well be taken care of by a doctor. If she comes home, then you can . . ."

Clarinda interrupted. "What do you mean *if*? Of course she'll come home. Why wouldn't she?"

"I can't answer for your daughter Clarinda. When she's ready to talk to you, I'll have her call you. For now you'll have to be patient."

"But . . ." Clarinda sighed.

Rhonda said goodbye and sat heavily on a kitchen chair, cradling her head in her hands.

***

Kate interrupted the story. "So did Penny stay with you through her whole pregnancy? Why didn't she go home to her mother?"

Jolene took a deep breath. "Well, you must understand that Penny and her mother didn't always get along . . . and that's putting it nicely. I don't want to speak ill of Clarinda, but I didn't blame Penny for not wanting to go home. Her mother expected the world to revolve around her and she didn't take kindly to anything that upset her routine . . . like an unwed pregnant daughter.

"How sad," Kate said softly.

"Yes very. After that first phone call, Clarinda decided that Penny would be better off in a home for unwed mothers." Kate could hear a quiver in the old woman's voice. "Mother would have none of that. She insisted that Penny needed to be with family and should stay with us." Jolene paused again. "Daddy and Uncle Frank finally intervened and persuaded Aunt Clarinda to let Penny stay."

Kate shook her head. "What about Christian? Had they planned to get married?" Kate was uneasy asking so many questions. Jolene didn't answer right away so Kate asked the question that was uppermost in her mind. "What happened to the baby?"

***

August 1956

The words on the page blurred as Penny's eyes filled with tears. Her hand dropped to her lap, the note from Christian still clutched in her fist.

"What does it say?" Jolene stopped brushing her hair and turned toward her cousin. "Is he still coming this weekend?"

Penny cleared her throat and shook her head. "No. He's not coming."

"Why not? Does he have to work?" Jolene set her brush on the vanity table and sat beside Penny on the bed.

Penny shoved the crumpled note toward Jolene. "I guess a baby wasn't part of his plan. He told me to . . . get rid of it." Penny felt her throat clog. She had never been so repulsed in her life by what her boyfriend was suggesting. Could he really want her to end their baby's life? She looked back at her cousin. "He found a doctor that's willing to . . . do the procedure. He even sent a check to cover the fee." Penny held up the check with Christian's signature at the bottom.

Jolene gasped. "Really? He would seriously have you," she swallowed hard " . . . do that?" Jolene looked up at Penny's tear streaked face. "But you wouldn't really kill your baby, would you?"

The younger woman stood abruptly. "I don't know what to do." Penny stepped to the closet and grabbed a light jacket. "I'm going for a walk."

"You're in your pajamas . . . and it's dark."

Penny shrugged and stepped into her shoes.

Jolene scrambled off the bed. "I'll come with you."

"You don't have to. I know you have to work early," Penny said as she zipped the coat over her growing belly. She hadn't felt the baby move yet, but the doctor said it could happen any time now.

"No. I want to come." Jolene pulled on her sweatshirt and shoved her feet into her slippers before hurrying after Penny. She stopped at her parents' bedroom door and peeked her head inside. "We're going out for a few minutes."

Her mother glanced at the clock. "Okay . . . What did the letter say?"

Jolene frowned as she heard the front door open. "I'll tell you later."

She hurried through the house and found her cousin standing under a tree in the front yard. They turned and moved down the block in silence, heading for the lamppost on the corner.

Jolene searched for words of advice, but came up empty. She had never known anyone that would consider having an abortion. She certainly didn't want her younger cousin to have to go through that. She'd heard horror stories of procedures that had gone terribly wrong.

Penny finally spoke into the darkness. "He seems to think it'll be easy and the best thing to do." She sniffed and swiped at her nose. "Easy for him."

"He doesn't want to get married?" Jolene asked gently. "Would you marry him if he asked?"

Penny shook her head. "I'm not even done with high school, and he's trying to get his career off the ground . . . we're not ready for marriage. Besides, I'm not even sure he wants kids." Penny stopped under the lamppost and looked up at Jolene. "What would you do?"

The older girl took several deep breaths. "I don't think I'm the person to ask. My advice would be to follow your heart," Jolene said as they started walking again. "What is your heart telling you to do?"

"My first instinct is to keep the baby. But I guess I could . . . let someone adopt him." Penny's voice caught. "Listen to me. I've already decided it's a boy."

The two women walked in silence, a cool breeze tugging at their hair and clothes. They turned the next corner and Penny spoke again. "One thing I know for sure is that I cannot abort him. That's just unthinkable."

Jolene nodded and released a sigh of relief. "I like that you're thinking of the fetus as a person. That says a lot. Some people don't get that connection and feel like it's just a bunch of cells that can be easily disposed of." A car drove toward them, its lights momentarily blinding the women. Jolene shielded her eyes and continued. "So adoption might be the right answer or you might even decide to keep him." Jolene stopped and turned toward her cousin. "But whatever you decide I'll stand by you." Jolene reached for Penny and gave her a hug.

"I love you." Penny murmured into her cousin's shoulder. "Thanks for listening."

Chapter 30

"I went with Penny to see the doctor for the first visit. Doctor Bernard was a very kind old man. He told Penny that he knew of a family that was hoping to adopt and he could arrange it—if that was what she decided," Jolene explained.

"This just breaks my heart. Obviously she gave the baby up right?" Kate asked as she walked back into the kitchen. "She never mentioned having a child." She pulled a glass from the cupboard and filled it with water from the dispenser on the door of the fridge. She took a big swallow as Jolene continued.

"That was the plan yes, but as you will see, not all plans work as we expect." She sighed and resumed the story she was spinning.

"In October of 1956 Penny was about five months along and she seemed to be progressing normally. She was feeling better and took walks every day. She could walk for miles. Mother wasn't sure she should be walking so far, but Penny was always so much happier when she returned from a walk." Jolene paused in her story and Kate heard another voice speak to the woman. Jolene seemed to cover the phone and said something about being almost done.

"I'm sorry. Am I keeping you too long?" Kate asked as she set her empty glass on the counter.

"No. My granddaughter was just saying goodbye. They are going home." The old lady paused and collected her thoughts. "Let's see where was I?"

"You were telling me how Penny loved her walks."

"Oh, yes. I recall one time while I was at work Penny decided to take a walk on her own. My parents were not even aware that she was gone until I returned from work and asked about her. Mother was instantly fearful and insisted that Daddy needed to take the truck out to find her. He had no idea which direction she'd gone so after driving around the neighborhood for an hour he returned home without her.

"Just as we were considering calling the authorities, she came walking through the back door. Mother scolded her for causing us to worry, but Penny insisted she was fine." Jolene chuckled. "It turns out she'd walked all the way to the neighboring town which was five miles away. She realized she'd gone too far and didn't have any money to call home. Instead she found a park bench and rested before turning back."

Kate smiled. "That sounds like the Penny I knew. She walked all over Spanish Fork. I worried about her too, so I know how your mother felt."

"Mother made Penny promise to take Teddy with her whenever she went walking. Not that he could do much, but it made Mother feel better." Jolene laughed. "Teddy was my dog, but you wouldn't know it. He hovered around Penny and never let her out of his sight, which was a good thing as it turned out."

Kate slid onto the couch and turned toward a noise down the hall. Jay was carrying their youngest daughter at arms length and both of them looked very unhappy. There were two large wet spots on the seat of Megan's pants where her diaper had leaked. Jay frowned and Kate could see he needed help.

"Are you almost done?" he asked in a whisper. "I think she needs a bath." Megan saw her mother and began to cry. Jay tried to shush her and that made the child even angrier. Kate reached for Megan and she immediately calmed down as she nestled against her mother's shoulder.

"Jolene? I'm sorry to interrupt, but I need to call you back. As you can probably hear, my baby needs me." She felt the baby's wetness seep through her shirt. "It has been so nice talking to you though. Would it be okay if I call again tomorrow?"

"Of course dear. I'll wait for your call. Thanks for letting me chat your ear off. It's been fun reminiscing about Penny."

Kate said goodbye and tossed the phone on the couch.

"What happened little girl? Did we forget to change you?"

"I'll start the bath," Jay said as he hurried away.

Kate nodded and lifted the child away from her side and inspected the large stain that had been left on her shirt. "I'm going to need a bath myself."

The girl giggled and clung to her mother, wrapping her tiny fingers in her mother's brown locks. After the couple's weekend away, the baby had been overjoyed to see her mother. Even Mitch seemed happy to see them, giving his stepmother a hug upon her arrival.

Kate stepped into the bathroom where the tub was beginning to fill with water. "Did you get some good stories to share about Penny?" Jay asked.

"Sure did. Jolene was a big talker and would have talked into the night if I'd let her." Kate stripped the baby down to her birthday suit and tested the temperature before setting her daughter in the warm water. "Once we get this munchkin into bed I need to start compiling my notes and scan in the pictures. I thought I'd make a slideshow and have it running in the foyer when people arrive. Can you help me with that?"

Jay knelt beside his wife and skimmed a toy boat toward Megan. "I could, but I think Mitch would be the one to ask. He is much sharper when it comes to computer stuff."

"That's true. I do want it to look good." She laughed at the offended look Jay gave her.

"That hurts." He splashed his wife with water.

"Hey! You're getting the baby," Kate grabbed her husband's hands.

Jay cringed and smiled at the little girl. "Oh sorry, Meggie, but your mommy hurt my feelings."

The baby looked up at Jay and laughed, splashing her tiny hands in the water.

"You said it," Kate said as she lathered up a washcloth.

"But you didn't have to agree so quickly." He kissed his wife on the cheek and stood up. "I'll let Mitch know you need help."

"Dadada!" Megan cried as her father slipped from the room.

"We'll see him in a minute baby. Let's wash your hair." Kate rubbed a bit of shampoo into the little girl's hair, recalling suddenly how much Penny had enjoyed getting her head massaged.

Kate couldn't believe it had only been a week since Penny had died. She also was amazed at all the stories she'd heard this week about Penny and the many lives she'd touched. Kate was certain that she had only scratched the surface of the good deeds that woman had done. She suspected there were countless other stories that she would never hear.

She rinsed the baby's head and let the girl play for another minute before wrapping her in a fuzzy blue towel.

"No. No!" Megan complained as her mother let the water escape down the drain.

"I'm sorry, but I have too much to do tonight. Let's go put on your teddy bear pajamas and read a story."

After a quick story and a song, Kate settled the baby into her crib and turned out the light. "Good night sweetie."

Kate hurried back to the kitchen and started sorting the pictures that she wanted to use. She searched through the box from Roberto and found a few more pictures of Penny and Jolene. She studied one photo closely trying to discern if Penny had a baby bump or not. According to the date on the back, Penny should have been about seven months pregnant, but the dog was sitting in front of the girls and obscured Penny's waistline.

The two girls were sitting beside each other in front of a Christmas tree. Jolene was smiling, but Penny had a scowl on her face. Kate decided not to use the Christmas photo and set it aside. She continued putting the other photos in order and gathered her notes and walked back to the office.

Mitch was already sitting at the desk. Kate set the stack of photos next to the scanner. "I need all of these scanned. Will that take too long?"

"Naw. I can get it done." The young man lifted the first photo and positioned in on the scanner bed. "I'll let you know when I'm done."

"Okay. I guess I'll start writing up the eulogy on my tablet."

Mitch nodded and scanned another picture.

Kate settled onto her bed and began outlining the life sketch. She started with Penny's birth and mentioned her parents. She hardly knew anything about Penny's parents or her upbringing, but she hoped Penny had a happy childhood. Jolene had said that her cousin didn't always get along with her mother, but that was typical of most teenagers.

She skipped to the first trip to Mexico and wondered if she should mention the pregnancy. She would have to ask Jolene what she thought about that. She didn't even know what happened to the baby. She put a question mark on the page and decided to come back to that time of Penny's life later.

After filling out a time line with as much information as she could, she realized she didn't know when Penny's parents had died. She wondered how she could get that.

"How's it going?" Jay asked as he sat on the bed beside his wife.

"Fine. But I don't know when Frank and Clarinda died . . . Penny's parents."

"Maybe you could find their death records online. You know like you used to do for family history and indexing."

"I still do that—" Kate said with a sigh. "Sometimes." Having a little one around had taken up most her free time. "But yes. That's a good idea."

Kate opened a tab for the Internet and went to the family search website where she typed in Penny's parents' names. Several records appeared on the screen including the 1940 census. She opened the census record and scrolled through the names until she found Penny listed as a young baby with her parents.

"Cool. I found them."

Her husband looked up from his book and smiled. "Good for you."

She read through the record and made note of their ages and where they'd been born. She closed the document and returned to the search results for other records that might have the date of their deaths. She was relieved to find an obituary for Frank. She read the news article and drew in a sharp breath.

"Oh my. Frank died in a boating accident in 1975. He was only sixty-five years old." She read further and then said softly. "Ahh. How sad. It looks like Penny's mother died in the same accident." She shook her head. "That must have been hard to lose them both at the same time."

Jay rested his book in his lap. "Wasn't she an only child? That would be extra hard to not even have siblings to help shoulder the grief."

Kate nodded. "She had Jolene though. They were like sisters from the way her cousin talks." She looked at her husband. "And she had Del."

"But they never had any children of their own. I think children always help heal the heart. Maybe that's why she took care of everyone else so carefully. She needed to be needed." Jay drew in a breath and began to read again.

Kate realized she hadn't told Jay about Penny's baby. She hated to tarnish Jay's opinion of their friend. "Jay?" She waited for her husband to lower his book again. "Jolene told me something about Penny that surprised me."

Jay put his book down and frowned. "What?"

Kate chewed on her lip. "Well, she said that Penny got pregnant as a teenager. I guess she had a boyfriend and you know . . . she ended up pregnant at sixteen."

"Really? What happened to the baby? Did she give it up?"

"Jolene was about to tell me that part when you brought Megan to me. I told her I would call her back tomorrow, so we could finish the conversation."

"I'm sorry. I had no idea." He took his wife's hand. "That's a huge secret for Penny to carry around her entire life. I wonder why she never told us about it."

"Yeah. I've been wondering if Del even knew about it. She would have told him don't you think?" Kate set her tablet aside and turned toward her husband. "I hope she did. That's one of the things I love about being married. Having someone to share my worries and heartaches with . . . and all the good things too, of course." She leaned closer and kissed her husband gently. "I love you, Jay."

Chapter 31

July 1957

Penny followed the path to the tiny structure that stood on the edge of the village. A section of the roof was missing and the door didn't close completely on the home. If they had time, she hoped to convince Del to come repair the roof and the door. As she drew closer she could see that the square of fabric covering the glassless window hung limp in the heat of the day.

She stepped from the low-lying shrubs, and found two dark haired children sitting in the dirt beside a mangy dog. The children grinned and scrambled to their feet as Penny approached.

"Penny! Penny!" They greeted her with squeals that startled the dog from his nap. They tugged at her hands and spoke rapidly in Spanish asking if she'd brought more cake. The day before she had brought a cinnamon roll for them to share.

"No cake today." Penny answered in their native tongue, relieved that the language came easier as she spent her second summer in Mexico. The two girls frowned momentarily, but their smiles returned as they led her to the front of the house.

"Where is Del?" the oldest girl asked.

Penny smiled knowingly. Del had played with the girls yesterday and five-year-old Teresita had become quite enamored by him. Penny knew from personal experience just how easily that could happen when you let your guard down. "He is still working, but he did say he might come see you later." She motioned to the shack they called home. "Is your mama in the house?"

The girls nodded and ran inside to find their mother. A moment later the three emerged, each carrying a bowl of pea pods. Lucia grinned at Penny and gestured for the petite blond woman to join her on the covered porch. The girls set the dishes on a small table and returned to their play in the yard.

The dark haired woman sat heavily in a chair. "How are you today, Penny?" Lucia asked as Penny removed her small backpack and took the chair opposite her. The girls' mother was expecting a third child and looked very uncomfortable in the heat of the day.

"Good. But the sun is very hot today." Penny said with a frown as she swiped her sleeve across her brow.

"Yes. You need a better hat," Lucia smiled and set a bowl on her belly and began to remove the peas from the pods.

Penny reached for a container and also began shucking the peas—something she'd learned how to do this week.

Lucia pointed at a small area beside the house where a barrel had been set up to collect rainwater. "We are so happy to have water. It will help my garden grow."

The main mission of this humanitarian trip was to construct systems to collect rainwater for the people of the scattered villages. But Penny and her friends only had a few more weeks in Mexico and there were so many more people that needed water. Penny sighed. "We are glad to help. We wish we could do more."

"No. It is enough." Lucia nodded and gave Penny another smile. "Thank you."

The women worked in silence as the girls found leaves and sticks to construct a house for the doll. Penny thought of the boxes full of toys in the attic at home. She hadn't played with them in years and with no siblings, the toys were almost like new. She should have brought them with her.

Penny studied the little girls' clothes, the same ones they were wearing yesterday. She had a feeling that the tattered dresses were most likely worn almost every day. There was a truckload of donated clothes and food on the way, but a rainstorm and muddy roads had delayed the truck's arrival.

"Oh, I forgot." Penny set the peas on the table and pulled two pieces of fruit from her pack. "Would you like an orange?" she called to the girls.

Rosa and Teresita ran to the porch, grinning and nodding their heads. "I love oranges," Rosa said taking the offered fruit. "Gracias." The girls sat on the rickety steps and began to peel the oranges.

Penny returned to her chair and removed a third orange from her pack. "One for you."

Lucia hesitated a moment, but smiled as she took the fruit and lifted it to her nose, inhaling deeply. "Gracias. You are too kind." The woman peeled the orange quickly and offered the first section to Penny. The younger woman began to shake her head, but graciously took the offered bite and popped it into her mouth.

"Thank you," she said before turning her attention to the little girls who were enjoying the sweet oranges. Rosa giggled as the dog licked at the juice that had dripped down her chin.

"Hola? Mis amigas," Del called as he advanced toward the humble home. "How are the monkeys today?"

The girls ran to Del and clung to his forearms as he straightened his arms and lifted them up. Penny's gaze traveled over the muscular man's torso, lingering on his bulging arms. She felt her face flush when Del's eyes met hers and he winked.

He set the girls on the ground and smiled up at the two women. "How are you feeling today, Lucia?"

"Bien," she answered with a smile as she put the last piece of orange in her mouth and chewed thoughtfully.

"And how's my lucky Penny?" Del asked as he flashed a smile in Penny's direction. "Are you surviving the heat here in the shade?" He stepped up onto the porch and crouched beside the women.

She reddened at the nickname, which was growing on her. "We're trying," she said as Del's smile made her insides quiver. Penny handed a bowl of peas to the man. "You might as well be useful." She laughed, attempting to conceal her nervousness.

Del took the bowl and struggled to fold his six-foot frame into a compact knot beside Penny's chair.

"Let me get you another chair," Lucia said with a grunt, only managing to rise an inch before Del waved her off.

"No. I'll be fine," the big man said with a grin. He sat on the edge of the porch and began to shuck the peas. Lucia's girls stood in front of him to help. "Oh by the way, I came to tell you that the truck has arrived." He looked over his shoulder at Penny. "We can start unloading when we're finished here."

Penny nodded. "Oh, I am so glad they made it." She looked at Lucia with a smile. "Shall I look for some little girl clothes and maybe some baby things?"

"Yes. Thank you." Lucia finished her peas and pushed herself up from her chair. "I need a blanket too, if they have enough."

Penny almost laughed at the woman's statement. Lucia could have two or three blankets if she desired. Someone had put together gift packs for the babies and Penny was sure they still had plenty. She planned to search through the boxes and find several dresses for the little girls that worked beside Del. She rose from the chair and looked over Del's shoulder.

"They're getting twice as many done as you are. You need more practice there, Big Guy." Penny laughed as Rosa took the last pod, opened it and removed the peas in one motion.

"Can't argue with that," he said as he stood and handed the bowl to Lucia. "We'll come back to see you before it's dark," he said with a smile at the girls' mother.

"Gracias," Lucia said as she lifted the bowls of peas.

Del reached for Penny, lifting her off the porch in one swift motion. "You're coming with me." He tucked her hand inside his and waved to the little family.

Penny's heart beat double time as his large hand encompassed hers. She breathed deeply, hoping he couldn't feel the sweat that was collecting on her palm. Del had never held her hand, but she couldn't say she minded. She looked up at the tall cowboy and found him watching her.

"Penny for your thoughts," he said stopping in his tracks and laughing. "Oh sorry. I'll never use that phrase again without thinking of you."

She laughed. "Yeah. My name's a curse to be borne."

Del squeezed her hand tighter as they continued down the path. "I like your name. It suits you. Small and shiny."

"And not worth a whole lot," Penny added as they reached the busy base camp.

The big man paused and turned the younger woman toward him. "Don't ever say that. You are worth a gazillion pennies if you ask me." He leaned down and kissed her cheek and then led her to a mud splattered truck. "Back to work."

The afternoon passed quickly as the group unloaded the truck and distributed the contents to the villagers. Penny and Del made a second trip to Lucia's home to deliver food, blankets and clothing to little the family.

"For me?" Rosa asked as she held the blue and white striped dress up to her chin, her eyes sparkling.

"Yes," Penny answered over the lump in her throat. "And one for you." Penny pulled a second dress from the box and handed it to Teresita.

"Oh! Que bonita!" the younger girl exclaimed as she pulled the pale green dress over her head and smoothed it into place over the dress she still wore underneath. She twirled and smiled shyly at Del. "I am a princess," she whispered softly.

"Yes. You are," Del answered with a brilliant smile. He set his box of food on the porch and spoke to the mother. "This will get you started, but someone will bring you more food soon."

"And I found a few things for the baby," Penny said as she lifted a green and yellow blanket from the carton and handed it to the expectant mother.

The woman accepted it with a nod. "Gracias."

Penny reached into the box again for an even larger quilt. "I brought you this pink one also in case you have another girl."

With a laugh, the woman smiled and accepted the two gifts. "My husband hopes for a boy, but the blanket will be used either way."

"There are a few other things in here that I hope you can use." Penny handed the box to the woman.

The older woman looked into the carton and shook her head. "May God bless you for your kindness."

Penny hugged the mother and kissed each of the girls on the cheek as she told them goodbye.

Del patted Rosa on the head and tickled Teresita under the chin. "You be good for your mama." He waved at Lucia and took Penny's hand, leading her back the way they'd come. "They're so cute. I'm going to miss them when we have to leave tomorrow."

"I know. But there will be more just like them in the next town." Penny looked over her shoulder and then up at the man. "I am always amazed at how happy these people are. They have nothing, but they don't even seem to care. Or maybe it's because they don't realize what they *don't* have." She shook her head in disbelief. "I have so much and I still find things to complain about." She turned away from Del's gaze. "I am an ungrateful selfish person."

"Don't be so hard on yourself. We all complain sometimes." He took her other hand and turned her towards him. "You're here doing what you can to help." He leaned closer, holding her attention. "That says a lot about you."

She shook her head. "You don't really know me."

"I think I am a pretty good judge of character." He lifted her chin. "I can tell you love people and you have a kind heart." Del pulled her into an embrace. "And as for getting to know you better . . ." He kissed the top of her head. "We'll have to work on that when we get back to the states."

Penny's Diner

Chapter 32

The phone rang several more times before it went to voicemail. Kate left a brief message for Justina saying that she was trying to reach Jolene, and that she'd try to call again later. The number Kate had called last night had been Justina's. She hadn't thought to get Jolene's own number until now.

"I guess we'll see if Justina gets home and calls me back," Kate said with a smile at the baby who was sitting on the floor with a pile of blocks. "Should we see what the big kids are doing and make some lunch?"

Mitch had finished scanning the photos into the computer last night and was now making them into a slideshow. Kate was amazed at how much he could do on the computer. He had taken a class in school and discovered he had a knack for creating power point presentations and slideshows—among other things. Kate was amazed at the streak of creativity that both of her stepchildren had. She couldn't take any credit for it, but neither could Jay. Because of his first wife's cancer, Jay and Renee had never had children of their own.

Kate picked up her youngest child and wandered down the hall. She peeked into the office. "How's it coming Mitch?" she asked standing behind the redheaded boy's chair.

"Almost done. I need you to listen to the music though. I added a couple songs that I liked, but we can change them if you want to." He started the slideshow and leaned back. Soft guitar music began to play in the background as the few pictures of Penny as a child appeared on the screen. Kate watched as the young girl morphed into a teenager and then into the elderly woman that they knew and loved. Megan seemed mesmerized by the pictures and the music.

"It's wonderful. You chose some good music. I wouldn't change anything." Kate patted Mitch's shoulder and the boy nodded.

"Cool."

"Grandma P would be very pleased with it. Thank you, Mitch."

"I'll save it on this flash drive and we can just pop it in the laptop when we get there on Wednesday." He inserted the small device and saved the presentation.

"We're getting hungry for lunch. Did you want a cheese sandwich and some soup? That's what Megan and I are having. Or there are leftovers."

"I'll take a sandwich. Do we have any sourdough?" Mitch asked as he swiveled in his chair and faced his little sister. The little girl giggled and reached for Mitch.

"I think we do. Can you take her while I make it?"

Mitch reached for Megan and turned back to the computer. "Should we play a game, Meggie?"

Kate smiled and moved down the hall to her daughter's room. Janae was lying across her bed with a sketchpad in her hand, several drawings surrounding her. "We're making lunch. Would you like some?"

Janae rolled off the bed. "Sure." The girl swiped at her face.

Kate could see she'd been crying. "Are you okay? What's wrong honey?" Janae stepped toward her stepmother's outstretched arms and Kate enfolded her in a hug.

After a moment the girl answered in a muffled voice. "I was just thinking about Grandma P." She hesitated and leaned away from Kate. "What do you think she's doing in heaven?"

"Oh, I don't know. She's probably playing music. She loved music. Hopefully she has a dog with her too. And of course she's happy to be with Del again." Kate smiled down at Janae. "I'm sure she's missing us, but I bet she's keeping busy taking care of people. She was always so good at that wasn't she?"

Janae nodded and sniffed. "I guess. It still hurts though that she's not here anymore."

Kate squeezed the girl again, feeling her own sense of loss. "I know." She stepped away from Janae and gathered up the drawings on the bed. "Wow. Is this Penny? It looks just like that picture we have of her," Kate said holding up a drawing of a young Penny on the back of a horse. "We should put this in a frame and take it to the service to display. I think Grandma P would like that."

"Can we take this one too? She loved Rudi." Janae touched a drawing of their little dog.

"Of course. You collect a few drawings that you want to take and we'll find a place for them."

"Okay." The girl brightened at the idea.

"Let's go eat. Can you make the tomato soup? Yours always tastes so good." Kate smiled as the girl nodded happily.

"Sure. The trick is using milk and a dash of basil," Janae said as she dropped the pictures on the bed and hurried toward the kitchen.

Kate followed Janae into the kitchen and pulled out the loaf of bread and the cheese. As she began to assemble the sandwiches, she thought about the life sketch she'd finished writing that morning. It still had a few gaps, but she hoped it would be adequate. She had decided not to include the part about Penny's pregnancy, but had summarized several of the good stories she'd heard about her sweet friend.

She'd also sent a photo to Louise at the funeral home via email, so she could put it on the program. Louise had replied by sending a copy of the outlined service indicating that Dotty, Clyde's wife, would be playing the organ and a woman named Karen would be performing a musical number. Kate was the only speaker listed. She still wished she could have convinced someone else to take part.

"Are we still going over to Grandma P's to clean her house?" Janae asked as she stirred the pot of soup on the stove.

Jay had suggested that they all go over tonight to sort through Penny's belongings. They were planning a yard sale on Saturday and there were still plenty of drawers and closets to go through. "Yes. We'll go after dinner." The girl nodded and continued to watch the soup.

Kate lifted the electric grill from the lower cabinet and plugged it in. "We'll have to take some stickers over and decided how much things should be sold for and we'll need to put up signs to advertise. I should probably put an ad in the newspaper." Kate buttered the sandwiches and then pulled three bowls from the cupboard. "I had to sell my grandmother's things a couple years ago when she died." She paused and looked up at Janae. "That was before I met you and your dad," Kate said with a smile.

After lunch Kate put the baby down for a nap and tried calling Justina again. She got the answering machine again and chose not to leave another message. She dialed the salon instead, hoping to find Connie.

"Hello, Tastefully Yours. How can I help you?" Connie said into the phone.

"Hey you. How's it going?" Kate asked as she sat at the dining table. She could hear the buzz of a hair dryer in the background.

"Good. How was your trip?"

"It was really nice. We met some great people that knew Penny. I came back with a bunch of stories to tell at the funeral. You're coming to the service right?"

"Yep. I found a sitter for the boys since Chris has to work and I'm trying to convince Robin to come with me. Tabitha and Barb are going to cover for us that day." Connie paused and Kate heard the cash register drawer open. "You'll be working tomorrow still right? I have you on the schedule."

"Oh right. Tomorrow's Tuesday isn't it. Yes. I've kind of lost track of the days." Kate reached for a pen and a piece of junk mail and scrawled the word "work" across the back, underlining it several times. She also jotted a reminder to put an ad in the paper for the yard sale. "I was calling to let you know that we are cleaning out Penny's house tonight and taking stuff to the thrift store. Didn't you say you wanted her couch?"

"Yes. I thought her sofa was in pretty good condition, wasn't it? I'll take it if no one else wants it. We need to replace the one in the TV room. Should we come get it tonight?"

Kate nodded. "Sure. That would be great. We'll be over there at about six o'clock."

"I'll see if we can borrow my brother's new truck. He may have to come with it." Connie laughed. "I don't think he let's anyone else drive it yet."

"That's fine. Maybe there'll be something he wants. I don't think I'm keeping much of the big stuff except maybe a dresser for Janae." Kate looked up as Mitch came into the room and stood with his hands shoved in his front pockets, waiting to speak with her. "We'll see you tonight then, Connie."

"Thanks. See you later."

Kate hung up and smiled up at her stepson. He was growing taller it seemed. "Are you going to Devin's now?"

"If that's okay. Yeah." The boy shrugged. "I'll be back in time for dinner."

"Sure. We're going to Penny's after dinner and we'll need your help."

The boy nodded and headed out the door.

Kate began preparing dinner and her little dog followed her around the kitchen hoping for a taste. Her mind settled on Penny as it so often did. She wondered if she would hear back from Jolene today. She was quite anxious to hear the end of Penny's story.

Chapter 33

There was more junk in Penny's house than Kate had first imagined. She hated to just toss everything out, but Jay didn't hesitate. The pile going to the dump was bigger than the keeping pile.

"Good thing you took that back seat out," Kate said as Jay stacked several boxes in the back of the minivan.

"I knew it would be this way. It's always a shock to find out how much stuff you've accumulated over the years. Some of this looks like it's fifty years old."

"Did you find out if you can borrow Steve's trailer on Saturday?" Kate asked as she handed him a laundry basket full of old bedding.

"Yes. We can use the trailer and he said he does want the washer and dryer as well."

"You told him he could just have them for free?"

Jay nodded and took another box from Mitch, squeezing it into an open spot.

Steve collected older appliances and refurbished them to sell. Kate knew that business had been slow lately and she was glad to help in a small way. The washer looked like it was almost new, but the dryer was an older model. She wondered if it was the dryer that had been bought to replace the set that had been given to Roberto's family.

"I hope he can sell them without putting too much money into them," Kate said as she watched a truck pull up to the curb.

Connie sat in the passenger seat, and Kate assumed it was her brother, Brock, driving the truck. The two climbed from the big vehicle. Connie gave Kate a quick hug and turned her attention to Jay.

"Hey. How are you?" Connie said reaching to shake Jay's hand before motioning to include her brother. "This is my brother Brock."

The other man moved up beside his sister and smiled. "Nice to meet you." He shook both their hands as Mitch and Janae came from the house, Megan on her sister's hip. The kids nodded silently as Jay introduced them.

"Wow. She's getting so big," Connie said leaning down to look into the baby's face. "Hi there sweetheart. Do you remember Aunt Connie?" The baby pulled away with a shy smile as the woman tickled under her chin.

"Well, let's get that couch for you," Jay said as he moved toward the house. "It's nice of you to take it off our hands."

Connie nodded and she and Brock followed the family into the house.

"While you're here, look around and see if you want anything else." Kate pointed across the room. "We are keeping the piano, but you don't know anyone that wants an organ do you?"

Brock shook his head. "No." He stepped to the organ and ran his hand over it. "That's going to be a bear to move."

"We have a piano mover coming on Friday, but we're hoping that someone will be interested in the organ and have a way to transport it," Jay said with a nod. "Mitch, will you grab the other end of the couch and we'll take it out to Brock's truck."

"Do you want the side tables or any of the lamps?" Kate asked as the men maneuvered the sofa through the front door.

"No. Those will probably sell pretty quickly on Saturday, I would guess." Connie picked up a throw pillow and set it on the recliner. "Does she have a full length mirror? I could use one of those."

"There's one in her bedroom," Janae said as she set the baby on the floor and hurried down the hall. Connie followed and paused in the doorway. "That's a beautiful headboard." She turned toward Kate who had stopped behind her. "Are you going to keep that?"

Kate shook her head. "No. I don't think so. The whole bedroom set is still nice, but we don't need it."

"I bet you'll get some good money for it." Connie nodded. "I'd buy it, but Brock made a headboard for Chris and me when we first got married. I will take the mirror though if you're sure you don't want it. How much?"

"I don't know. Make me an offer."

"$50?"

"Sold." Kate laughed. "Penny left instructions for us to donate the money from the estate sale to Primary Children's Hospital."

"Well then let me give you $65 for it. You should tell people where the money is going and you might get more that way." Connie lifted the oval mirror to test its weight. "I think we can carry it."

Kate grabbed the other side of the framed mirror and the two women carried it into the living room.

"That's a good idea. I'll put that in the ad and on the flyers," Kate said as they set the mirror beside the front door. Megan crawled to her mother's side and Kate adjusted the mirror so the baby could see herself. "She always loved to play in front of this mirror. Penny babysat her once and said they spent the whole time in her bedroom." Kate smiled at the happy memory.

"Maybe you should keep it then." Connie looked down at the baby.

"No. I have a nice mirror. We are keeping a few mementos for the kids and lots of pictures. I know Megan won't remember Penny, but I want to keep her memory alive anyway." Kate scooped up the baby. "Lets go see if they got that couch on the truck."

Jay stood on the curb talking to someone Kate didn't know. The young man wore a baseball cap and a faded sweatshirt. He glanced up at Kate and Connie as they walked down the path. He ducked his head and turned toward his car. An uneasy feeling passed over Kate as she realized it was the same black jeep she'd seen earlier in the week. She hugged the baby closer.

"Brock might need help." Connie said as she brushed past Kate. "His leg is still bothering him a bit."

"Oh. Okay," Kate said as she followed Connie to the truck where Brock was working to secure the couch.

"Have you got it?" Connie asked.

Brock nodded and tightened the strap around the piece of furniture. He carefully hopped down on his good leg and shoved the couch further into the bed. "That should hold."

Brock stepped closer to the women and eyed Jay and the other man. He drew in a sharp breath and frowned.

"Who is that?" Connie gestured toward the young man talking to Jay.

"I don't . . . how would I know? It's not like I know *everybody*." Brock made a noise in his throat, glanced over his shoulder at the men on the curb and started back toward the house.

Connie shook her head. She had the feeling Brock did know the guy. "Settle down. It was just a question," she said as she followed her brother up the walkway.

Her brother ignored the comment and asked, "Are we taking anything else?"

Kate fell into step with Connie unable to shake the uneasy feeling that seemed to be associated with the stranger talking to her husband. She shifted the baby to her other hip.

"Yeah. There's a mirror just inside the door. It might fit in the back seat," Connie replied.

"Hey Kate. Hold on," Jay called as she reached the steps to the house.

Kate turned to find Jay coming toward her. The young man standing beside the now open rear door of his Jeep. She glanced at Connie and walked back toward the street. "What's up?"

"I think you'll want to see this." Jay smiled, took the baby from her arms and led her to the mysterious black Jeep. The young man nodded briefly and stepped back as the couple drew closer to the open door.

Resting on the backseat were five boxes of diapers, two large boxes of wipes, several packages of newborn sleepers and a stack of blankets. Kate rested her hand on the car and leaned inside. "That's a lot of diapers." She looked up at her husband with a puzzled expression and smiled weakly at the young man. "Did someone have a baby?"

"Someone had *three* babies." Jay laughed and nodded at the young man. "Kate this is Guy. He's been driving around for the last week wondering what to do with all these baby things he was told to buy."

Kate shook her head still perplexed and peered through the rear glass into the cargo area behind the seats. She counted three baby swings, three baby bouncers and several other bags of paraphernalia. "I don't get it. Who asked him to buy all this stuff?"

Jay smiled and looked at Guy, waiting for him to answer.

"Well, ma'am . . ." Guy cleared his throat, hesitant to speak. "I had been told to keep it a secret, but I suppose I can tell you now." He swallowed and looked down the street before returning his gaze to Kate. "Miss Penny asked me to buy the baby stuff and said to bring it back to her. She was going to give me the address of where to deliver it, but then she wasn't answering her calls and she was never home," the man's voice trailed off.

Kate put her hand to her mouth and looked at Jay.

Her husband nodded. "I just told him the news."

Kate stepped closer to the young man. "I'm sorry you hadn't heard." She looked at her husband. "It was a shock to all of us."

The group fell silent as Kate looked into the car again. "This is one of her random acts of kindness, isn't it?" she asked with a smile as her gaze swung between Jay and Guy. "That is so cool. But you have no idea who they are for?"

"I know it's for some family that had triplets. She said something about the husband being out of work, but I don't have a name or an address." Guy removed his hat and scratched at his head.

Kate shook her head. "How are we going to find out who had triplets? For all we know it might be someone living up in Salt Lake City," Kate said with concern.

Jay tapped his chin. "We could search through her things in the house. Or maybe we should just see if there's an article in the news about the birth. I mean how did she hear about this family anyway?"

Guy smiled at the baby in Jay's arms and replaced his hat.

"I asked her the same question when she first asked for my help. She said that sometimes she finds articles in the paper, but other times she just hears about situations from people she talks to. She's like a really good detective," the young man laughed and shook his head.

Kate nodded. "Yeah, she has a bunch of news clippings about people that were hurt in car wrecks and house fires. She's like a magnet for finding people that need help." Kate nodded at the men. "While she worked at the diner, she seemed to help anyone that came through the door."

A silence fell over the group except for the baby's babbling. Kate squinted at Guy who was chewing on his lip. "You seem really familiar. Have we met before?"

Guy said, "I've seen you before, but no, we haven't actually met." He turned his face so she could see his profile and held a serious pose. "I've been told I look a lot like my sister."

Kate studied him further before exclaiming, "Robin!" The young man had the same nose and dark coloring as the hairdresser that Kate worked with.

Guy pointed at her with a wink. "Very good." He turned as Connie and Brock came down the path with the mirror between them.

"So what do we do now?" Kate asked.

Jay smiled and looked at his wife. "We finish what she started."

Connie helped Brock push the large mirror into the backseat of the truck and then headed to the small group standing beside the black Jeep. Brock slammed the door shut and stood beside his truck, a hesitant look on his face.

"Come see this," Kate said as she waved her friend closer.

Connie leaned into the backseat of the jeep and looked into the space behind the seats. "That's a lot of baby stuff. Who's it for?"

"That's the question of the day," Jay said with a laugh as he bounced Megan to keep her happy. "Have you heard of anyone having triplets recently?"

Kate and Connie exchanged looks.

"Not that I can think of," Connie said as she turned back toward Brock, who was still standing a few yards away. "Brock? Come here. Have you heard about anybody having triplets?"

Brock took a step toward the cluster of people and shook his head. "Emily might know. She pays more attention to stuff like that." Brock stepped to Guy's vehicle and looked into the backseat. "Nice."

Brock stepped into the circle and Kate gestured toward Guy.

"Hey Brock. Have you met Guy?"

The two men acknowledged each other with a nod and Guy reached for Brock's hand.

"Actually we have met. Penny sent me to his house a few weeks ago." Guy smiled at the stunned expressions of the group.

"Oh!" Connie inhaled sharply and then nodded in understanding.

"You're looking better," Guy said as he patted Brock on the shoulder. "How's the leg?"

"It's good," Brock said with a small smile.

Janae and Mitch came out of the house and stopped beside Jay.

"What's going on?" Janae asked as Megan reached for her big sister.

"We have a mystery to solve," Jay said, handing the baby to his older daughter. "We need to find a family that just had triplets to give all this stuff to." He motioned to the car's interior.

Mitch stepped to the open door. "Triplets? That's like three babies at the same time, right?" He looked up at his dad. "One of the teachers at the high school was expecting triplets. She wasn't my English teacher, but I heard she had to quit before the . . ." The boy paused in his explanation as Kate interrupted with a little squeal.

"Yes! I heard about that from Penny a few months ago. She was telling me about this couple that had been trying to have a baby for years and finally they were getting three. She mentioned that it was a teacher and that the lady had been put on bed rest. What's her name, Mitch?"

Mitch smiled and said, "Mrs. Montoya."

Chapter 34

Guy stepped into Penny's house with the rest of the group and waited by the door as Connie searched the Internet for Mrs. Montoya. "Do you know her first name, Mitch?" she asked as she scrolled through all the Montoyas in the area.

Mitch shrugged. "No. But you could look her up on the school website."

Connie grinned. "Good idea."

"Do you think she had all the same kind of babies or can triplets be both girls and boys," Janae asked as she sat on the piano bench with Megan on her lap.

"They can be mixed—both boys and girls. I don't know what she had. We'll have to wait and see," Kate explained.

"Can I come when you take the stuff to them?" Janae looked up shyly at Guy.

"Uh. I suppose a few of you could come help me carry it into the house." He looked around the room. "We probably shouldn't all go."

"I found her on the school website," Connie said into the room. "Lacy Montoya. But it doesn't give her personal information, so I'll have to go back to Google. I'll have it in a sec."

Jay picked up some boxes and started for the door. "Lets load a few more things in the van and then we can decided if any of us will go with Guy."

Guy opened the door and stepped aside. "What can I do to help?"

Jay nodded at Kate. "She'll tell you."

Kate directed the clearing of the rooms and getting the last few things packed away. Guy and Brock dismantled the bed and stood the mattress and box springs against the living room wall. Mitch and Jay set the headboard and frame along another wall. Kate, Connie and Janae moved the lighter things into the dining area and thirty minutes later all the furniture was in the front part of the house.

Kate swiped at her brow with the sleeve of her shirt and sighed. "Thanks everybody. That would've taken much longer without your help."

Jay patted Guy on the shoulder. "Yeah thanks. You saved my back."

Kate stepped up beside her husband. "Is there anything that you could use, Guy? We are selling most of it on Saturday, but of course you are welcome to take anything you might need." Kate gestured to the furniture-packed room as the young man looked around

"Uh. I don't know. Penny's already done so much for me." He shuffled his feet before glancing at the kitchen table. "Robin and I don't have a table really. We just sit on the couch to eat." He shrugged and looked back at Kate. "We can keep doing that though."

Kate shook her head. "No. That's silly. Take the table. You know Penny would have already bought you one if she'd known you needed it." A warm chuckle filled the room.

"Well, that's probably true. Okay. Save it for me and I'll come get it on Saturday," the young man agreed with a smile. "Did you find the address for Mrs. Montoya?" he asked in Connie's direction. "It's getting late, but I was hoping to drop all this off tonight." He ducked his head and took a deep breath. "I've had to park on the other side of campus for the last week just so the guys wouldn't see all the baby stuff in the back of my car."

That brought another round of laughter.

Connie pulled out her phone. "I have her address. She lives in Springville." The hairdresser strode across the room to Guy and showed him the phone. "Here's her address. Should I text it to you?"

"Sure."

Guy gave Connie his number and she sent the address to him.

"Well it's been fun, but I need to get home," Connie said as she tucked her phone into her back pocket and moved toward the door.

Brock nodded. "Yeah. I've got to drop off the couch and pick up some things for work tomorrow." Connie's brother stepped in Guy's direction and rested his hand on the young man's shoulder. "You have fun dropping off the gifts. The Montoyas are going to be ecstatic." He smiled broadly. "I would love to be there to experience the giving side of what you're doing," he paused and cleared his throat, "because I'm positive it's even better than being on the receiving end."

"You got that right. Giving you the truck was my first experience, but it was pretty great," Guy said with a chuckle.

"I would have to agree," Brock pulled Guy into a quick embrace and Brock walked out the door.

Kate could tell that both men had been affected by the experience they shared.

Jay broke the silence. "We should get this baby home." He picked up Megan and started turning off lights in the house.

Janae picked up the diaper bag and put it over her shoulder. "Are we going to help deliver the gifts? She lives in Springville. Maybe it's close to our house."

Kate looked at Jay. "It's up to your dad."

Jay took a breath and looked at Guy. "Would you mind having my wife and daughter along?"

Guy smiled. "Sure. They'd have to follow me, since I don't have much room, but it would be nice to have a little help." Guy walked out the front door and down the path with Jay and his family close behind.

Jay paused on the front walkway. "How about you Mitch? You interested in going?"

Mitch nodded quickly. "Yeah. I'd kind of like to go too."

"Alright." Jay nodded and spoke to Guy. "Follow us to our home and I'll put the baby to bed while the rest of you find the Montoyas."

"Are you sure, Jay? Maybe you should go," Kate said.

"No. You go. We'll be fine, won't we, Meggie?"

Janae let out an excited squeal, ran ahead to the van and climbed inside. Guy headed for his own car and the Lundquists went to theirs. Jay handed Megan to Janae who buckled her in the car seat and Mitch went around to the other side.

"Are we going to tell Mrs. Montoya who gave her everything?" Mitch asked as they started down the street.

"It's up to Guy. I don't think it would hurt, but we'll do whatever he thinks is best," Kate answered.

The baby began to cry as they took the exit to Springville. Kate glanced at the clock. "She's really tired. You can skip her bath if you want. Just change her diaper and put on her pajamas." Kate looked over her shoulder and tried to shush the baby. "She'll want a bottle and maybe a story."

Jay touched his wife's arm. "I've got this. I've been doing this for a long time."

"I know . . . I just hope she'll go down without a big fuss."

The family pulled up in front of their home. Kate and Jay climbed from the vehicle and Janae lifted Megan from the seat and handed the fussing baby to her father. Kate came around to the driver's side and kissed the toddler on the cheek. "Goodnight little girl. You be good for daddy."

Megan reached for her mother and began to cry harder when her mother didn't take her. Jay hugged the child against his chest and tried to soothe her.

"We'll see you in a bit."

Kate nodded and climbed into the car, waiting as Guy pulled back into the street. She followed the black Jeep as they made their way to the other side of town. They stopped in front of a small twin home where both porch lights were off. She hoped they wouldn't be waking the family. What if they'd just gotten the babies to bed?

She and her kids hurried to Guy's vehicle and started unloading the gifts. They followed Guy and placed them on the porch, working in silence. The entryway was so tiny that they started laying things on the walkway, keeping a clear path to the door.

"Are you going to knock or leave it for them to find?" Janae asked in a whisper as they removed the last box of diapers.

"I think we better knock. I don't think it should be left out all night." Guy stepped to the front door and knocked softly. They waited, but all was quiet in the house. Guy grimaced, but knocked a little bit louder. After another minute, Kate heard a noise from inside.

A man in his thirties cracked the door open and flipped on the light.

"Hello?" he said in a weary voice.

Guy smiled and held out a box of diapers. "Hi. Are you Mr. Montoya?"

The man nodded, but kept the door mostly closed.

"Great. I hope I didn't wake you. I have some gifts for you and your family." He motioned to the items on the porch and gestured to the boxes lining the walkway.

Mr. Montoya pulled the door open wider. "Gifts? From who?"

Guy looked at Kate. "Well, it's a long story, but a woman I know asked me to get these things for you. She heard you were out of work and thought you could use a little help. Can we bring them in?" Guy asked as he pointed with the box of diapers.

"Wow." The man looked mystified as he ran his hands through his messy hair. He stepped aside. "Uh, yeah. Come on in."

Janae grabbed a box and followed her mother and Guy into the house. A few minutes later, Mrs. Montoya stepped into the living room as she pulled the belt of a robe tighter around her waist. She started gathering clean laundry from the couch.

"What's all this?" Mrs. Montoya asked as Kate added to the growing pile of boxes.

"Have you heard of Christmas in July?" Kate laughed. "Someone wanted you to have a few things for your new babies. We are fortunate enough to be the elves."

Mrs. Montoya's mouth fell open and she seemed speechless. "Uh . . . seriously?"

Kate nodded and walked back to the front door as Mitch stepped into the house. "That's everything," the boy said.

The group of six stood in the tiny living room surrounded by boxes. The new parents inspected each item unable to hide the joy they felt at having received so many gifts.

"Who would have done this?" the wife asked as she held a blanket to her cheek. "I can't believe it."

"Someone that saw a need," Kate answered as a tear slipped down her cheek.

Janae looked around expectantly. "Are the babies sleeping?"

"Yes, but you can come see them if you'd like." The woman motioned them into a back room where there was one crib. Mrs. Montoya turned on a small lamp as Kate and her children crowded around the crib. Three little bundles slept side by side in the bed—one pink blanket and two blue.

"Oh! They're so tiny," Janae whispered. "How old are they?"

"Two months. We just brought Sammy home this week," Mrs. Montoya said as she pointed to one of the blue blankets. "He was the smallest and needed extra time in the hospital."

Kate nodded and looked around for Guy.

"I'm going to get . . . um . . . our friend."

Mitch followed Kate back to the living room where Guy and Mr. Montoya were starting to open up the boxes. "Do you want to see the babies?" Kate asked Guy.

"Sure." The young man nodded and leaned the partially opened box against the sofa. Kate led him into the tiny bedroom and stood by the door as he peeked into the crib.

Mrs. Montoya was softly answering Janae's questions.

"They only weighed about three pounds at birth, but now they are all close to six."

Janae nodded. "I wish I could hold them."

Kate stepped into the room and spoke quietly. "Not now honey."

Janae turned. "I know, but maybe we could come back sometime," she said hopefully.

Mrs. Montoya touched Janae's shoulder. "That would be great. I can always use another set of hands. Do you live close by?"

"Yes. We live here in Springville. Can we come back Mom?" Janae asked pleadingly.

"We'll talk about it later. Let's go out before we wake them."

The small group filed back into the cramped living room. Mitch and Mr. Montoya were setting up the first swing. "I don't know where we'll put all these things. We might have to push the couch against that wall," the man said as he studied the room.

"Are you sure you can't tell us who to thank for all these beautiful things?" Mrs. Montoya asked as she ran her hand across the top of the swing.

Kate turned her gaze on Guy who was pulling a bouncer from its carton.

"It was supposed to be anonymous, but . . ." Guy paused and looked at the woman who was lifting a quilted blanket from the pile. "Her name was Penny. She . . . um . . . actually died last week before I was able to bring all this over."

Mrs. Montoya dropped her hands. "Oh no. I'm so sorry. Was she sick?"

Kate shook her head. "Not really. She died peacefully in her sleep. She was such a good lady. She was always taking care of people." Kate motioned to the people in the room. "We have all been blessed by knowing her."

Chapter 35

Janae was still talking about the babies the next morning, chattering nonstop about how she couldn't wait to see the babies when they were awake. Before they left the Montoya's home the night before, Kate had taken down Lacy's phone number, so Janae could help the new mother some afternoon.

"Surprising them with those gifts was so much fun," the girl said as she unloaded the dishwasher. "We should do that again. You know how sometimes people do that sort of thing at Christmastime? I think we should do it *all* the time!"

Kate nodded and took a glass pan from Janae and set it on the shelf. "That's probably why Penny did it. Once you've experienced the joy that comes from helping people, I bet it's hard to stop. But it takes money to buy gifts like that. I don't think we could do it every month, but we should definitely do something like that once in a while."

The girl nodded. "How much do you think all of that cost? A thousand dollars?"

"I don't know. Probably not that much." Kate grabbed her purse and kissed the baby on the head. "I better go, honey. You call me if you have any trouble. Mitch will be here until noon and then he has to work. He'll take his bike."

"Okay. Bye Mom."

On her drive to work, Kate's mind wandered to the events of the evening before. She had been as thrilled to see the triplets as her daughter, but the amazement on the parents' faces was even more fun to see. What pleasure Penny must have felt each time she assisted someone. What a wonderful thing for Guy to experience as well. Kate had wanted to ask Guy how he had started working for Penny, but she hadn't had a chance. Maybe she'd get to speak with him at the memorial service.

Kate pulled into the parking lot of the salon and her phone began to ring. She picked it up and saw an unknown number from California. She answered it quickly.

"Hello?" Kate climbed from her car and walked toward the back door of the salon.

"Kate? This is Jolene. I'm sorry I couldn't call yesterday. I had doctor's appointments all day. Is this a good time to finish my story?" Jolene asked breathlessly.

"Actually, I'm just heading in to work. But I can call you this afternoon. Would that be okay?"

"Oh yes dear. I will be here all day. Do you need my number?" Jolene asked.

"It's on my phone now that you've called me," Kate said with a smile as she walked to the employee break room and put her purse in a cupboard.

"Oh, of course. These new phones are just amazing. Okay dear. I'll wait for your call then. Have a good day at work," Jolene said before she hung up the phone.

Kate pulled her apron over her head. She stepped to the front counter and checked the appointment book. She would be busy today. Her regular clients only had Tuesdays to come in, so the day was always full.

Connie was already at the sink with her first haircut of the day. She rinsed the woman's hair and began to towel dry it as Kate stepped to her station.

"How was the drop off? Were they happy to see all the gifts?" Connie asked as she helped her client into the chair and put the drape around her shoulders.

A smile lit up Kate's face. "Yes. They were stunned and so thankful for the swings and clothes. The babies were sleeping, but we got to peek in at them. They were precious and so tiny. Lacy said they were only about three pounds when they were born." Kate unwound the cord on her hair dryer as Connie combed through the woman's wet hair.

"Wow. My kids were never that small. Both of my boys came out half-grown weighing eight and a half pounds each." Connie shook her head and began cutting her customer's hair.

The bell at the front rang and Kate's first client walked through the door. "Gabby. Hi, come on over."

The morning sped by as Kate had one customer after another. She finally had a break and sat down in a chair with a bottle of water. Connie waved goodbye to her latest patron and dropped into the seat next to Kate.

"I got a call this morning from Jolene." Kate took a swig of water.

"Jolene?"

"Oh. I guess I haven't told you about her. She's Penny's cousin. She lives out in California." Kate paused and drank the rest of the water. The bottle crinkled as she tossed it in the small wastebasket. "Her daughter messaged me while we were in Ephraim and I called her on Sunday when we got back. She practically grew up with Penny, so she had some great stories to tell."

"Oh really. That's good. Are you ready to give the life sketch tomorrow then?" Connie asked as she pulled a laundry basket closer to fold the clean towels.

"It's getting closer to being finished. I have been waiting to hear the rest of Penny's story though." Kate stood and carried a stack of towels to the shelf. "I had to end our conversation early because Megan needed me, so that's why Jolene called me back this morning."

Connie took the basket into the break room and Kate followed her. "You'll hear about her life tomorrow, but one thing I may not mention is the fact that Penny became pregnant when she was a teenager," Kate said with a frown.

"No way." Connie stopped and studied Kate. "Really?"

Kate nodded and pulled her purse out of the cupboard. "I'll tell you about it when I get back. What are you doing for lunch? Should I go grab something? I don't have anyone coming in for about half an hour."

"A turkey sandwich." Connie pulled a bill from her pocket and handed it to Kate. "Hurry back."

The line was short at the sandwich shop, so Kate got the two lunches and rushed back to the salon. "So all I know," Kate said as she unwrapped her lunch at the break table, "is that Penny was pregnant when she was sixteen, and she ended up living with her aunt and uncle during the pregnancy."

"Why would she stay with them?" Connie wrinkled her brow as she pulled the tomatoes from the sandwich.

Kate took a bite and swallowed before continuing her tale. "She didn't get along very well with her mother and apparently her boyfriend wanted her to get an abortion."

Connie paused in her chewing and waited.

Kate shook her head. "Jolene said Penny didn't do that, but I don't know anything else. That's where the story ended."

"Did she give the baby up for adoption?" Connie asked before taking another bite.

"I have no idea."

"Maybe her kid is out there somewhere." Connie pointed at Kate. "What if he is the rightful heir to all her stuff?" She swallowed. "Wouldn't she put that in the will though?" Connie took a drink of her water before continuing. "I guess if she gave up the baby then she probably wouldn't leave anything for him . . . or her."

"Right. For all I know, the child never knew her. It wasn't as common back then for kids to find out who their biological parents were. And some kids just don't want to hurt the parents that raised them." Kate finished off her sandwich and wiped at her mouth. "I'll call Jolene when I'm off today and find out what happened."

Connie crumpled her wrapper and drained her water. "Call me. I'd like to know what she says."

The two women returned to work just as Robin stepped through the front door.

"Hey Robin. What brings you in?" Connie asked.

"I'm covering for Tabitha this afternoon. She has the stomach flu."

"Oh no. I hope it's only the 24 hour kind. She supposed to work tomorrow so we can go to the funeral," Connie said as she swept around her station.

"She thinks it was something she ate last night at her mother-in-laws. She's already feeling better, but I told her to stay home."

Robin organized her station and nodded at Kate. "I hear you met my brother." Robin chuckled. "He finally told me about his job with Penny. Crazy, huh?"

Kate smiled. "Yeah. Crazy is right. So you had no idea he was delivering trucks and baby clothes to people?"

The younger woman smiled and shook her head. "Nope. He's pretty private. I only just found out that he quit the pizza place. I guess Penny has been paying him to help her."

The door chimed and two women came through the door. Robin greeted her customer and Kate helped the second one, but she continued to think about Guy. She hadn't even thought about Penny paying Guy, but of course she must have been. She wondered what he would do now. Hopefully he would get that job he was applying for at the auto shop.

The remainder of the day passed quickly and Kate collected her things before heading to the car. "We'll see you both tomorrow right?" she said to Robin and Connie.

"Yes. Robin says Guy wants to drive, so I am happy to let him. It starts at one? Somewhere in Ephraim?" Connie asked.

"It's pretty simple to find. Just head down Main Street and you'll see it."

"Sounds good."

The door chimed as Kate passed through the door and walked to her car. She looked up at the sky at the dark clouds that were forming. A flash of lightning in the distance caught her eye as she climbed behind the wheel. It looked like they might get some rain before the day was over.

Kate decided to call Jolene as she drove home, knowing she may not have time to speak to the woman once she got to the house. Dinner and children would need her attention. She hit the send button and waited for Jolene to pick up.

"Hello?" the woman answered on the third ring.

"Jolene. This is Kate. Is this a good time? I'm on my way home and thought I'd call."

"Yes perfect. Let's see where were we? You know Penny was pregnant and living with us, but did I tell you about her accident?"

Kate's breath caught. "Penny was in an accident?"

Chapter 36

California October 1956

A sigh escaped as Rhonda came into the house and dropped her purse on the table. Jolene's mother had spent the last three hours volunteering at the hospital, something she did every Wednesday afternoon.

"Boy, am I beat." She dropped onto a chair and propped her aching feet on a second one. Jolene set a stack of clean plates in the cupboard and turned to face her mother.

"Do you know if Penny had any plans this afternoon?" she asked, worry in her voice. "I haven't seen her since I got home an hour ago. I assume she went for a walk, but with the storm coming, I'm starting to worry."

"Did she take the dog? She said she'd take Teddy when she went out." Rhonda let her feet fall to the floor and groaned as she stood up.

"I think so. He hasn't been in here bugging me so I figured she and Teddy were together." Jolene dried the last glass and set it in the cupboard beside the plates. "I guess I'll take my bike out and see if I can find her. She's probably on her way home even as we speak."

The younger woman grabbed a hat and sweater from the hook by the door and wheeled her bike out of the garage. She waved at her mother and headed down the street.

"Oh Penny. Why can't you be satisfied with lazing around the house like a good expectant momma."

Jolene smiled to herself as she pedaled through the neighborhoods and turned down the side roads that she knew Penny liked to take. She scanned the streets she passed, hoping to catch a glimpse of her cousin and the big golden retriever. As she neared town, she slowed her bike and paused at a corner while a big van rumbled by.

"Maybe she's getting her hair done today. She did mention that a few days ago, but I doubt she would take Teddy along for that."

Jolene decided it wouldn't hurt to look. She began pedaling again and made her way to the salon on Main Street. She peered through the glass door as she straddled the bike. She could see Margie inside, but no sign of the dog.

"Teddy would have had to wait outside," she murmured and climbed back on the seat, continuing down the block.

She stopped at the city park where she knew the dog liked to run and left the bike under a tree as she wandered past the tennis courts and play area. Two teenage girls were walking toward Jolene and stopped when she stepped in front of them. "I'm looking for my cousin. Have you seen a young woman with a big yellow dog? She's blond and kind of short . . . the woman, I mean."

The girls frowned and shook their heads. "No. Sorry. Good luck."

She thanked them and returned to her bicycle. "Maybe she's made it home by now."

Jolene decided to take a different way home on the off chance that Penny had done the same thing. She turned her bike in the opposite direction and clutched at her hat as the wind began to pick up in intensity. She would have to hurry to beat the storm clouds that continued to mount on the horizon. As the hill became too steep, Jolene climbed off the bike and began to walk it up the incline. She paused to catch her breath and was startled when a horn honked at the curb. Her father opened the door to his truck and came to her side.

"Let's put that in the back. Mother called me soon after you left. I can't believe she's done this again. I thought she would have learned by now." Her father's brow furrowed and he shook his head. "Where have you checked?" he asked as he lifted the bike into the bed of the pickup.

"I came the usual way and then I stopped at the park and the hair salon."

"I checked the library and the market but she wasn't at either of those places." Garret climbed into the front seat of the truck and waited as Jolene slammed her door shut. "Let's continue home and see if she's arrived yet."

Jolene chewed on her lip and stared out the window as tiny raindrops began to fall on the glass. She shivered involuntarily as she watched the sky darken further.

Oh dear Penny. Where are you?

She reached to turn up the heat and sat back against the upholstered seat. She was probably worrying for nothing. Her cousin was most likely sitting home with her feet up wondering what all the fuss was about. Garrett slowed and turned down a road to his left.

"Where are you going?" Jolene asked as her father took another turn.

"I just had the thought to drive by that old house on Cedar. Penny made me stop the other day so she could take a picture of it."

Jolene nodded. Penny did love that historic building with its intricate wood trim and the iron finials that topped the castle-like home. They'd driven by it more than once this summer.

The rain began to fall harder as they turned onto Cedar and came to a stop in front of the two-story home.

"Well she's not here." Jolene sighed. "Now what?"

Her father put the car in park. "I'm going to walk down the block. Just wait here."

Jolene started to protest, but her father pulled his collar up and shoved his hands in his pocket. Garrett walked several feet in one direction, stopped and let out a whistle that he used for calling the dog. He seemed to listen before he turned and headed up the street the other way. Jolene heard him whistle a second time and call Teddy's name.

"This is never going to work." She muttered as she watched her dad continue to call and listen.

She leaned forward, straining to see through the rain-smeared glass as her father turned his head and jogged toward the last home on the block. Garrett climbed the steps to the home and disappeared behind an overgrown hedge. Jolene looked over to the ignition, hoping her father had left his keys.

"Good thing." She slid across the bench and started up the engine. "He's got to be soaked to the skin already." She put the truck in gear and pulled it forward until it was idling in front of the house where she'd last seen her father. She looked up at the home, but the hedges obscured anything more.

"Of course," she muttered.

She turned off the engine and gathered her coat around herself before scrambling from the car. She splashed through a puddle on the sidewalk and groaned as the water soaked through to her stockings. She hurried up the steps and through the small opening that led between the hedges.

On the other side of the bushes, Jolene found her father kneeling beside Penny who was curled in a fetal position, the loyal dog lying beside her. Teddy looked up as Jolene let out a cry and fell to her knees.

***

Kate's breath caught. She pulled into a gas station worried that she wasn't paying enough attention to the road.

"What happened?" she asked as she put the car in park.

"Penny started having pains, so she stopped a few times to catch her breath hoping it would pass. When it didn't, she knocked on the residence where we found her, but no one was home. The pain became too much and she couldn't go any further. Teddy stayed with her until my father found them."

Kate shivered as she thought of Penny lying on the ground in such unbearable pain. "But how did your father even find her?"

"That was a miracle," Jolene exclaimed. "Daddy said for years that it was inspiration, pure and simple. He had the impression that he should go to that neighborhood and once he was in the right area, he began to whistle for the dog. Teddy had barked and whined, but would not budge from Penny's side. Thankfully Daddy heard him."

Silence filled the phone line for several moments.

"Did she lose the baby?" Kate asked in whisper as she backed out of the parking space and returned to the road.

"Yes," Jolene matched Kate's whisper, "and the ability to ever have children of her own. Because of the hemorrhaging they decided to remove her uterus. That was the hardest part for Penny to reconcile."

Kate sped toward her home as Jolene painted a picture of the days and weeks that followed in that difficult time in Penny's life.

"Clarinda, Penny's mother, came to see her while she recovered, but that didn't go well." Jolene took a ragged breath. "I was at the hospital, but left the room when she arrived to give them privacy. Clarinda had only been in the room a minute or two when I heard the sounds of raised voices coming from inside. I retreated down the corridor as her mother stepped back into the hallway and left the hospital in a hurry."

Kate exited the freeway and stopped at a red light as Jolene continued.

"Several days later when I asked if her mother was coming back to take her home, Penny said she would never be going home again. She started crying and I felt terrible for even bringing it up. Through her tears she explained that the first words out of her mother's mouth had been, "What a relief. Now you can get on with your life.""

An audible gasp escaped Kate's mouth. "No! She really said that?"

"I wouldn't put it past her." Jolene said quietly. "Clarinda was very caught up in high society and quite snobbish really. She would not apologize to her daughter and could not even fathom why Penny was so upset with her. The whole situation caused an even larger rift in their relationship. They didn't speak for many months after that."

"What a shame," Kate said as she pulled into her neighborhood.

"Yes," Jolene continued, "but I believe what bothered Clarinda most was the embarrassment she felt at having to explain why her only daughter wouldn't come home."

Kate parked in her garage, listening as the story continued to unfold.

"Penny stayed with us and eventually finished high school. Her grief lessened as she started working at the hospital with my mother after school. The patients loved her and she loved them. She devoted many hours as a volunteer and found great joy in the service she was able to give. It was a time of healing for Penny and made her into the loving generous woman that she was."

Kate could hear Jolene's voice fill with emotion. She waited as the woman regained her composure and then said, "But they must have made up eventually. I remember seeing pictures of Penny's wedding and her parents were there, right?"

"Oh yes, but what a showdown they had trying to plan that wedding." Jolene chuckled. "Penny wanted things done simply and her mother insisted on a big to-do. Clarinda won that battle—as she often did, but I was just glad Aunt Clarinda finally accepted Del."

"What? She didn't like Penny's husband?" Kate asked as Janae peeked out the door and saw her stepmother sitting in the car. Kate held up a finger as the woman on the phone spoke again.

"Well, Del had plans to be a cattle rancher and Clarinda wasn't sure that line of work would provide well enough for her daughter. My aunt still held out the hope that Penny would come to her senses and embrace a lifestyle that was more befitting of her . . . from Clarinda's point of view that is." Jolene said with a sigh. "She just couldn't' understand that Penny had chosen a different path—one filled with helping the less fortunate and making do with less. It was a shame that Clarinda never realized how happy Penny was."

There was break in the conversation, so Kate climbed from her car and ascended the steps into the house. "Jolene? I need to say goodbye. I'm sorry. The kids need me."

"Yes, of course dear. Thank you for listening to me ramble. I've enjoyed remembering my sweet cousin. I wish I could be there for the funeral, but I can't. I know Penny would understand."

Janae looked up as Kate walked into the kitchen. "I appreciate you talking to me. It has been such a pleasure hearing about Penny." It was

Kate's turn to swallow the lump in her throat. "We loved her like family. Our only regret was that we lost her so early."

Chapter 37

"Did you put the seat back in the van?" Kate asked as she styled her hair. Jay and Mitch had just returned from dropping off the unwanted items at the thrift store while Kate finished writing the speech she would be giving today. They would be leaving for Ephraim in a few minutes.

"Mitch just helped me with it."

"Good. Did you get the computer? And the pictures?" Kate turned toward her husband. "We'll need the diaper bag too. I don't know if there are snacks in it."

Jay stood behind Kate. He slid his arms around her and kissed her neck. "I checked for snacks and put everything in the car. Mitch is putting on his tie and Janae is dressing Megan. We can leave as soon as you're ready."

Kate sighed. She was a bundle of nerves, but she was glad this day was finally here. "Thanks sweetie."

"You look nice. Where'd you get this pretty shirt?" he asked running his hands over the silky sleeves of the blouse. "Someone has incredible taste."

Kate set down her brush and turned in his arms. "It is nice. Make sure you tell Amber that I love it."

Her husband frowned. "I told her what color to look for." Jay's secretary was also his personal shopper when it came to wearable gifts.

Her laugh was cut short as he kissed her again.

"Are you coming? The girls are in the car," Mitch said from the hallway.

Kate stepped out of Jay's arms and reapplied her lipstick. "Be right there."

The couple hurried to the garage and climbed into the van. "Does anyone need to use the bathroom? It's only an hour drive, so I don't plan on stopping." Jay put the car in motion when there was no response from the back seat.

Mitch put in his ear buds and hummed along to his tunes while Janae read a book. Megan fell asleep as soon as they were out of town and Kate read through her notes again.

"I hope people saw the announcement in the paper and someone shows up," Kate said as she tucked her papers back into her purse. "Connie and Robin are coming with Guy and Penny's neighbor Kim said she'd be there." Kate sighed. "Or maybe I don't want anyone to come. I don't really like talking in front of a huge crowd."

Jay took her hand. "It's going to be fine. You'll do well."

An hour later Jay pulled into the parking lot of the funeral home. "We're thirty minutes early," she said, surprised at the number of cars that were already there. "You think these cars are for Penny's service?"

"I doubt they'd have anything else going on right before a funeral." Jay helped the kids from the car and followed his family to the door of the building.

A man in a dark suit and a woman in a soft green dress greeted them as they stepped into the dim interior. "Welcome. Are you here for the Penny Haws memorial?" the woman asked.

Kate stepped forward. "Yes. I'm Kate Lundquist and this in my husband Jay. Are you Louise?"

"I am." The gray-haired woman smiled and touched Janae's shoulder. "What lovely children you have." Janae smiled and Louise turned her attention to the man beside her. "This is Troy Atwood. He'll be conducting the service today."

Troy grasped Jay's hand and nodded to the rest. "Let me show you to your seats."

Kate accepted the program that a young man offered her as she walked into the chapel, Penny's face smiling from the front cover.

"Thank you." She nodded.

The family was seated on the front row beside a man and woman who smiled as the children got settled in their seats. Kate read through the program as soft organ music filled the room. The woman seated behind the organ had to be Dotty, Clyde's wife. Kate looked over her shoulder at the crowd and found Ernie sitting beside a silver haired woman a few rows back. He lifted a hand in a discreet wave.

The chapel was almost full, but more people continued to file in. Several young men were busy setting up additional chairs in the back and along the sides of the room.

"They heard you were speaking," Jay said with a chuckle as he surveyed the growing crowd.

"Hardly. They just loved Penny." Kate pulled her tissues from her purse along with her notes. "Don't get me started." She dabbed at her eyes and blew her nose.

The butterflies in her gut multiplied as the clock edged closer to the start of the service. She leaned toward her husband. "I'll pay you if you'll do this for me." She tapped the papers in her hand. "Honestly. Anything you want."

Jay reached for Megan who was beginning to squirm on Janae's lap. "Sorry. I'm on Meggie duty today."

Kate frowned and took a deep breath. Troy stood at the pulpit and the organ music faded.

"Welcome friends. We are so glad to see so many wonderful people here to pay tribute to Penelope Crawford Haws. We'll begin with an opening hymn and then Mr. Ernie Hollingsworth will give us an invocation."

Music filled the crowded chapel as the voices joined in singing. Kate felt her nerves calm as Ernie stood to pray. Troy returned to the microphone and announced the order of the program. Kate was first. Her knees wobbled as she made her way to the stand and looked out over the enormous gathering.

"What a sight," she said feeling her throat close. She dabbed at her eyes again. "I hope I can do this. I'm sure Penny is looking down on us wondering what all the fuss is about." The crowd murmured their agreement and Kate began the synopsis of Penny's life.

A feeling of peace fell over Kate and the entire room as she recapped Penny's generosity and the many hearts that she had touched. She looked into Roberto's face as she told of the washer and dryer incident. She found Laurie in the audience when she mentioned the hospital bills that were secretly paid for and smiled at Ralph and Nora as she mentioned mortgage payments that were taken care of for months at a time. Kate finished her prepared speech and paused for a moment.

"I talked to some of you while preparing this life sketch, but I obviously couldn't talk to everyone. If it's okay with Mr. Atwood I would like to invite a few others forward that would like to share briefly any additional stories." She returned to her seat as a line started to form in the aisle.

The first man in line stood at the microphone and tried to speak, but found it difficult with the emotion he was feeling. A woman hurried to the stand, put her arm around his waist and began to speak.

"This is my husband Charles Finnegan. Better known as Finn to some of you. He was only in town for a few days, but was blessed to meet Penny Haws."

Kate smiled as she recalled Luther's story of the homeless man that Penny had fed and clothed. "My wonderful husband was down on his luck and struggling with . . ." the woman paused as the man reached for the mike.

He looked out over the audience and began to speak in a soft voice. "I wasn't sure I had a reason to live," Finn said as his wife looked on. "I'd lost my job and my pride. I'd come to town looking for work, but

I'd had the same bad luck." He sniffed and pulled out a handkerchief. "I found myself sleeping behind the diner where Miss Penny worked. I was very hungry and hoped to find something to eat in the dumpster." He ducked his head. "Yes, I was that desperate.

"Penny caught me scrounging through the trash. I was afraid she was going to call the cops on me, but instead she brought me a bag of food." He swiped at his nose with the hankie. "After feeding, then clothing me, she encouraged me to not give up. She said there was always something better down the road. She was right of course. A week later I met my sweet Annie and found employment on the very same day." He looked at his wife. "The rest is history as they say." Finn and Annie walked arm in arm back to their seats.

A dozen people stepped to the stand and shared more of the same type of experiences. They spoke of groceries being left on porches, alert neighbors the eyewitnesses to Penny's acts of kindness. One man explained that when he had been out of work for several months he had received a free meal delivered from the diner to his door every evening. The delivery boy had been unwilling to divulge Penny's secret, but the story had finally leaked out several years later.

Over forty-five minutes later Troy finally stood to close the meeting.

"What a remarkable woman our Penny was. We shall truly miss her." He cleared his throat and glanced at the woman seated beside Mitch. "Our concluding musical number will be performed by Karen Shields and then the benediction will be offered by Grant Smith."

The couple at the end of Kate's bench stood and walked to the stand. The woman went to the podium and the man sat at the piano.

"Good afternoon. My name is Karen Moore Shields," the woman began. A low murmur emanated from the audience. "Yes, some of you may recognize my name. I spent a few years here with my mother and had the privilege of getting to know Penny. Before I sing today I would like to tell my own experience with our beloved friend."

"I'm sure some of you folks that knew me then will remember that I was," she looked at Mitch, "as this young man might say . . . pretty messed up." Several people chuckled as Karen continued," but Penny loved me anyway."

Chapter 38

Ephraim 1984

"The tables must be wiped down after every customer, even if you don't see any visible food," Penny explained to the newest waitress. "We keep the towels and cleaner in this cupboard."

Karen sighed. "Shouldn't there be a guy that clears the table for us? A bellboy or whatever?"

Penny smiled sweetly at the teenage girl. "A busboy. Yes, we have one but he gets very busy. You don't want to let your tables sit empty. I find it's easier to clear and wipe down my own tables."

The young woman blew a bright pink bubble and popped it with her teeth. "Right."

"And one more thing, Karen." Penny handed her apprentice a spray bottle and a damp towel. "We'd rather you didn't chew gum while you're waiting tables." Penny smiled and waited as the girl spit her gum into a wastebasket. "Now today you'll be helping me and by the end of the week you'll be on your own, so pay attention."

Karen had just turned fifteen and the last thing she'd wanted for her birthday was a dumb job at this diner. Her mother had dropped her off an hour earlier for the interview and for some reason Penny had hired her on the spot. She followed the waitress to a table in the back and watched as Penny stacked the plates and cups and balanced them on her tray.

"Be sure you wipe the salt and pepper shakers and straighten the sugar packets in the box. Then wipe down the seat and check the edges of the table for anything sticky." Penny ignored the soft grumble that came from the young woman's throat. "The last thing we need is someone getting jam on his tie." Penny chuckled as if she'd made a joke.

Karen began wiping down the table as Penny carried the full tray back to the kitchen. The young woman ran her towel over the seat and pushed the condiments against the wall. She pulled a straw wrapper from the vase and returned the fake flower to its container before standing back to check her work.

"Excuse me. Can I get some ketchup?" a man at the next table asked with a smile.

"Uh sure," Karen said reaching for the bottle on the table she had just cleaned.

"Thank you. Are you new? I haven't seen you before," the man said with a smile.

"Yeah. First day." She pushed her hair behind her ear and smoothed her apron. She looked down at her mismatched socks below her cuffed pants. She hadn't expected to get the job let alone be working today when she'd dressed this morning.

The man extended his hand. "John Carol. Nice to meet you."

Karen took John's hand and felt her face warm as the man held it firmly and gazed into her eyes. "I'll have to request your table next time I come in."

Karen smiled weakly, pulled her hand back and turned away almost bumping into Penny who stood behind her.

"John, are you bothering Karen?" Penny laughed and refilled the man's glass with ice water.

"We were just getting acquainted." The man grinned. "Karen. What a pretty name to go with a pretty face."

"Enjoy the rest of your day," Penny said to John as she steered Karen to another table. "He's a charmer. Good tipper though." Penny took the spray bottle and rag from Karen and handed her a pad of paper and a pen. "You can take this next one."

The new waitress stepped to the next table. "What are you drinking?" Karen asked as Penny looked on.

The woman at the table raised her eyebrows, stealing a glance at Penny before answering. "I'd like a lemonade please."

The scruffy bearded man across the table smiled at Karen. "I like your style. I'll take a coffee."

Penny smiled pleasantly. "We'll be right back for your order."

The two waitresses moved toward the counter where Penny pulled a mug from a shelf and pointed at a pot of coffee. "Be careful, it's hot."

Karen lifted the carafe and filled the cup to the brim as Penny filled a tall glass with lemonade. "He'll want cream. Three," Penny instructed as she placed the two drinks on a tray

Penny's Diner

and handed it to the younger woman.

As they headed across the dining room, the tray wobbled in Karen's unsteady hands, sloshing some of the coffee. Karen looked up with grimace.

"Don't worry. It'll take some practice, but you'll get the hang of it."

Karen delivered the drinks and successfully took Don and Mabel's food order. Thirty minutes later she happily tucked her first tip into her pocket.

The day continued in much the same way until a young man with purple hair and a ring in his eyebrow came through the door and requested Karen's table. The younger waitress let out a small cough as she saw him slide into his seat.

"Someone you know?" Penny asked as she wiped off her tray.

"Uh yeah. My boyfriend." Karen took a deep breath. "I guess he found out I got the job."

Penny followed Karen to the table. "Hey Sly. What are you doing here?"

The young man licked his lips and grinned up at Karen. "I was hoping for some lunch, but I don't have much cash on me."

The young woman shook her head slightly and glanced sideways at Penny.

"You must get tips, right?" Sly asked as he opened the menu. "I'd like a burger. Maybe some fries on the side." He handed the menu to Karen. "Oh and a coke."

"Uh . . ." Karen slid her hand into her pocket and fingered the cash she'd collected throughout the day. Penny took the menu and ushered Karen into the kitchen.

"You keep that money darlin'. I'll cover Sly's lunch today, but I'm thinking you might consider finding a new boyfriend."

***

Karen looked out over the audience as the memory faded and continued her story.

"As the months passed, I learned to love that diner—the people who came in to eat and the people that worked there. Penny was my biggest cheerleader. She encouraged me to make changes in my life including dumping Sly." The crowd murmured.

"She also encouraged me to follow my dreams of making music," Karen glanced over her shoulder at the man at the piano, "which led me to finding my husband, Adam." The man winked at his pretty wife.

"Even though my husband has taken over the role of cheerleader and supporter, Penny Haws will always remain in my heart. I could not imagine what my life would be like if I hadn't taken the path that Penny helped put me on."

The woman at the podium swallowed several times to regain her composure. "This was the first song Penny ever taught me." Karen lowered the microphone and began her song.

As the first notes rang through the small chapel, even the baby stopped tugging at Jay's tie.

Karen's strong clear voice blended with the piano and filled the room. Kate closed her eyes and let the music wash over her. The hymn was one that she had grown up singing, but she had never heard the arrangement as Karen was performing it.

Kate was certain there were no dry eyes in the room as Adam played the final chord and Karen blew a kiss heavenward. The singer smiled radiantly at her husband, grasped his hand and let him escort her back to the front row. The closing prayer was said and a soft buzz filled the room as people greeted each other. Dotty played a final hymn as the congregation filed into the lobby.

Jay stood and handed Megan to Mitch and turned to find Karen. "That was beautiful. Thank you so much for sharing your talent with us today," Jay said clasping Karen's hand. He reached for Adam's hand and shook it as well. "You are both so talented. That was just the perfect conclusion to the meeting."

Kate stepped closer and reached for Karen. "I know we haven't really met, but I just have to give you a hug."

Karen laughed. "I'm always up for a hug."

"Thank you for sharing your story. It touched me deeply. I only knew Penny for a few years, but her impact will stay with me forever," Kate said as she stepped out of Karen's arms.

The Shields were stopped several more times as they made their way up the aisle as Kate and Jay followed close behind. At the back of the chapel Kate paused to talk to the friends that had come from Utah

County. Robin, Guy and Connie along with Penny's neighbors Kim and Gigi stopped to speak with Kate.

"Good job, Kate," Connie said with a quick hug. "Penny would have been embarrassed to hear all the nice things people said about her."

"Yes she would," Kim, Penny's neighbor, said with a laugh. "But her life needed to be celebrated. She was such a wonderful example of love and concern for her fellow man."

The group fell silent as the chapel continued to empty. Kate smiled at Gigi. "I'm so glad you could come. How's your little dog doing?"

"Good." The woman nodded and turned her gaze on Guy. "You're the guy in the Jeep," she said suddenly.

Guy looked stunned, but nodded. "Uh . . . yes I do drive a Jeep."

"I live on Penny's block so I saw you parked in front of Penny's house last week." Gigi replied boldly. "Made me kind of nervous to be honest."

"Oh. Sorry. Yeah that was me." Guy didn't say anything more, so Kate spoke up.

"I guess I should introduce you guys." Kate turned to her two coworkers. "This is Connie and Robin, they work with me at the salon and this is Guy, Robin's brother. He was working for Penny," Kate hesitated, "doing odd jobs."

Jay stepped forward to shake Gigi's hand. "And I'm Jay, Kate's husband."

"Oh, yes I'm sorry." Kate pointed to the three children beside her. "And these are our children. You've met Janae and Megan, and this is Mitch."

"Nice to meet you all." Gigi turned to Guy. "I'm sorry I was suspicious, but I like to keep an eye out for my neighbors."

Guy nodded. "That's okay."

The organ music stopped and Kate watched Dotty gather her music and descend the stairs of the stand.

"I want to meet Dotty and her husband," Kate said to Jay as she motioned to the organist.

Robin touched Kate's arm. "We have to go anyway," Robin said. "Guy has a class later."

"I'm glad you came." Kate smiled and leaned in for a quick hug with both of her salon buddies. Connie waved and followed Robin and her brother into the foyer.

"Us too," Kim said. "You ready?" she asked Gigi. The women said goodbye and hurried out the door.

The family turned and went back toward the front of the room where Dotty and Clyde were standing. "Kate," the man said as she reached them. "How nice to meet you in person. This is my wife Dotty."

"Good to meet you," Kate said turning to introduce her family. "This is Jay and our kids. Mitch, Janae and Megan."

Dotty touched the baby's head and beamed. "What a sweetheart." The woman turned to Kate. "You did a fantastic job with the service," she said as she placed a kiss on Kate's cheek. "And oh how sweet was

Karen's song . . . ." The woman shook her head. "I had a hard time seein' the music through my tears."

Clyde nodded in agreement. "Quite a day."

"Yes. It was a very nice meeting," a voice acknowledged from behind Kate. Ernie stepped into the circle. "I'm certain Penny would have especially loved the music," he smiled at Dotty.

"I'm just glad it's over." Kate sighed.

Dotty took Clyde's arm. "Well good day to you. Stop by next time you're in town with your lovely family." The couple moved slowly up the aisle of the chapel.

Ernie rested his hand on Jay's shoulder. "I need to speak with you and your wife for a few minutes if you don't mind."

Jay exchanged a curious look with Kate as the banker explained. "It concerns some unfinished business that Penny left behind."

"Of course," Jay said as Ernie ushered the family out a side door.

Chapter 39

The side door led to a hallway with several offices. Ernie opened one of the doors and peeked inside. "Let's step in here." He seemed to reconsider. "I wonder if your older children might wait here in the lobby."

"Of course," Jay said pointing to a couch and addressing his older children. "We'll just be a few minutes. You guys wait right here."

The banker paused and smiled as the teenagers dropped onto the sofa. "Penny often spoke of her beautiful *grandchildren* with such pride. She told me about Mitch and his basketball prowess and how talented Janae was on the piano." The banker nodded and followed the couple into the room before he closed the door. "Her favorite topic was little Megan though. She said she was the cutest baby she'd ever seen . . . I can see why she thought that," he said as he touched Megan's cheek.

Kate felt tears begin to collect in her eyes. "We did love her like our own," she sniffed and swiped at her nose.

Ernie handed her a tissue from his pocket.

"I'm sorry. I didn't bring you in here to make you cry, but we do have a bit more to talk about." The man unfolded two chairs that were leaning against a wall and motioned for the couple to take a seat. Jay hesitated to take the last chair. "No. I'll stand. You sit," Ernie said.

"Thank you." Jay took the baby onto his lap and turned his attention to the banker.

"I'm not sure how much you know about Penny's parents." He looked at Kate with raised eyebrows.

She nodded her head. "I found their obituary online. They were in a boating accident, right?"

Ernie rubbed at his chin. "Yes, her parents were sailing with friends and were lost in a storm. The empty boat was discovered some time later with no trace of it's four occupants." Ernie frowned and took a breath. "I didn't know Penny at the time, but she told me about it several years later when she asked me to handle her inheritance."

Kate looked up in surprise. "Inheritance?"

"Yes, despite their strained relationship, Penny received a rather large inheritance."

Jay looked at his wife. "We wondered how she had the means to do some of the things she was doing, like paying people's mortgages."

"So her parents had money and left it to her when they died?" Kate asked.

Ernie nodded. "Quite a bit of money, actually." He folded his arms over his chest and leaned against the small table by the door. "Let's just say you could live off the interest quite well and never touch the actual money from her parents."

Kate was stunned by the notion of Penny having that kind of money.

"You're talking millions then," Jay stated as Kate looked his way, her mouth hanging open.

"Yes," the banker said softly.

"How did her parents get that kind of money?" Kate asked trying to recall if Jolene had mentioned her uncle's line of work.

"Penny's father was a movie director and a very shrewd businessman from what I gather. He also invested well in the stock market."

Kate inhaled deeply and shook her head. "I would never have guessed that Penny was a multi-millionaire. She lived so simply."

Ernie nodded. "Yes she was very sensible—even in the way she assisted people. She could have easily lavished gifts upon people and helped them beyond their needs, but she decided not to do that. She understood that an overly generous gift would not be appreciated the same way that a simple offering would be. She certainly didn't want to draw any attention to herself." Ernie crossed his arms and smiled at the couple. "Besides most folks don't take kindly to being a charity case, so she always tried to strike a balance. As you can see, she had a knack for providing just the right amount of help to get people on their feet again and still maintain their dignity."

Ernie pulled a sealed envelope from his pocket. "Penny left a letter explaining how she wanted the money used after her death." He handed the envelope to Kate who took it with shaking hands. "This is just a copy of the letter, the original is with her attorney."

Jay spoke, "Rob has it? He never mentioned this."

"Yes, he knows that there is an inheritance, but not many of the details. Penny liked to keep things under wraps. She asked that I be the one to tell you about it since I had managed the money over the years." He shrugged.

"So you knew who we were when we stopped by your house?" Kate asked.

"Yes, once you told me your names. I was really glad to meet the famous Lundquists." Ernie laughed and continued. "I remember the day she told me she'd found the perfect couple to take over her business."

Kate looked perplexed. "Her business?"

Ernie laughed. "Yes, her business of finding people in need and giving them a hand."

Kate was shaking her head, letting it all sink in. "You mean that Penny wants Jay and I to give away *her* money?" she asked incredulously." She paused and glanced up at Ernie. "How can I suddenly be in charge of millions of dollars?" she wondered out loud.

Ernie laughed at the look on Kate's face. "It'll be fun. You'll see. The hardest part, I imagine, will be that you can't help everyone. This labor of love may be the most enjoyable work you'll ever do, Kate. Well next to motherhood." He smiled at the baby. "I know it brought Penny a great deal of joy."

Kate gripped the envelope tightly and read her name across the front. How was this possible? This was a huge responsibility. Did Penny really think she could do this? Kate thought about the delivery they made at the home of the Montoyas the other night. She smiled at the memory. It could be fun.

Ernie interrupted her thoughts. "The only condition that Penny insisted upon was that it should be done anonymously . . . whenever possible."

He motioned to the envelope in her hands. "You can read the letter now or wait until you get home. I'm sure you'll have questions, so here's my card." He pulled a business card from his pocket. "I'll continue to handle the banking end of things for as long as I'm able."

The baby began to fuss, so Jay stood up to pace with her. "Is there some paperwork to sign? Should I have our lawyer, Rob, call you?" Jay asked as he let the baby get down.

"Yes. We'll need to take care of some things over the next few weeks. I have Rob's number." Ernie opened the door and the couple joined the teenagers in the hall.

The family filed down the hallway toward the lobby. Kate stopped and turned to face Ernie. "What about Guy? Can I keep using his help?"

Ernie looked surprised. "You know about Guy?"

"Yes," Jane interrupted with a smile. "We helped him take swings to the new babies on Monday." Megan squealed and took off running down the hall as Janae and Mitch hurried after her.

Ernie's gaze followed the two older kids as they corralled the youngest child. "I haven't actually met Guy yet, but Penny told me about him a few months ago when I helped her set up the scholarship for him."

It was Kate's turn to be surprised. "Oh of course. She would be the one paying for," she covered her mouth and lowered her voice, "his schooling."

The man spoke softly as they entered the foyer. "Yes she is."

"Was that why he's working for her?" Jay asked.

"Oh no. There are no strings attached to his scholarship. She set up the fund for his tuition without him knowing. He may suspect, but I'm not sure he's ever been told," Ernie added quietly as he looked at the three children standing by the table with the slideshow still looping on the screen. "She did most of her work in secret, but as she got older it became harder. It rankled her that she couldn't do it all by herself anymore. I suggested she find a younger person that could help her. That's how Guy came to work for her."

Kate nodded and tucked the envelope in her purse. She couldn't believe the turn of events. "I don't even know where to start?" she said as she lifted the baby into her arms.

"You'll figure it out," Ernie said. "She trusted you and so do I."

Kate sighed as her family collected the computer and the framed photos from the table. She picked up a photo of Penny and her children that had been taken at Megan's birthday party only a month prior.

"Gamma," the baby said as she touched the picture.

Kate's eyes grew wide. "Yes. Grandma Penny. Did you hear that?" she asked her husband and children.

Janae pointed at the picture again. "Who is this Meggie?" the girl asked, laughing when the baby repeated the word two more times.

"Oh. I wish Penny could have heard her," Kate said with a sigh.

Ernie smiled. "Maybe she did."

Epilogue

Kate's phone startled her from the crossword puzzle she was trying to complete. She reached for the phone and answered.

"Hi Brock."

"I'm just taking the exit. I'll be there in ten minutes," the handyman said as Kate grabbed her purse and slipped on her coat.

She tapped the steering wheel impatiently as the garage door lifted, her anticipation building as she backed across the driveway. She headed down the block and checked the clock on the dash. She had an hour until the kids came home from school. Megan was spending the afternoon with Grandma because Kate had plans.

It had been two months since Penny's funeral and Kate had been perusing the newspapers and the online news compiling a list of people in need. She was surprised at how many people could use a helping hand.

Today's delivery wasn't for someone she'd found in the paper. Kate had known this person for several years. Elsie Swenson lived a few blocks away and was a good friend. Elsie owned a catering business and was in fact the very caterer that Jay had used for his first date with Kate over two years ago. The woman was in her seventies, but continued to provide her scrumptious food for gatherings, large and small. Unfortunately, Kate had heard recently that the caterer's oven was on its last leg.

Kate turned onto the Swenson's street and put her car in park. She could see Elsie's home from where she waited, but hoped the older woman wouldn't see her. She shut off the engine and waited for Brock to arrive.

A moment later the handyman's truck stopped in front of the Swenson's home. She could see the large box in the back of the truck that contained the brand new oven that she and Brock had purchased yesterday. Brock stepped from the truck and glanced in Kate's direction. He didn't wave, but Kate raised her hand in recognition, her heart racing as she saw Brock amble up the walkway to the front door.

The front door opened and Brock spoke to Elsie gesturing to his truck at the curb. Elsie stepped onto the porch and put her hands on her hips. Kate found herself ducking lower in her seat as Elsie glanced her way. Brock said something more to the woman and then Elsie's husband, Jim, appeared on the porch.

Kate watched as Jim and Brock used a cart and wheeled the new appliance into the house. Elsie followed the men inside and closed the door. Kate smiled and started the engine.

"I do enjoy spending your money, Penny," she said as she hurried back to her own home.

About the Author

Marianne Elder Gowers was born in Seattle, Washington as the middle child in a family of ten children. She is an avid reader and always has several books waiting on her nightstand. She didn't realize her dream of writing until her five children were grown and having babies of their own. She loves spending her days bringing to life the many characters in her imagination.

To learn more about Marianne and her upcoming books go to www.mariannegowers.com

Made in the USA
Middletown, DE
10 February 2019